AF071565

In Love with Love

Ella Risbridger is a writer and editor from London. Her bestselling books range from poetry anthologies to children's stories and cookbooks. Her debut cookbook, *Midnight Chicken (& Other Recipes Worth Living For)*, was named a Book of the Year in multiple publications (among them *The Times*, the *Daily Mail*, and the *Washington Post*) and won the Guild of Food Writers Award. She is a frequent contributor to the *Financial Times* and the *Observer*, and has written for most places at one point or another. She has never written a romance novel, but she has read approximately ten thousand of them. She is excited to talk about every single one.

Her newsletter, *You Get In Love And Then*, was an instant Substack bestseller, and can be found at ella.substack.com. Apart from romance novels, she likes poems, gardens, and Marmite toast. She has one orange cat.

IN LOVE WITH LOVE

The Persistence and Joy of Romantic Fiction

Ella Risbridger

Sceptre

First published in Great Britain in 2025 by Sceptre
An imprint of Hodder & Stoughton Limited
An Hachette UK company

The authorised representative in the EEA is Hachette Ireland, 8 Castlecourt Centre, Dublin 15, D15 XTP3, Ireland (email: info@hbgi.ie)

3

Copyright © Ella Risbridger 2025

The right of Ella Risbridger to be identified as the Author of the Work has been asserted by her in accordance with the Copyright, Designs and Patents Act 1988.

Extract from 'Peanut Butter' in I *Must Be Living Twice: New and Selected Poems 1975–2014* by Eileen Myles © 2015, Eileen Myles. Reprinted with permission of Profile Books

All rights reserved. No part of this publication may be reproduced, stored in a retrieval system, or transmitted, in any form or by any means without the prior written permission of the publisher, nor be otherwise circulated in any form of binding or cover other than that in which it is published and without a similar condition being imposed on the subsequent purchaser.

A CIP catalogue record for this title is available from the British Library

Hardback ISBN 9781399749220
Trade Paperback ISBN 9781399749237
ebook ISBN 9781399749244

Typeset in Sabon MT by Hewer Text UK Ltd, Edinburgh
Printed and bound in Great Britain by Clays Ltd, Elcograf S.p.A.

Hodder & Stoughton policy is to use papers that are natural, renewable and recyclable products and made from wood grown in sustainable forests. The logging and manufacturing processes are expected to conform to the environmental regulations of the country of origin.

Hodder & Stoughton Limited
Carmelite House
50 Victoria Embankment
London EC4Y 0DZ

www.sceptrebooks.co.uk

for my sisters:

for Floss, half-fae, half-human, all woman;

*for Bee, new cowgirl in town with
leather chaps and a shady secret;*

*and for Cia, now and always, a wanton-looking
redhead clutching a Save the Seals collecting tin.*

Contents

Introduction: Friends Fear She's Reading Romance Again — 1
1. What If We Kissed in the Community Library? — 17
2. A Truth Universally Acknowledged — 33
3. The Hot Billionaires Are Back — 53
4. The Fox, the Hedgehog, and the Aliens — 83
5. Cowboys and Horses — 107
6. Daisy Bacon and the Fifty-Fifty Girls — 131
7. The Hometown Hero — 147
8. Sex and Text — 165
9. Two Tickets for the Love Train — 189
10. Gay Boys, Straight Girls, Queer Awakenings — 211
11. The Infinite Weird — 239
Epilogue: What If We Kissed at the Funeral Home? — 261

Endnotes — 263
Acknowledgements — 275

Introduction

Friends Fear She's Reading Romance Again

This is not an exhaustive history of the romance novel. Nor is it even a comprehensive summary of the romance novels of now.

It is, if anything, a romance novel itself – or, at least, a love story. Maybe it's a love letter? If it's a love letter, it has a message-in-a-bottle quality: I'm flinging this out into the world hoping that it's going to wash up at exactly your feet. Writing is always like this, I have to tell you. To write anything you have to believe, somehow, that it's all going to work out ok. You have to believe that out there, somewhere, is the person who will really see you, and love you for what they see. You have to believe, basically, that the things you believe – however earnest or embarrassing or exposing – are the things that will make someone out there go *Yes. Yes. That's it. That's how I feel too! That's me!* You are looking for the person who gets it: the person to whom you do not have to explain anything, the person who understands everything you give them.

This is why so many writers are hopeless romantics.

So here I go.

Here's my heart; please be careful with it.

In Love with Love

You can picture me the way so many heroines start off their stories: stripy pyjamas, glasses, messy hair up in one of those grabby claw-clip things. An orange cat (I love him; he tolerates me). A blank page full of promise; so much to say, and no idea how to say it. Heart all in knots because something is just beginning. "Dreams" by The Cranberries playing.

And you?

Since I'm on the sofa under a blanket, you're probably a high-powered professional in the big city (in which case I'll teach you to breathe out), or a wholesome outdoorsy profession in your small town (in which case, you'll teach me). If I'm stressed on the way to a meeting, you're baking brownies in a blizzard, Miles Davis on the record player. If I'm too scared to write what I feel, you're a painter who always speaks her truth or a deep-sea fisherman who knows that the salt sea will take my breath away and bring me back to life. If I just lost my job, you don't know it yet, but you're about to start a business. If my wife died six years ago, leaving me with a little daughter I would give my life to protect, you're the first person she's warmed to in all that time. She wants to try your lipstick – will you let her? Will you laugh with her on the swings?

Maybe we hate each other, in which case, maybe there's only one bed. If we think we might like each other, there will be two beds in only one room, and we'll go to sleep in chaste pyjamas listening to each other breathe. It's eminently possible we'll have to pretend to be in love, for some reason: I won't inherit my father's mill unless he sees me settled down, you can't let your ex's new lover show you up at a wedding. Maybe we get married so you can stay in the country, or so your grandmother can see you walk down the aisle – even though we're best friends, or still total strangers. Maybe we mean to get divorced right after, because we hate each other, but for some inexplicable reason we can't unless we live together, or take a trip together, or gaze into each other's eyes because of magic or a curse or a promise. Maybe you get ill, or get hurt, and I gently bathe your forehead, because even though I hate you, I can't let you die. I'll die if you die. While I'm bathing your forehead and making you soup, I understand, at last, what you mean to me. Or maybe it's the other way round: I'm lying in bed, and someone – a shadowy, familiar figure – is feeding me soup from a spoon. Through the haze of my fever, it dawns on me: it's you. It's always been you.

I should have realised so long ago! I should have realised when we were locked in the janitor's cupboard hiding from the assassins! I should have realised when they sent us on that road trip together for work, and we had the same taste in obscure road-trip snacks! I should have realised when you were the only person to remember the thing from my childhood that meant everything to me! I didn't realise, or you didn't, and now everything is falling apart. You think I'm in love with someone else; your fiancée showed up at my work to tell me she's back on the scene. I know I'll never be good enough for you, because I'm traumatised in ways nobody could ever understand; you know you'll never be good enough for me, because *you're* traumatised in ways nobody could ever understand. (Wait a minute . . .) Perhaps you have secrets you're not ready to share, or perhaps – and memorably – a false leg you don't want to talk about.* Perhaps someone – one of your friends, even! – has put a dead fish inscribed with obscenities in my bed, hoping to chase me off.† (I'm too poor to love you; or are you too rich to love me?)

For some reason, we don't talk about any of this. We don't try to make things better; we don't call or text or ask each other what the fuck just happened. We just have one perfect night – or almost one perfect night – or a single brief (and perfect) kiss – and then we fall apart, because we're human, and we're fallible, and this is the third act, and everything is as bad as it could be. This is the worst part.

Sometimes, if things are particularly bleak in the world outside the book, this part is too much for me. I can't bear it: the idea that anyone should suffer, when *everything* is suffering, makes me fall apart. I have to put the book down and read a different book, but I always come back.

No: not true. I always come back *if* I trust the author to bring us home somewhere better than we started. I always come back if I trust we're going somewhere good, whether that's me off the sofa, you unwinding your city-girl bun and taking out your fierce hairpins, or both of us walking down

---

* *A Photo Finish*, Elsie Silver, 2021
† *Crazy Rich Asians*, Kevin Kwan, 2013

Friends Fear She's Reading Romance Again

the aisle with your half-orphan daughter and my orange cat as, respectively, bridesmaid and best man. I want our best friends to agree we're so much happier like this, however this is. I want my mom at the dry cleaning shop to approve of you; I want your dad at the mill to tell you that this is the kind of person he always dreamed you'd bring home; I want your aunt to murmur, quietly, that your dead parent or sibling would have loved this, loved me, loved us. I want someone in the department to mutter *oh, about time!* and us to realise, with a shock, we've been observed this whole time – our secret romance played out to everyone who's known us both for years – or I want the department to gasp in real, honest shock at the Christmas party when we appear hand in hand. I want to kiss in a corner while big band music plays and the credits roll. I want to end with a dot dot dot, or an epilogue, or a promise ... I want to end with the future.

I don't know if I need a Happily Ever After – we'll unpack *that* in a bit, I promise – but I need a happy for now: I need to know we're coming into safe harbour and nobody is going to drown before we get there.

I need to fall asleep thinking: *When's she writing another one? And what's going to happen next?*

I need to wonder what's going to happen, even though I know what's going to happen. It might happen in, you know, a slightly different way – see above re. false legs and dead fish – but it will happen, more or less the way I think it's going to happen, every time. When it doesn't happen how I think it's going to happen, I think it's a bad book, and I'm annoyed. I don't want you to knot me up like a pretzel; I want to eat my buttered toast and fall asleep happy. I don't want to be tricked. I don't want a twist. I don't want to be surprised, only delighted.

In this way, romance novels are not like other novels: or maybe only like mystery novels, where an ending without a criminal unmasked is no ending at all. Nobody laughs at mystery novels for this. I think that's weird! I love mystery novels, probably almost as much as I love romance novels, but it doesn't escape my notice that when it's a boy thing (murder), it's cool to have a formula, when it's a girl thing (kissing), it's sort of humiliating. We are supposed to be embarrassed by the way romance novels follow the blueprint. We are supposed, at least, to acknowledge it with a self-deprecating nod of the head and a shrug. People love to tell you that the best romance novels are the ones that break the formula, and then follow up by recommending books that would give nobody the cosy buttered-toast feeling.

Listen: I hate when people get prescriptive about genre. Genre (like gender) is at its best when it's a playground instead of a prison: here are your new toys, let's see what we can do with them. Here are the Barbies, here are the Beanie Babies, here is a large teddy bear you're going to need to be your one's boyfriend because we don't have nearly enough borrowed (stolen) Action Men to go round. I'm allergic to authority and hate all kinds of rules. The word "technically", as in "technically, a romance novel should...", brings me out in hives. The word "should" is even worse. I am, in theory, up for all kinds of ideas about the way we write, and what we read. And yet there's something about the way people who *don't* read romance talk about romance that makes me, myself, want to put up the exact kind of gatekeeping boundaries I hate.

I want to defend my Happily Ever After with both hands.

The term "feminist" is so broadly used and abused that it's almost more trouble than it's worth at this point: overexposure has made it almost meaningless. It has, I think, been essentially divorced from its political roots, as perhaps all useful words eventually are, and splintered into dozens of factions and a slogan t-shirt factory. If anyone can wear a *This Is What A Feminist Looks Like* t-shirt, no matter who they are and what they do, does that make anyone – or everyone – a feminist? Is it useful to group the trans-exclusionary radical feminists with the queer liberation feminists? Is it useful – has it ever been useful – to group together everyone based on the single common belief that women should be treated as people? Perhaps I ran into too many "male feminists" who groped girls at parties in the noughties; perhaps I've seen too many women use "feminist" as a cover for anti-immigrant or anti-trans beliefs now in the 2020s; or perhaps I've simply got into too many arguments about Judith Butler where nobody has done the required reading: whatever it is, I'm a little nervous about applying it to my own arguments.

And yet it's impossible to think critically about romantic novels – why we love them, why people hate them, why we write them, why we read them – without a feminist lens. To turn critical attention on romantic fiction is, I hope, a feminist act: to give these works, chiefly by and for women, the thoughtful and careful unpacking that other literatures might take for granted. Equally, it's impossible to credibly call yourself any kind of feminist while dismissing romantic fiction. If you want to take the rights of women seriously, particularly in times where it seems that the rights of women are being eroded from all sides, you must also take seriously the art that women create and consume – now as much as in the past. You must take the living woman as seriously as you take the dead woman, whose opinions have been made safe by time.

With certain notable exceptions (a lecturer I had at college in – yes! – the twenty-first century), we all accept that the literary work of great women is just as mighty as the literary work of great men. Nobody could scorn the work of the Brontë sisters as frivolous.* Yet if you like the yearning, the longing, the troubled past, the passionate kiss in *Jane Eyre*, then it's a short step to romantic fiction more generally.

Romance fans know this all too well. But you must be wary of people who tell you that their favourite romance novel is, for instance, *Villette* by Charlotte Brontë. (And I *love* that book. The Brontë sisters, or most of them, were pretty good at the high-intensity kissing.) Because when

---

* Yes, I know people have tried. Those people are beyond my help. They are beyond any help, and you should not let them occupy a moment of your thoughts.

Friends Fear She's Reading Romance Again

someone tells you the best romance book is *Villette*, then you can be pretty sure that person thinks they are too good for romance books. They often follow it up by explaining that they don't really read romance books. But of course.

What this person is telling you is that the thing you love was best in the past, when it was Art, and before it was yours. Back then, people understood what a book was *supposed* to be.

And this is true, I suppose, as far as it goes.

And this is true provided what you mean is: there has never been a time when novels were separate from romance novels, and there has never been a time when these two types of book weren't under scrutiny. *Reading romances* and *reading novels* are two interchangeable crimes: the French word *roman* means "novel", and it's not a coincidence. Two of the very earliest novels in English are *Love-Letters Between a Nobleman and His Sister* (1684) and *Pamela or, Virtue Rewarded* (1740), and they are exactly what they sound like. *Pamela*, by Samuel Richardson, is (sorry not sorry) essentially an epistolary Jilly Cooper, complete with problematic employer–employee age-gap non-con relationships (that nonetheless end in marriage); *Love-Letters*, by Aphra Behn, is a bonkers romp about a man, his wife's sister, and everyone they know.

Both books – obviously – came under immense scrutiny when first published. Both books, when read by women, became scandalous.

In Love with Love

So yes. Books were best in the past, provided what you mean is: there has never been a time when women could read novels without comment.

Gender (like genre) is a playground, but when we talk about romance novels we'd be remiss not to understand this as a woman's world first and foremost. To be honest, it's sort of a wilful misreading – wishful thinking, if you will – to consider novels *as a whole* as ungendered. Men – and the statistics will bear me out here, although I'm not the kind of writer to put them in myself – don't read. Oh, they look like they do. They carry one heavy tome around with them, if they are that sort of man. They can *talk* about books. But they don't read like women read. They don't buy books like women buy books. And they don't read books that women write either. Writing is gendered, reading is gendered, and the way people think about novels is gendered. Men can write for women, but can women write for men? Will men read women? The Bell brothers weren't sure they would. Nor was George Eliot.

Then again, I would rather not hold up George Eliot as any kind of hero here. George Eliot, actually, is exactly the kind of person who makes me want to cling onto my Kindle deals. "Silly Novels by Lady Novelists are a genus with many species, determined by the particular quality of silliness that predominates in them—the frothy, the prosy, the pious, or the pedantic," begins a bitchy little essay of 1856. Eliot likes the phrase "Silly Novels by Lady Novelists" so much that it is also the title of the essay, in which the author tears viciously and happily into a stack of romance books.

Friends Fear She's Reading Romance Again

There is, essentially, nothing about romance novels that Eliot seems to like (although it must be said, she does appear to have read *a lot* of them). Me? I could fall into these mid-Victorian romps that Eliot loathes and live there gladly for a week. Everything she quotes *is* silly. The writing is overwrought, underbaked, and also irresistible. Do you not seek to submerge yourself in a "pot pourri of Almack's, Scotch second-sight, Mr. Rogers's breakfasts, Italian brigands, death-bed conversions, superior authoresses, Italian mistresses, and attempts at poisoning old ladies"? Who could *help* wanting this?

Eliot, apparently: not only are these books supposedly beneath us in literary terms, but they will more broadly impede the whole course of female emancipation and education. Men will think badly of women, on the whole, because these books exist – which is reason enough, for Eliot, for these books not to exist.

I think this might, on the whole, be the worst reason to dislike romance novels that I've ever heard.

At least men have the wide-eyed boldness to come out and accuse women who read novels of being sex workers: "*she who can bear to peruse them,*" thunders the eighteenth-century bestseller Reverend Fordyce, "*must in her Soul be a Prostitute*". Like so many bestsellers, though, it would be unwise to take his as the voice of the people. After all, Fordyce, now, lingers on as the favourite writer of literature's most odious man:

In Love with Love

A book was produced; but, on beholding it (for everything announced it to be from a circulating library), Mr. Collins started back, and begging pardon, protested that he never read novels. Kitty stared at him, and Lydia exclaimed. Other books were produced, and after some deliberation he chose Fordyce's Sermons. Lydia gaped as he opened the volume, and before he had, with very monotonous solemnity, read three pages, she interrupted him—

This, to me, is extremely charming.

Mr. Collins, much offended, laid aside his book.

And *Pride and Prejudice* continues.

Isn't that so great? Isn't that completely wonderful?

There is this bit in the Eliot essay where she gets scathing about the idea that reviewers "tell one lady novelist after another that they 'hail' her productions 'with delight'". Well, I do hail these productions with delight. I hail lots of things with delight. I love to be charmed by things that don't exist.

I love to read about clothes and jewels and gardens and horses. I love to read about woolly hats and wild storms in small Canadian towns, and perfect cups of coffee and autumn leaves in middle America, and freshly painted walls in tumbledown cottages in the Cotswolds or Cornwall or Cape Cod. I love to read about objects and fabrics and textures and sensations. I love the part in a

Friends Fear She's Reading Romance Again

romance novel where the author describes the love rival's clothes because they are always so immaculate and coordinated; I love the part where the hero gives the heroine some kind of perfect and thoughtful present; I love the part where they eat together, sushi or soup or a picnic or a box of heritage strawberries from a local farm co-operative hand-picked by the hero in his wholesome outdoor work. I love when someone builds something for someone they love. I love when there is woodwork involved. I love when there is crafting involved. I love when there is a little magic. I love when there are breakfasts and death-beds and second sights.

And all these things delight me.

Maybe Eliot was not big on delight, but I am.

I think, in a funny way, the whole thing hinges on delight: the whole thing being romance novels, the whole thing being reading for pleasure, the whole thing being a sense of joy that is not tied to moral or intellectual betterment.

Women's delight – *especially* when it's bound up with sex – is a tinderbox to a certain kind of thinker, because it's a threat to a certain way of life. It's dangerous to let women think about making their own choices; it's dangerous to let women choose their lives based on what delights them, enchants them, makes them happy instead of anyone else. It's dangerous to let women think too much about happy endings, because then they might look twice at what you want to give them instead. When women write for pleasure, read for pleasure, they aren't thinking about what men might think. They are thinking about themselves: themselves, and the women in the books they read.

Here is a woman I think about a lot: a girl named *Sarah Oakey*. Sarah lived two hundred years ago, if she ever lived at all. I don't know anything about her – can't find anything out about her, although I have tried. She exists, if she ever did, only for this story.

Sarah's story is very short and it goes like this: *Once there was a woman they sent to the madhouse for reading too much.*

It sounds like a joke, doesn't it?

It sounds like the kind of joke people used to say to me when I was little and went everywhere with a paperback in each hand. It sounds like the kind of joke old men say to young women who aren't paying enough attention to them.

I found out about Sarah on the internet about fifteen years ago, and I've thought about her on and off ever since. Her story is the kind of thing people like to talk about, when they talk about the past: every so often she crops up on one of those lists of reasons men called women crazy in the past. These lists always go viral. *Too much crying; too many snacks; wilfulness.* People love these lists because they love to think of how narrowly we avoided this kind of life ourselves – a hundred years, in the grand scheme of time, being nothing at all.

Novel reading, Sarah Oakey, Gloucester.

The madhouse was Gloucester Asylum, which did exist. You can look it up, see pictures of it. It is hard, harder than

Friends Fear She's Reading Romance Again

you would think, to imagine being taken there because you cared too much about people who didn't exist. You are here, probably, because you care too much about people who don't exist. You are here because you want to be around people who also care too much.

This book is for Sarah Oakey, and all the Sarah Oakeys.

This book is for everyone who cares too much; everyone who ever cried at the third-act crisis or got breathless at a fictional touch on a fictional cheek or tilted their screen away from a stranger on the Tube. This book is for everyone blushing on the bus.

The world is very bleak, lately. Maybe it always has been, and this is just our particular bleakness, but nonetheless: it's bad out there. It's a hard world. Sales of romance used to go up after a tragedy; now they are up all the time. I don't know what this says about the world, but I know what it says about us: in times of darkness, we seek the light. In times of darkness, we find joy where we can: *silly novels by lady novelists*, or whatever you want to call them. Chick lit. Romcoms. Kissing books. I said from the top that this wouldn't be a comprehensive history of the romance novel, or even an extensive bibliography of the great romance novels. And it is, perhaps, comprehensive and extensive in one way only: it is a field guide to delight; not a defence, or a counterattack, but a love song.

This is a book about things I love and I hope you love it too.

I

What If We Kissed in the Community Library?

The summer I worked at the library I read at least one, probably two, romance novels a day.

It was a community library, which is to say, the local authority had withdrawn funding several years before. They let us use their books, and their computers, and we – or rather, the charity who ran the place – funded everything else. The building itself was elderly and graceful, like an old aristocrat fallen on hard times. The furniture was mostly wipe-clean and functional. The sash windows were rotting gently in their frames. But there were a lot of books, and there were people doing their best. It was an important place.

In between stamping books for toddlers, or logging old ladies into their emails, or trying to figure out what, exactly, the semi-nude man (loin cloth, denim visor) was doing in the Naturalists section of the basement (had he misread the sign?) – and what, exactly, *I* could do about it* – I sat behind the desk, and I read.

I read so many romance books that the library itself – huge bubbles of damp plaster peeling from the walls,

---

* Nothing!

uncomfortable hard plastic chairs – became kind of romantic to me. I started writing library romances to entertain myself; worse, started matchmaking library patrons. How could I help it?

June came on Thursday mornings to change her books; May came on Thursday afternoons. I learned fast not to shelve anything June returned, because May invariably took them out again hours later. When something disappointed one, it always disappointed the other, too. They lived on opposite sides of town; they were different, according to their saved demographic data, in every way.

But they were soulmates. If it hadn't been a breach of every regulation in the GDPR handbook I would have told them about each other; instead, I just propped June's returns prominently on the trolley for May, and kept anything new May found behind the counter for June.

There were tired parents taking out the same books to learn *how to talk so kids will listen, and listen so kids will talk*; there were expectant mothers taking out the same *what to expect when you're expecting*; there were teens, different schools, different lives, taking out dark fantasy mangas and graphic novels about urban witches kissing under the Brooklyn Bridge. There were so many romance readers, all kinds of romance readers, I wanted to start them some kind of club: some kind of silent reading club. Every day they brought back books and took them out again, and every day I took the best ones from everyone, made a stack of their books on my desk, then read them instead of shelving them.

What If We Kissed in the Community Library?

I loved reading romance books, but I really hated shelving them. I hated shelving them because the romantic shelving system was, to me, a disaster.

While "Crime" had three big bookshelves and a constant supply of new books, the single official shelf for "Romance" held mostly agèd Mills & Boons, languishing unloved and unlucky and rarely borrowed. The vast majority of romance books – the books that I thought of as romance – were scattered across other categories of fiction. Some went to Classics. Some went to Young Adult, or even to New Adult. Most went to General Fiction, lost in the vast mass of every kind of novel.

This was phenomenally annoying to me: the Crime people could expect new books to arrive, neatly shelved, on a semi-regular basis. The Crime people would know where to find their new books, just as the Cookery fans could always wander down to the basement (we meet again, Mr Loincloth), and the Celebrity Memoir gang could check the row of shelves to the left of the big bay window. The Crime people got prime real estate. We, the Romance crew – and by now I felt myself to be one of them – had to forage. Our desires were overlooked.

And there was no solution. It was not permitted for a day supervisor to change even a single label on a spine, let alone to rearrange whole swathes of the shelving system. Also, frustratingly, I did not think I actually *had* a solution; at least, not one that could be applied broadly. *I* knew what romance should be. I knew romance when I saw it. It was in my head, but I struggled to define my beloved genre.

It was, as the little boy in *The Princess Bride* says, *a kissing book.*

It was a book about romance. Which did not really help pin things down.

It wasn't enough for a book to be a love story. A romance novel is always a love story; but a love story is not always a romance novel. A romance novel is something else. It is something like what used to be called "chick lit", but not exactly. (Also, now nobody said "chick lit" except the worst kind of man.) It's definitely more specific than the amorphous category of "women's fiction" – as distinct, I suppose, from real fiction, by men? Women wrote all kinds of fiction; women were *in* all kinds of fiction. It was overwhelming. (How, for instance, do you solve a problem like Marian Keyes?*)

But my instincts knew.

Some books in Classics – *Jane Eyre*! *Pride and Prejudice*! – felt right to me. Others – hello, other Brontë sister – did not.

There were YA books – Becky Albertalli! – that felt right; then there was the baffling classification of "New Adult", which seemed to mean a book about a person in their twenties having sex, and that was almost entirely romance.

Then there were writers like Jilly Cooper who defined the genre so completely that she was almost beyond genre.

---

* Romcom? Family saga? Issues-driven contemporary fiction? Very good, funny, smart books?

What If We Kissed in the Community Library?

There were writers like Jill Mansell, with bare kicked-up legs on the cover; there were writers like Jasmine Guillory and Emily Henry with the big bold fonts and the big bold colours; there were fantasy romances like Sarah J. Maas's *A Court of Thorns and Roses*, which needed to be shelved next to *The Priory of the Orange Tree* by Samantha Shannon (fantasy, drama), but also really needed to be lifted out of the General Fiction and into something like Erotica. (We did not, in the community library, have an Erotica section.) There were one million books with swirly writing and beach huts on the covers; and books with stark fonts, flowers and titles like *Hopeless* in which definitely one party was going to die; and black and red covers with maybe a skull or a syringe or a rose in which if one party died, the other party might well bring them back to life in some new, changed form. All of these were shelved in General Fiction, trapped between the slim Nobel-winning volumes translated from the French and battered paperbacks about abused kids called things like *Suffer the Little Children* or *Daddy, Please Don't*.

There was nothing wrong with the slim volumes or the paperbacks. It was just that they weren't my books – or my way of dealing with trauma. I didn't, and don't, love to be confronted by the world in a way that feels out of control. Life is already out of control!

I want to read something that gets me out of here.

I don't want to read something that ignores the fact that life is hard – but I do want to know how to live that hard life lightly. If love is the most important thing, and to me it was and is, I want books that think that too.

I want books that know love is enormous and vital and frightening: love is always frightening, because love is always the same shape as loss. Love is the same shape as loss, and desire has the same all-consuming hunger as death. There's something embarrassing about such big words, maybe about such big ideas. I feel slightly defensive about them, and their right to be here: they feel almost adolescent. *Hunger, death, desire, love.* Too much for grown-ups! Too much for everyday living! They demand to be written in red and black and Tippex across a schoolbag.

The singer Lorde wrote, once, that she had always been fascinated by teenagers: the way they *know something that adults have forgotten.* I think about this a lot when I think about romance novels. It is probably why so many of them end up shelved in YA. Romance novels give us back the things we used to know, or hoped we would get to know. They restore to us the world the way it was when it was all new to us: new and shining and terrible. The writers and readers of romance are scholars of the human heart: they know how hungry it can be, how much it wants, how much it needs. It's hard to see why people belittle romance novels so fervently when they contain all the most vital elements of being alive, including the beginnings and the endings.

And yet they do it without pretentiousness, or gatekeeping, or intellectual showing off. They just do it. And they do it in a way that makes you want more. They do it in a way

What If We Kissed in the Community Library?

that is, above all, funny. Funny, even when your heart is breaking; sweet, even when you're falling through the sky.

Funny, sweet, heartbreaking, delicious: I suppose what I am looking for, always, in romance, is a book that feels like popular '90s sitcom *Friends*. I wanted a book that was about looking for your lobster, and finding them. I wanted something deceptively light, full of big feelings and, ideally, a happy ending.

It wasn't that I thought *all* romance had to have a happy ending. Did I?

I was clear, for example, that *The Time Traveler's Wife* was a romance novel. It had big ideas about science fiction, but it was a romance novel. It was a romance novel the same way that Dorothy L. Sayers' Golden Age detective story, *Busman's Honeymoon*, was a romance novel: as Sayers said, it's either a detective story with romantic interludes, or a romantic story with detecting interludes. *The Time Traveler's Wife* counted, but it didn't offer – unlike Sayers – a happy ending. Or, at least, not exactly a happy ending. Or – wait, was it? I couldn't think about the ending without crying even after nearly twenty years, but it was an ending that believed in love above all things.

It believed in the lightness of love, and the weight of it. It believed that love mattered. It believed that love was the only thing that really mattered; and it believed that love could overcome all things. Which was, I supposed, something that all the romance I loved had in common. It wasn't the happy ending, per se; it was the belief that happy endings were possible. It was the belief that happy endings were important, and that to strive for them was not just a good thing but the only thing worth doing. It was the belief, I suppose, that striving for happy endings is not a single plot but a state of mind.

I wanted to read about people *trying* to be happy.

It isn't exactly that all romance novels have to have a happy ending. It's just that the ones I love mostly do. And it seems, too, that we're in a happy ending phase of romantic fiction right now.

We probably won't always be. In the past it was fashionable for romantic fiction to end badly and sadly and weepily, but perhaps the world was less bleak then. Comedy and tragedy kind of take it in turns to come in and out of fashion. Writers want to write something new, which is by necessity something old: there are no new stories, especially not in romance. What changes is the way you tell the story; and the way you tell the story changes depending on the emotional socio-political climate. We would be forgiven if the desire for a happy ending rose with each tick of the second hand on the Doomsday Clock. Our awareness of the increasingly bleak global climate shifts the national (and indeed international) mood further towards darkness; the reader reaches for a writer who can carry her, if only for some little time, in the opposite direction.

Which is tough, for romance, because the reader and writer are so often the same person. I sat in the library reading romance books, scribbling romantic stories on the back of the printed Holds List, just for myself. When you read a lot of romance, the world starts to feel romantic. When you read a lot of romantic stories, the world starts to feel story shaped.

In the late 1970s and early 1980s, the academic Janice Radway spent several years working with a group of romance readers in the American Midwest. Radway, an anthropologist, studied romance reading not as a literary text, but as an act in and of itself worthy of study, and distinct from other forms of reading. The women – and the group was entirely formed of women – filled out surveys and spoke with Radway at length and over time about their *complex feelings* on romance reading: not just the place it held in their lives, but the function it served. It seemed that it was not – as assumption would have it – a question of "wishing they had a romance like the heroine's", but rather that "romance reading is valued by ... women because the experience itself is *different* from ordinary existence."

Romance novels are, by design, a space for dreaming: they function as a wish-fulfilment station. But the wishes are, perhaps, not always straightforward. Like Radway's reading group, I don't seek either the "strong, virile heroes" or the "romance like the heroine's". I don't seek to be them; I don't seek to possess them. But I want to live in their world for a little while: a world in which I understand all the rules, a world in which I know where we're going. I want to live in a universe where things make sense: where a third-act break-up has a satisfactory resolution, where cruelty has a reasonable rationale and results in a good solid grovel, where the perfect moment is not fleeting but caught forever on the page (which is no longer blank).

The world of the romance novel is the world of *all* romance novels. The rules of one are the rules of all, and therefore it's only necessary to be a newcomer once. Your first romance novel is not a visa, it's a passport: your presence in one romance novel grants you access to any other, a friend instead of a foreigner, safe even in the strangest of set-ups. This is why romances span universes like no other genre: aliens, cowboys, gargoyles, oil barons, regular barons, secret countesses and fraudulent dukes, fairies and faeries, farmers, fishermen, monsters, monster-truck drivers, dancers, hockey players, soccer players, single dads, single mothers, surprise mothers, surprise mothers to infant vampires or a litter of wolves, woodsmen, mathematicians, scientists, scholars, school teachers, time travellers, mermaids, astronauts, carpenters, café owners, waitresses and – obviously – writers. They can be in outer space or in your own backyard. The romance novel can be set in literally any location, with any cast of characters, and the romance reader will find herself immediately and comfortably at home.

The experience is different from ordinary experience – but not because it's pirates or cowboys or whatever. The thing that is different between our world and the world of romantic fiction is that in the world of romantic fiction there are rules – and we understand the rules. Furthermore, and so far away from real life it's laughable, we understand that those rules are bringing us, always, to a place of love.

Critics of romance novels love to laugh at us because the same things happen book after book, but they don't understand that that's the point. A sculpture isn't less impressive because I've seen a ball of clay before: it's not the colour on the palette, but the way the painter puts it together that makes the picture. A Bernini sculpture, the one with the hands pressing into the thighs and the billows of transparent gauzy cloth, is more impressive because I know what a block of marble is and what it looks like when fingers press into soft skin: I know what he started with, I know where he wanted to end up; I love to see it and feel like it's really real.

You could give ten painters the same ten-paint palette and the same still life composition, and they would paint ten different pictures. A Rachel Ruysch tulip is not the same as a Georgia O'Keeffe tulip, even when the pinks and oranges and scarlets and golden stamens come from the same colours and the same shapes and the same desire to convey the perfect singular sexy inside of a fleeting floral moment. I want to see both! I want to see it all. I love to see how a writer will put the pieces together this time around. It's obvious, to me, that it's writing on hard mode to keep a reader's attention when she already knows not just the ending, but the beat-for-beat structure the story must have to feel satisfying. If you don't have the pull of plot to keep the narrative tension, your characters and setting have to be so very vivid; your dialogue so sharp; your jokes so good. The emotions have to be pitch perfect. It all has to feel real. It has to feel like you made it real.

Anyone can play here: here are the tools, here are the tropes, what will you do with them? What will you make with them?

This is why, I suppose, one of my most favourite kinds of romance novel is the romance novel about the romantic novelist. Or editor! Or publicist! Consider: basically every Emily Henry ever written. Her work makes plain something which often stays under the surface: *all* romance novels exist in the context of other romance novels, and all romance novels exist in awareness of themselves. It's the most self-referential, and also perhaps the most intertextual, of genres. I love the kind of romance novel which is about romance novels, because *all* romance novels are about romance novels in a way: no romance novel is romance-novel indifferent.

No romance novel can be romance indifferent. It is probably more fair to say that nobody in a romance novel is anything indifferent, at least not by the end. Indifference, in a romance novel, is a disease to be cured; left untreated, it's always fatal.

The romance novel is a playground for feelings for the reader (and, perhaps, for the writer), and so the people who live inside the romance novel will never stay neutral. They can't. Neutral feelings are the territory of the sparse, slim literary volume, and I barely buy the idea of neutrality there either. People aren't neutral, not really. They might have mixed feelings, or contradictory feelings, but not no feelings.

What If We Kissed in the Community Library?

Never no feelings! Even – especially – the kind of people who would like to pretend so. A cold-hearted billionaire, for instance, who self-medicates his childhood trauma by keeping everyone at a distance; the girl jilted at the altar who can't let herself be swept away again, one way or another. Still waters never run deeper than in the closed-off characters of romantic fiction; and sense and sensibility, sooner or later, will be gone with the wind. You can try all you want to be Miss Dashwood, but you'll end up as Mrs. Ferrars. However silly you think romance is, romance has other ideas.

A heroine in a romance novel knows perfectly well the shape that romances take. We all do. Boy meets girl, boy loses girl, boy wins girl, and sometimes vice versa. She knows either what she's missing out on, or eschewing with a firm hand. She knows what she's lost, if she's the kind of heroine who starts by being betrayed; she knows what she's never had, if she's the kind of heroine who starts by leaving rather than being left. Whether you are a reader or a writer of romances, you know the shape of stories. You know the pull of stories.

The romance-writer romance novel is always an experiment in metatext: any story which begins with a writer and a blank page is either a confession or a journey. But let me tell you a secret: a story that begins with a writer staring at a blank page is *also* always a love story. This is because the kind of story that begins with a writer staring at a blank page is always a story about a writer trying to fall back in love with writing; and it's always a story with a happy ending

– or, at least, a satisfying ending? – because we know the writer will triumph by the end. If not the writer, at least *a* writer is going to triumph: we are holding the proof in our hands. Such things, such happy endings, are possible. These endings are the ultimate striving towards happiness; they are the ultimate in attempts to make something good out of a brand-new, fresh page. Which is, of course, all love stories ever are. Maybe that's why I love them.

The definition of a romance novel continues to elude me. I still don't know how to tell you what counts, except that what counts for me might not count for you. And yet, maybe this is as good a working definition as I can get to right now: romantic fictions are stories that believe the arc of the universe bends towards love, and they will use all the building blocks at their disposal to make you believe it too.

Love for friends, for family, for chosen family; for Twiglets and cut grass and bobbly jumpers and sky-high Manolos; for buttery soft leather jackets and the wide open sky of the prairie; for your scatty best friend or your elderly aunt or your grumpy co-worker; for your home, and for far away; for the new guy at work or the girl on the bus. For the people in the library. For the peeling paint. Maybe even for the guy in the loincloth taking out twenty-two books about frogs and toads, now thickly littered with Post-it notes and scraps of notebook paper. (So that's what he was doing in the basement!) For the people around us; for community; for things we know, and things we don't know. For everything, in short.

What If We Kissed in the Community Library?

Romantic fiction tells us that there is a space for love in this world, and I, for one, want more than anything to believe it.

These books – these are the ones I mean. But you already knew that.

2

A Truth Universally Acknowledged

It is a truth universally acknowledged that any essay about Jane Austen, or even one which merely touches lightly upon her works – the smallest, most fleeting reference – must be in want of a poorly rendered paraphrasing of her most famous opening lines.

Actually, as opening lines go, it is perhaps not just the most famous of Austen's, but the most famous in all literature; and certainly the most parodied, mimicked and retold. "It was the best of times; it was the worst of times" may resonate in every terrible century, but it tends to be lifted wholesale, like an illustrative picture, rather than copied like a template (the "blurst of times" notwithstanding). The same is true of surprisingly calibrated clocks and instructions to call him Ishmael; the opening might be iconic, but the shape of the line lives only in the specifics of that sentence.

A truth universally acknowledged, however, can run and run. For a novel more than two hundred years old, *Pride and Prejudice* can lend itself to practically any modern-day situation: the Labour Party's plan to clean up Britain's waterways, for example, or the idea that "C-suite executives" need more friends. The linguist Geoff Nunberg, in a radio show marking two centuries since Jane Austen's death, managed to find it used to sell emergency contraceptives, business class flights, and pension schemes.

It acts as a marker that the person writing the piece is clever, but not too clever; has read at least one book, or at least is familiar with one *line* of at least one book, but not a book – like *Ulysses* or *Gravity's Rainbow* – that might intimidate anyone. A book, in other words, so often adapted, retold and mimicked that it feels like it belongs to us already, whether we've read it or not.

The tone is knowing, wry and just a shade ironic.

(And this knowing tone is, of course, also ironic, because in the hand of a writer other than Austen *a truth universally acknowledged* becomes shorthand – in real terms – only for the fact that the author has read that line before.)

When a writer of newspapers, or blogs, or whatever, tells us that a truth is universally acknowledged, they mean just what they say. When Austen tells us that a truth is universally acknowledged, we question every word in the sentence. What, for instance, comprises the "universe" in *Pride and Prejudice*? And what, exactly, is the nature of "truth"?

When we read those words in an article, we're being invited to understand that we, ourselves, are the universe in question. The Austen parody serves as a cheat code to connection. We both understand the allusion; we understand each other; therefore we are, from the start, already on the same side.

The writer is a smart and thoughtful person because they have mentioned Austen! The reader, who recognises the

A Truth Universally Acknowledged

Austen reference, is also a smart and thoughtful person! We are of the same universe; we acknowledge the same truths, ideally those which are about to follow. Whether that's the need to clean up Britain's waterways, take action on emergency contraceptives, business class flights, C-suite executives or pension schemes, we who understand the same literary references, are on the same team. The line gets used, I suppose, as a kind of shibboleth for a social class system: we understand each other, and so we understand these truths together.

Which is, of course, the *exact opposite* of Austen's writing. You can read all of Austen as a series of tests of the social order. What are the boundaries here? What could break them? Who could break them, and what would happen if they did? The opening of *Pride and Prejudice* simultaneously makes and unmakes the world for the reader: there are rules to play by, which means there must also be players to test those rules. We walk right into a world of reason and rationality, of sense and sensibility, of acknowledged truths, yes, but also the subtler questions of social order that somehow simultaneously undermine and underpin them. It's almost metatextual: this is a story in which people tell themselves stories about the ways other people tell stories. This is a story *about* story; a narrative about the narratives of romance, sex, money, class and the social order.*

---

* Which is, of course, why she's not just the mother of romance novels – but, in some ways, all modern novels. This is how pretty much all modern novels work, which is perhaps why Austen remains so startlingly current.

(Which are, of course, all myths in and of themselves. What's money but a narrative to make sense of the world? What's class but a narrative to make sense of the narrative of money?)

The scholar Rachel M. Brownstein argues that if Austen skipped the first seven words, and went straight in with *a single man in want of a wife*, we would expect something more akin to a modern romance novel. We can take from this, I think, that Brownstein means something less rich, less complex and ironic and thoughtful than Austen; and also that Brownstein has not read very many modern romance novels. Austen is the mother of romance novels precisely *because* she holds the heaviest and lightest of ideas as if they weighed just the same. We can call her the mother of romance novels because these things that she pioneered – the richness, the complexity, the idea that people move in trackable patterns and that those patterns are worthy of our attention – are the things that are common to all good romantic fiction.

The mistake people who don't read romance novels make is that they think that people who *do* read romance novels don't understand what romance novels do. We do understand it. I actually think – and this is daring – we who read romance, and we who love it, might understand it better than people who do neither.

What Brownstein means, I think, is that the first seven words of *Pride and Prejudice* are key to our understanding that what follows will not be a simple romance; what

Brownstein's analysis misses, maybe, is that no romances are ever simple.

A romance in which the two leads meet, find each other perfect and perfectly suited, and encounter no further friction is a romance that's going nowhere on the first page, let alone on the three hundredth page. No romance, fictional or otherwise, comes without a single complication (even the first-love teenage sweethearts are bound to run into a hiccup once in a while); all fictional romances are freckled with trouble. Always have been. *The course of true love*, as someone wise once said, *never did run smooth*.

The thing about quoting Shakespeare – much like quoting Austen – is that when you pluck the pithiest words from their surrounding context, something usually gets lost along the way.

For aught that I could ever read, Lysander explains to his would-be wife, *or could ever hear by tale or history, the course of true love never did run smooth.*

A Midsummer Night's Dream is the ultimate romantic fiction (even romantic comedy), and like almost all romantic fiction, it's self-aware: romantic fiction knows itself, knows its own history. Lysander's line is not just about love, but about representations of love. It tells us again what not only Austen but every romance writer before or since has made clear: if it's not a *difference in blood* (social position; financial position; racial or religious or cultural difference), it's *misgraffed in respect of years* (age-gap books, come through), *or else it stands upon the choice of friends*; *or if there were a sympathy in choice, war, death, or sickness [do] lay siege to it.* Romantic fiction is mostly about two people, but it's also always about the world in which they live, and the ways the world shapes and scars and marks the people within it.

We are, in some ways, everyone we've ever met; we carry them with us in fragments, building selves out of the things they left behind and the things we took. We are walking libraries; catalogues of everything that's ever happened to us. We are galaxies in animal skins, and when two people fall in love they also bring with them everyone they've ever loved, and everyone they've ever hated, and everything that's ever happened to them, and everything they have ever known. You can't fall in love in a vacuum.* You carry with you all your baggage; there is always blood, years, friends, war, death, sickness. There are always complications.

You cannot write about people in love as separate from the world that made them.

We love in context.

Every romance writer knows this; every romance reader knows it too.

It is a truth perhaps rather less universally acknowledged that every romance novel is a social history of the time that made it. No romance novel, however commercial, can be divorced from the socioeconomic background of its characters and its creation. The "romance novel", as we understand

---

* Metaphorically speaking. I'm sure someone has written an incredible black hole romance.

romance novels, has to wrestle with class and money and work and friends and death and desperation; the romance writer has to hold all of these threads together in the shape of two people, and never let them go. The romance writer has to hold the *universal truths* as lightly as she holds the *single man in possession of a good fortune*, along with his putative future wife. This holding of threads, lightly, is what romance novels do; this is why they are so compelling.

Romance novels are, by design, a space for dreaming, but does that make them a wish-fulfilment station? Many people have tried to draw direct parallels between the kind of stories women buy, and the kind of lives they want to lead, the kind of people they want to love, the kind of sex they want to have. It's true that most people, I think, would like to be loved; it's true that most people would like to feel safe; it's true that most people would like to have good sex. (It is also undeniably true that there was a two-thirds increase in admission to American emergency units for kink-related accidents the year that *Fifty Shades* got big. Draw your own conclusions.)

But it's not as simple as that.

The tension at the heart of *every* romance novel lives not just in the space between what we have and what we need, but in the space between what we want, and what we want to want. It is, I think, a feature of pretty much all romance novels that the key characters are kept apart by some powerful force: the force might be internal (like a past trauma), or external (like an overbearing father or a war), but even when the force is external, it's more often an emotional, interior response to such agents that is the real reason for their separation.

The heroine, for example, *wants* to be the kind of person who can please an overbearing father; the heroine *wants* to be the kind of person who can stay away from love to avoid ever getting hurt again. The hero wants to be the kind of person who doesn't fuck things up for his politician mother. He wants to be the kind of person who doesn't let anyone make his life unduly complicated. He wants to want the right kind of woman, or any woman at all; she wants to want the nice, boring boyfriend she's had every day of her adult life until the first, already hot page of this sapphic romance novel. He wants to want to marry the fiancée he secretly proposed to as a teenager, despite the people they've both grown up to be; she wants to be the kind of person who wants to marry the man carrying the family entail.

The type-A med student *wants* to want an equally high-flying doctor, but she falls for the warm and smoky woodsman in the town where her car breaks down; the kind-hearted bookshop owner wants to want to save her store, but the big-time bookshop magnate is going to buy her out – and she can't stop loving him. A haughty millionaire meets a clever girl from an unsuitable family. Her family stress him out; he's rude to her; she snubs him. In vain he will struggle! It will not do! He doesn't want to love her; she doesn't want to love him. The world is full of complications, and it seems we carry most of them inside ourselves.

A Truth Universally Acknowledged

This is what romance novels are for: they are for exploring the gaps between who we thought we were, and who we actually are. All romance happens in that space, because that's the space of possibility – and love is above all an exercise in possibility. One function of reading romance, then, might be self-revelation. Would I want this? What do I want? And who am I?

Romance novels are, too, an exercise in possibility. It's that paint palette again: how will the colours come together this time? How will you keep me guessing, even as I know all the answers?

Which is, of course, the same question we ask ourselves about all relationships, especially long-term ones, especially monogamous ones, especially ones that feel like a romance novel themselves. How will this stay new when I know? How can something be both familiar and erotic, when – as the therapist and author Esther Perel says – the erotic is the opposite of the familiar? Desire, she says, needs mystery to thrive; and intimacy is the opposite of mystery; and yet intimacy is what we crave. Perel's Paradox (as surely it must be known by now), based on her book *Mating in Captivity*, is designed to understand why people have affairs, but it's also helpful in understanding why people read romance novels – even though, as our detractors love to point out, we already know the ending.

And, in some cases, we know every beat of the plot.

And we still can't get enough.

* * *

If the opening lines of *Pride and Prejudice* are the most parodied, repurposed and retold, the plot of *Pride and Prejudice* is surely not far behind in the re-creation race. The opening lines might now sell everything from contraception to political allegiance, but the characters, or the setting, or the plot, have sold millions and millions of romance novels. *It is a truth universally acknowledged*, writes Jane Austen; but so too do Helen Fielding, Ali Hazelwood and Julia Quinn, among many, many others.

My searches through Amazon, Wikipedia and eight million Reddit threads threw up nearly two hundred authors publishing over a thousand books explicitly marketed as *Pride and Prejudice* retellings. This is categorically an understatement. These – often in ten- or twelve-book series – are only the ones that blare it on the covers. It's impossible to find them all: you would have to read every romance novel ever written (and I have done my best, but I'm only human), and carefully map each plot against Austen's original to dig them all out.

There are, of course, dozens of adaptations for the stage, screen and little screen that cleave fairly faithfully to Austen's original text. But what is interesting to us, in this experiment of trying to understand the ways we read romance, are the stories that take Austen as a starting point, then run with it. If we're trying to unpack the reasons romance readers seek out tropes, what better place to begin than the story which in some ways created the modern sense of trope?

Of course, there are tropes in Austen that existed *before* Austen. The arrogant man, the clever girl who outwits him,

A Truth Universally Acknowledged

the many sisters and the ambitious mamma might all come straight from a fairy tale. You could read Mr. Darcy as an upside-down Bluebeard, or a tameable wolf. Lizzy Bennet as a plucky goose girl, a Red Riding Hood, a Little Red Hen ... doing it herself, her own way. Leaving your many sisters behind is a time-honoured fairy-tale tradition; so, too, is falling in love with something that frightens you. So, too, is a happy ending in which not everything can be saved: Longbourn is always lost, because you *can't go home again*.

Which is itself – as the writer Daniel Handler notes in his memoir – the title of a 1940 novel by Thomas Wolfe which "most people have never read" and which, certainly, "nobody has read in decades". A title that has been endlessly reused, paraphrased and borrowed – and was itself borrowed from an Australian British activist named Ella Winter. The sentence – any sentence – lives outside of the text and the context from which it emerged. The "death of the author" (used mostly now to reassure people it's all right to consume art by bad people) really means only that the things we create have a life independent of their creators.* They belong not to their authors, but to their readers. Some works never live;

---

* A question Claire Dederer's *Monsters* unpicks with panache. Ironically, one might describe the premise of this book as a defence of *"bad"* art by *good* people: a defence of much-derided art made for, with, by, and about joy. One thing I love about romance novels is that I don't worry about their artistic credentials: I just love them, and understand them, and take great comfort from them, and absorb their meaning into my life forever. The thing, in fact, that art is supposed to do. "Good" and "bad": tough categories! Tough calls!

others go on being reshaped forever. We are not tired of retelling Greek myths, stories of Roman gods, or the books of the Bible. Some stories run and run.

Literature is all a series of borrowings, references, repurposes and reimaginings of ideas – and yet it's really only in genre fiction that people worry about it. It's hard to know how to define a "retelling", exactly, but let's say there's a spectrum with "fanfiction" at one end and "all literature" at the other.

The psychoanalyst Carl Jung thought that all stories come from somewhere deep in the human psyche; that we share, as human beings, a kind of collective unconscious full of universal inherited ideas. We all have, Jung argued, a universal sense of *father*, of *child*, of *flood*; we all know what it means to *love* and to *belong* and to *fear* without needing to be taught. We know *maiden* and *mother*, we know *shadow* and *self*, men know women and women know men. These universal ideas, drawn together, form our dreams; our dreams form our myths; our myths form our stories. All stories come from these stories. All stories are retellings, one way or another. It's kind of a strange idea, if you think about it, closer to the nature of a story itself than to scientific study. How could we know if we would have Jung's story-shapes in our minds without the stories we are already telling and retelling? How could we know what came first?

Many cultures have romantic folktales. Many cultures have romantic myths and legends, tragedies and heroines and the stars and the sun. All cultures, I think – though I'm not an expert by any means – have love, sex, possession and passion as key and driving forces in their narratives. These cut right to the heart of who we are as living things, competing for warmth, and light, and a future. No wonder, then, that these are the stories that we can't stop telling. No wonder that these are the stories that have lasted forever.

The stories we told as cave people around those first campfires became legends, and legends became songs sung by bards, and songs sung by bards became songs sung by everybody. Orpheus and Eurydice, Lancelot and Elaine, Tristan and Isolde: these are the Greek myths and the Arthurian legends – big, beautiful, tragic love stories – which Lysander read, the stories that convinced him that the course of true love never did run smooth.

We can say now that a romance demands a happy ending, but these romances demanded a sad ending: a broken heart, a correct punishment for stolen kisses, an enduring sense of justice and of fate. They were the same; they were different; and yet the need to tell stories about romance is as old as time and wide as the world.

Proof of this: Bolu Babalola's extremely good romantic short story collection, *Love in Colour*, which updates a dozen myths from all over the globe, and all of remembered history. Osun! Psyche! Nefertiti! Zhinu! Romance abounds. Kissing abounds. Disaster abounds. And yet it takes Babalola's deft hand to bring them into the shape of a modern-day romance. It takes Babalola, a writer raised on *The Notebook*, *Bridget Jones's Diary*, and above all Jane

Austen, to shape these ancient love stories into something that fits the "romantic fiction" template.

Because this thrilling rollcall – from Nigerian goddesses to Celtic princesses, Greek nymphs to Chinese butterflies, Shakespeare to Scheherazade – doesn't *really* register as "romantic fiction" otherwise. It just hits different! I know it, and you know it too. Nothing really registers as *actual romantic fiction* until Austen.

She was simply the first, I think, to string these tropes together in the way we have come to know as romantic: she gives us the meet-cute, the third-act crisis, the last-chapter grovel just when we want them. The shape of the story is irresistible to the romance reader – and the romance writer. The story just *feels* true. It just feels right. It's compelling – an Escher painting of a thought – to wonder how much that *rightness* comes from the constant presence of Austen. It feels impossible to tell now whether Jane Austen simply excelled at the telling of romances, or if our conception of excellence in romance stems from the way Austen told them. Do we have Jung's archetypes in our heads because we tell each other these stories, or do the stories come from our deep need to express those inner archetypes? Does our understanding of how romantic fiction functions stem from her work? Do we think of romantic narratives as we do *because* of the way Austen wrote them? And is this why we retell her novels so amazingly frequently?

The retellings span all of time and space, and pay varying levels of homage. There are the obvious ones – *Pride and*

Prejudice and Zombies – and the beloved ones – *Bridget Jones's Diary*. There are the straightforward sequels – *Mr. & Mrs. Fitzwilliam Darcy* – and alternative universes (what if Elizabeth accepted Darcy's first proposal? See *Unequal Affections*, by Lara S. Ormiston). *Falling for Mr Darcy* by KaraLynne Mackrory carries the subtitle "A Pride and Prejudice Variation": same characters, same setting, a completely different plot. (She twists her ankle and has to be carried home: more Marianne Dashwood than Lizzy Bennet.)

There are many retellings from Darcy's perspective (*An Assembly Such as This,* Pamela Aidan); from the perspective of Charlotte Lucas, Georgiana Darcy and Anne de Bourgh (a minor character at best!); *Longbourn*, by Jo Baker, is a retelling from the perspectives of the servants of the house. *Pride and Prometheus* matches up Mary Bennet with Dr Frankenstein (!), while *The Other Bennet Sister* merely gives Mary the happy ending for which all damp squib sisters were holding out the whole time. (Neither book, by the way, is played for laughs.)

Mary Bennet also steps into a starring role in *Miss Bennet's Dragon*, the first of a trilogy by M. Verant, in which Lizzy can talk to dragons. This is, increasingly unsurprisingly, one of many dragon-related retellings of *Pride and Prejudice*. "Some may call the stories wild and say that they bear no resemblance to the original, but Wilson finds Miss Austen's characters timeless and inspirational," announces the blurb on Enid Wilson's collection of short stories *My Darcy Mutates* ... before following it up with a warning that "this title contains explicit adult content, leather kilts, ropes and flying dragons". If you prefer your retellings to be explicitly faithful, but still full of dragons, there is also *Heartstone*, by Elle K. White. If you have no time for fantasy – and no time for history – Curtis Sittenfeld's *Eligible* casts Liz Bennet as a magazine writer in Cincinnati (with Chip Bingley as reality TV star; Fitz Darcy as a neurosurgeon). In *Just As You Are*, Camille Kellogg casts her as a gender-queer magazine writer, this time in New York, whose beloved lesbian magazine is bought out by mean butch Daria Fitzgerald (who *hates* Liz's listicles). Ann Herendeen goes back to the Regency era, but makes everyone gay (Lizzy/Charlotte, Darcy/Bingley); Rachael Lippincott sends just one modern-day teenage heroine back to Georgian England and lets her fall for the Lizzy Bennet stand-in all by herself.

Every Bennet sister gets her own retelling – often multiple retellings. Kitty Bennet has *What Kitty Did Next* and *Her Summer at Pemberley*; *The Scandalous Confessions of Lydia Bennet, Witch* does what it says on the tin. Settings range from "Bennet House, the only all-women's dorm at Longbourn University" to a shabby burlesque club and "a small moon in the Londinium lunar system".[*]

There are mysteries – *Death Comes to Pemberley*, by the greatest to ever do it, P. D. James – and big social themes: *Pride: A Pride and Prejudice Remix*, by Ibi Zoboi, transplants

---

[*] *The Bennet Women*, Eden Appiah-Kubi, 2021; *A Certain Appeal*, Vanessa King, 2021; *Pride and Prejudice in Space*, Alexis Lampley, 2024.

the story to modern-day Afro-Latino Brooklyn (will Zuri Benitez fall for "judgmental and arrogant" Darius? Can they together stand in the path of gentrification?); *Unmarriageable: Pride and Prejudice in Pakistan*, by Soniah Kamal, sees Alys Binat and Valentine Darsee grapple with the impact of Partition and British colonialism while (of course) falling in love; and DJ Liza would never, ever fall for evil property developer Dorsey in Nikki Payne's *Pride and Protest*.

And this, of course, is to say nothing of all the fanfiction: set in legal offices, Lovecraftian swamps, restaurants in upstate New York and "Nassau (1719)", featuring "*genuine* apologies this time!!!", "non-consensual blood drinking" and a "bad idea taken seriously". All told, there must be upwards of ten thousand reworkings of this single novel, some faithful, some – as the fanfic community would put it – "crack".

And listen. While writing this, I added so many of them to my TBR.

I want to read – not *all* of them, to be fair, but – so many of them. The pirate crossover! The Lydia Bennet witch! The trans academics! I want to see how people shuffle the cards, and what story they can play out from the story I know inside out. I know the rules here; let me use those rules to measure other worlds, other societies, other ideas. Let me use the shape of the thing I know to better understand the thing I don't. The story becomes an outline through which to see the colours of other lives; the trope becomes a yardstick by which to measure the depth of feeling.

We understand innately that life is chaos; that romance is never free of complication; that love is always in context. All good romantic fiction understands this, and one reason we find romance so compelling is surely *because* of these complications. We know vividly the ways in which these complications crowd us in our own lives. There is always something else happening: some trauma, some trouble, some fight between the hero and heroine, between society and self. There is so much going on, and yet in romantic fiction, one clear emotion cuts through the noise. It lends us a clarity that we can use, maybe, to make sense of our own personal narratives: there will be many things that happen to you, in your life, and you will feel many feelings, and here are some ways to fold them in.

If romance novels are, in some ways, a reshuffling of tropes, then romance novels also allow us to play with existing narratives and come to satisfying conclusions every time. Maybe, in some ways, we're learning from them how to play the hand we're dealt. We're learning how to reshuffle the cards we have into something that suits us better. As for the women in Janice Radway's survey, romance reading is not a mere exercise in escape, but an exercise in more fully inhabiting the self we have, and the world we have.

Which is why, I suppose, we continue to retell Austen. The more often we retell her stories, the more power they gain as a machine for making things anew. The more we retell *Pride and Prejudice*, the deeper Lizzy Bennet goes into myth, and the more useful she becomes as a vehicle for ideas and for the

A Truth Universally Acknowledged

self; that is, the closer she becomes to a trope in and of herself, as a character. And as a trope, she is useful for this clarity of thought, and for the creation – unsought on her part and probably on Austen's – of intangible community that comes from knowing yourself among hundreds of thousands of other people who see themselves and their lives in one of the ten thousand Lizzy Bennets out there.

Pride and Prejudice has, by dint of all these retellings, almost become a fairy tale itself, extant from Austen's work. We use her opening lines, perhaps, in the same way we use *once upon a time*. We set a mood; we make a society; we understand each other when we say her words.

We can't be far off the first Bridget Jones retellings coming into bookshops: would they still count as an Austen retelling? How far can we travel before Lizzy and Darcy become legend? But no, wait – we're already there. If there are 167 authors, as per my hasty bookshop trawls, writing direct retellings, there are thousands more writing in Austen's shadow. Or rather, thousands more writing in her light.

You can see Lizzy in every bright, frustrated romance heroine; you can see her in everyone hanging up on their mum, everyone with a troubling younger sister and a much more beautiful older sister (hello, Jo March!), everyone turning down the person they love out of sheer vengeance and spite. You can see Lizzy Bennet everywhere.

And as for Darcy?

Consider every grumpy billionaire book you've ever read, and see Darcy live forever.

3

The Hot Billionaires Are Back

If you trace the lineage of Fitzwilliam Darcy all the way back, you get to the Beast.

If you run the lineage of Fitzwilliam Darcy all the way forward, you get to Rupert Campbell-Black.

This is the ancestry of the Hot Billionaire.

It is, perhaps, the most enduring of all tropes.

"Dude! Forbes just named you the World's Hottest Billionaire!" might be my favourite opening to a romance novel of all time (it is, of course, by Elsie Silver), because it so perfectly gives the people what they want. There is no pretence; there is no subtlety. We don't need it. Romantic fiction is the true home of the Hot Billionaire; when I see a Hot Billionaire rise up unbidden in some other, more heavy-going work of fiction I always wonder whether the author knows how neatly their serious novel fits into other, lovelier genres. Because it always does: the emergence of a Hot Billionaire basically tips any novel into a romance novel. Not a regular billionaire, of course, but a Hot Billionaire. There is a clear difference, and you know it – like pornography – when you see it.)

Is money inherently sexy? I suppose that depends on whether power is inherently sexy, which, of course, it is. Or:

power is inherently tied up with the erotic. The sex/money/power triad is pretty close to being eternal: the prospect of swapping "crushing financial worries" for "hot sex with someone who loves you" has, as an economic and social proposition, never quite gone out of style. Indeed, the simple trade of sex for money is as old as it gets.

Sex work is called "the oldest profession" for a reason, and some Hot Billionaire books do feature sex work: escort-turned-spouse is a fairly familiar pathway, and fake dating tropes, while not explicitly about sex work, often have an undeniable sex-work-y quality when there is money involved. But the boundaries around sex work can be profoundly porous: a permeable membrane through which various Hot Billionaires and their humble lovers can pass at will. And what is inescapable, once you step onto this train of thought, is the degree to which all heterosexual relationships have historically been very difficult to define in a way that definitively excludes sex work. The trade of sexuality for economic freedom is entwined with the most fundamental structures of our society: the traditional middle-class heterosexual nuclear family, for instance, in which he goes out to work, and she stays home with the babies; or the still-prevalent expectation that he pays on a first date, and in exchange she puts out. There remains an economic imbalance within almost all modern societies that is given counterweight only by female sexual power: women often find themselves famous for being the wives, girlfriends, lovers and even concubines of men in ways that are rarely true in reverse. (Taylor Swift's boyfriends honourably excepted.)

Even queer sexuality is queer in a world structured around this fundamental truth: men tend to have significantly more power, and more money, than women. To be a woman in love with a woman, or a man in love with a man, or to excuse yourself from the gender binary altogether, is to at least attempt to reject these strictures. It is to step away from the edge of the cliff and ask yourself why everyone else continues to cheerfully hurl themselves over. (Even as nobody is entirely exempt from misogyny.)

Heteronormativity is a self-replicating process. Even the most alert and awake of straight couples struggle to escape it: who does the bulk of the housework? who drives? who buys cushions? who remembers birthdays? Even if you have deliberately defaulted from gendered stereotypes, you can't escape the ways you *have* paid up, and been made to pay up: you can't help but know the things you feel smug about, or the things you feel weird about, or the things you wonder whether you should feel weird about, or the things you feel you have to fight for despite how absurdly, obviously right and useful and ordinary they feel in your own life. (For a fairly uncontroversial example: shared parental leave.)

You cannot engage romantically with men without engaging with the systems and structures put in place explicitly and implicitly to keep *you* in *your* place: it's simply not possible. It has to be addressed, one way or another: you can lean in, you can fight it, but you cannot pretend that you're exempt. Like the wind in a desert, the great sweep of heterosexuality has built us sand dunes to climb, and gaps to fall into, and hollows to hide in. It could have been neutral once, but now it's a landscape and that landscape needs to be navigated somehow.

None of this is new information, and the degree to which you're appalled by it is up to you. It is perfectly possible to find these structures rational but not erotic, or erotic but insane. Or even neither, though it is, I think, quite difficult to imagine a thesis of straight sex that is not erotically entangled with gender politics. The interchange and exchange of power for sex for money for sex for power is so woven through the intimate relationships between men and women that it is, I believe, fundamentally impossible to attempt to entirely unweave, or separate, the two. Can straight sex ever escape the power dynamics of heteronormativity? Can the personal ever overcome the political? And would we want it to? The trope of the Hot Billionaire says not.

Or, at least, not right now.

There are, at the time of writing, about four hundred female billionaires in the world. There are almost three thousand male billionaires. I suspect that this percentage (almost 90 per cent male) is *still* more diverse than the Hot Billionaires of modern romance.

The Hot Billionaire is a strongly gendered ideal, but it's worth noting that it has not always been so.

The 1980s, for instance, gave us Shirley Conran's bonkbuster-defining *Lace*: four women, their lust for power, and the men they leave in their wake. Having met at boarding school in Switzerland, Maxine, Pagan, Judy and Kate (Conran's alter ego) go on to become a hotel magnate, society fundraiser, America's most successful PR woman and the editor of the world's most famous women's magazine (*Verve*!) respectively. It's sex all the way down. Some of the sex is good; some of the sex is terrible; some of the sex is insane. Some of the sex is consensual; some of the sex is consensual by the standards of the 1980s and questionable by those of today; some of it is explicitly non-consensual. Some of it is romantic. Much of it is not. But our heroines rarely lose focus for long.

My own introduction to *Lace* came in the school library. Not that the school library possessed a copy, you understand; *Lace* was not the kind of thing they wanted us reading. But I was in the library: it was PE, I was pretending to have a hurt foot or something. I was in the library, eavesdropping on a teacher and the librarian talking.

The teacher was holding a confiscated copy of Philippa Gregory's *The Other Boleyn Girl*. I knew instantly that it was the copy from our class. You could tell it was the copy from our class because the spine was cracked in a very specific place: it was cracked at just the right place so that the book would fall open to reveal Anne Boleyn in bed together with her brother and their shared lover. The spine was cracked at that page because every girl in class – maybe even in school – had read it. Not the whole book, you understand: just the sex scene. Just the incestuous threesome scene. This was why the novel had been confiscated. My friend Sarah had been the first to find the *sex* – she had marked it neatly with a bookmark, then brought it back for everyone to have a look at. We were rabid for it. We could not believe it. It felt like a cold clean shock to the heart. You can write that? In a *book*? A book you can buy in a normal *shop*? We were thirteen years old and it was like looking up on a cold clear night: terrifying, vast, unfathomable.

The teacher was laughing. "I don't know what to do with it," she confessed to the librarian. "I took it off them but I don't know what I'm supposed to be telling them off for. They're all reading it. I can't give them behaviour reports for *reading*, can I?"

The librarian was laughing too. She flipped the book open to the page and read it. I couldn't see her face but it sounded like she was raising her eyebrows. "Listen," she said. "It could be worse. We used to do that with the goldfish scene in *Lace*."

"Oh my God," said the teacher. She sounded like we felt: like she had just seen too much of the sky. "Oh my God. *The goldfish scene in* Lace*!*"

I had to find it. I had to know. I was thirteen years old and everything was about to get a whole lot weirder.

This is, I think, the most perfect way to experience *Lace* – aside, perhaps, from having someone in your Year 9 class actually hand it to you, and tell you it's the dirtiest book you'll ever read. Instead, I got to be the person handing it round. "She actually does it! With a fish!" I said. This is not what is happening in that scene, but I was thirteen. I didn't know anything about anything. None of us did, but we were all wide-eyed and fascinated. It is true and bonkers that Conran actually started writing *Lace* as a guide to sex for schoolgirls, an origin story so compelling that it feels like a story in its own right. What kind of schoolgirls? What kind of guide? Who commissioned that book, and what in the holy gender dynamics was going on there? Presumably it was not intended as a friendly "boys and girls have different parts" type business, with fact-based, line-drawn pictures. Presumably one would not ask Conran to write *that*. Anyway: it immediately sold three million copies.

It's hard to know if *Lace* counts as a romance novel. Much like Danielle Steel, Conran has said on record that she would rather be removed from this narrative. "I write about the human condition," Steel told CBS a few years ago. "I think of romance novels as more of a category and I write about the situations we all deal with." While most romances also handle "the situations we all deal with", it's true that there's something about Steel – and Conran – that sets her apart from the kind of romance novels I mostly reach for. Even with a happy ending, there's something separate about them: the bonkbuster as a genre overlaps with romance, but isn't always entirely the same. (Jilly Cooper, I think, straddles both. Classic Jilly.)

Passion's Promise and *Matters of the Heart* (two standout Steel novels) might sound like romances, but they don't hold precisely the same function: if sex is implicitly about power, then in the bonkbuster the implicit is made explicit. For a woman to sleep with her boss in sole pursuit of a pay rise would, in a modern romance novel, be viewed as surreal: a reason for the reader to think less of her (and less of the hero), a reason to see her not as an avatar for ourselves, but as another and more desperate kind of woman.

In a bonkbuster, however, such an act is applauded. How else would you get to the top? Why would you not use every weapon at your disposal in pursuit of your own power?

There's a certain kind of '80s shoulder-pad feminism that finds the art of the romance novel to be a backwards step, and sometimes I wonder if such feminists might be right. To read *Lace* now is to marvel at the idea that there could exist a book for women, by women, in which women fuck and fight and generally claw their way to the top of their professions, *and that book would be a huge commercial success, beloved by everyone from adolescents to OAPs.* I do not think *Lace* would be published today. And if it were, I think there would need to be a beautiful love story at its heart. *Lace* is concerned with (in this order) power, female friendship, and sex. Slow-burn romance it is not. The Hot Billionairess is not interested in bestowing money on a humble man; she is interested in making her own money and hanging onto it, regardless of the terrible things men continue to do. The Hot Billionairess is a billionairess entirely outwith her sexuality, *even when her financial success directly correlates to her sexual exploits.* And the Hot Billionairess is no longer in vogue.

The Hot Billionairess, now, is pretty much exclusively a figure of lesbian ("sapphic") romance, if she is anywhere – which she mostly isn't. Perhaps this is simply a reflection of reality; perhaps, though, the reality is more complex.

The reality is that there is no ethical way to be a billionaire.

Or without sugarcoating it: *there is no ethical way to be rich.*

There is not even an ethical way to be a tiny bit rich, not really.

To be rich – rich in the way that a Hot Billionaire has to be rich, rich in the way of smoothing over every problem, rich in the way of buying apartment blocks and flying on a private jet – is to be, fundamentally, complicit in all the worst abuses of capitalism. The Hot Billionaire, then, gives us as readers access to capital without the shame of acquisition. It is power without responsibility; it is wealth without shadow.

Even more so than the Hot Billionaire, the Hot Billionairess begs the question of the origin of her money – and to be frank, why aren't we reading *that* story? If a woman is going to rapidly acquire wealth, I want to see how she does it. I want to be in on the rags-to-riches climb. I want to see how Cinderella makes it happen. I want to see the Shirley Conran of it all. Which is not the point of a Hot Billionaire book. The point of a Hot Billionaire book is to imagine money; the point of a Hot Billionaire book is *not* to imagine toil.

There are, it must be said, quite a lot of excellent books (C. W. Farnsworth!) where the Hot Billionaire and the Hot Billionairess must get together for the good of their respective empires. These are, I posit, not true Hot Billionaire books. They are, in fact, *marriages of equals*, and are therefore simply regular romance novels that happen to be set in the universe of money.

The thing is, the heroine of every true Hot Billionaire romance is a Cinderella – basically hard-working, generally put upon, and totally deserving.

She is, for instance, often a journalist writing a story about the Hot Billionaire (see Cat Sebastian's *You Should Be So Lucky* for the gayest, cutest, most trouble-free version; see Mhairi McFarlane's *Who's That Girl?* for *Game of Thrones* actor fanfic, plus extremely nice "but how does this actually *work*" celebrity-regular-gal sequel). She might be the flight attendant on his private jet.* She might be his ex-girlfriend, accidentally hired to decorate his house.† She might – to really go rogue – be the cheerfully freckled bicycle courier delivering papers to his office, whereupon she immediately becomes the willing fourth in his existing queer knife-play BDSM triad. (Name! That! Book!)‡

While she is not always technically poor, she's certainly not in the same financial league as the Hot Billionaire.

---

* *Mile High*, Liz Tomforde, 2022.
† *Head Over Heels*, Jill Mansell, 1998 – interiors that shaped my entire taste.
‡ The truly insane – and dark erotica – *The Perfect Fit*, Sadie Kincaid, 2023.

The Hot Billionaires Are Back

She might be, in fact, working exclusively for him: is it possible to have a Sexy Nanny/Hot Single Dad book which doesn't follow the patterns set out by the Hot Billionaire? The power dynamic – he has power, she has none, until the sudden role reversal three quarters of the way through – seems to sketch out the same tropes and shapes as those of a Hot Billionaire.

Sometimes it's obvious. Liz Tomforde's *Caught Up*, for instance, is the story of Miller, a pastry chef in trouble, who is reluctantly hired by Kai as the nanny to his small son (who's been abandoned by his mother). Kai is a very wealthy baseball player; Miller needs his money, and his kitchen.

Or there's R. S. Grey's *Three Strikes and You're Mine*: Chloe is also a pastry chef in trouble, who is reluctantly hired by Luke, a very wealthy baseball player, as the nanny to his small daughter. She needs his money, and also his kitchen ... Oh, man, I love this genre. I love that I loved both of these books separately and didn't realise until right now that they share *the exact same plot*.

Caught Up is clearly a Hot Billionaire book. It is also clearly a Hot Single Dad book. It has the same power dynamic, beat for beat, as something like Talia Hibbert's *Untouchable*.[*] Nathaniel is a (normal, rich!) widower, and Hannah is his disgraced nanny. He may not have as much money as Kai or Luke the baseball players, but what he has,

---

[*] Talia Hibbert is good across the board, but my true favourite is *Get a Life, Chloe Brown*. Recommend!

she needs. She has to stay on his good side; he can lift her out of the world she's made for herself. The power dynamic is the same.

What is it, though, with the recurring themes of motherlessness in these books about powerful men? What is it about this kind of set-up that allows us to explore alternative ideas of family? Sadie Kincaid's *The Perfect Fit* is, on the surface, a book about three Hot Billionaires seeking out a penniless fourth – but it's also a book about the family we choose for ourselves.

E. L. James's *Fifty Shades of Grey* is the most famous Hot Billionaire book of the last twenty years – but it's really a story about maternal abandonment. "You're a sadist?" Ana asks her lover, shocked, in the first book. "I'm a dominant," he corrects her, sternly. "I want you to willingly surrender yourself to me, in all things." Three hundred pages, and several movies later, Christian Grey is on his knees. "I'm not a dominant," he sobs. "The right term is a sadist. I get off on punishing women who look like my mother." He holds up a photograph of his mother, a "crack addict". She looks, of course, exactly like Ana. It's not, shall we say, subtle. But subtlety is surely not the point: *Fifty Shades* kickstarted not just the aforementioned array of kink-related ER admissions, but a new avalanche of Hot Billionaire romances. Few stories, if any, are original; few authors embrace that truth as blatantly as E. L. James does; indeed, her global *Grey* phenomenon began life as *Twilight* fanfic. It's easy to think of this provenance scornfully, even snobbishly, but it's more interesting, I think, to cast it as a toolbox handed to the reader. Here's how you build a Hot Billionaire. Here's every individual Lego piece. He's frightening. He's frightened. His deep, unprocessed feelings about his mother are barely concealed beneath his expensive bespoke suit.

James, like Conran and Steel before her, does not see herself as a romance writer. She also does not see herself as part of the romance community in any way. She responds angrily to suggestions that she belongs there; that she belongs to us. And perhaps, if she had identified as a romance writer, she might have worked a little harder to conceal the joins in her narrative; and perhaps she would have inspired fewer others to take up their own stories. Perhaps, if she had understood more exactly what she was doing, if she'd worked more tightly to conventions, she might have been less successful.

But what of her hero? To position Christian Grey in the world of romantic fiction, we need to think first about Georgette Heyer. Most Georgette Heyer heroes can be classed as Hot Billionaires, if you adjust for inflation. She famously described her heroes as being either Mark I or Mark II: Mark I, "rude, overbearing, and often a bounder"; Mark II, "suave, well-dressed, [and] rich". Mark I: *sexy*. Mark II: *sweet*. (Or, in my opinion, at least *sweet-adjacent*.) Heyer scholars E. R. Glass and A. Mineo further break these Marks down into Type A: Darcy-Rochester; Type B: Rochester-Darcy; and Type C: Knightley. (The difference between A and B, should you be wondering what is implied by the neat little switch, is that a Darcy-Rochester is aloof and sarcastic; whereas a Rochester-Darcy is blunt and frank.)

These categories are delicious. But I think we can go further – deeper – for a more general classification. And to do that, we need to go right back to basics: right back to the start.

The Hot Billionaire, generally, takes many forms – dukes, princes, sports stars, tech kings, tortured mobsters, etc. – but these many forms can be simplified down into these two key *types* of Hot Billionaire: Prince Charmings, and Beasts.

You can roughly classify this as Good billionaires, and Bad billionaires. Charmings are good. Beasts are bad.

We are currently in a Beast era.

(We might even be in a Bluebeard era.)

This is because billionaires, as a category generally, are not currently in vogue. However, *no longer suffering financially* has never seemed a more delightful and appealing prospect.

Beasts, of course, have been cursed in some way – usually, but not always, generational trauma – and require a lover to break the spell. It could be a literal curse, as in from a witch; it could be childhood trauma, as in from a mother. (When fathers inflict childhood trauma – as they frequently do – it somehow still tends to be the mother's fault for not intervening. But of course. She's the one who features in his nightmares; she's the one he obsesses over; she's the one Christian Grey is still taking it out on, voodoo doll-style, twenty years later.)

So let's say that Beast!Hot Billionaire has usually been abandoned by his own mother, or at least raised neglectfully by a socialite who cared more about parties than about her innocent offspring. And Beast!Hot Billionaire: Single Dad type emerges frequently enough that the abandonment of his own offspring by *their* mother, his former lover, feels notable too. It's very fairy tale, isn't it, all this? Jung's archetypes of maiden and mother rise up and meet us.

The "crone" (Jung's delightful phrase for postmenopausal women) is often also present as an elderly aunt or best friend's mum. There is something profoundly interesting in how the Hot Billionaire trope, and romance novels taken as a whole, so often use the most traditional of heterosexual relationship structures to celebrate non-traditional and non-linear familial arrangements. We want, I think, both the nuclear family, and the wider village that the model of the nuclear family replaced.

Which is, of course, the kind of scope and generosity that we can only really find in romance novels: romance novels give us the ability, in many ways, to *have it all*. And the Hot Billionaire offers a practical, financial mechanism for having it all.

We want great wealth; and we want the freedom that comes with great wealth; and we also want the clean hands which could never have accumulated great wealth. We want power without the responsibility of power.

And yet, I think, we are *not stupid*. We are not naïve: we understand that there is no truly ethical way to be rich.

In Love with Love

Someone almost certainly had to suffer for all this: there is, inevitably, a price that must be paid.

The Hot Billionaire has had to pay the price. There is always the *curse*: he is a man with a terrible secret, a man suffering under the yoke of all this cruel and dreadful money. He is a man who doesn't *want* the love of a good woman but needs it all the same. He doesn't know he needs it, but, oh, how he needs it. The heroine has rocked up on his doorstep, uninvited. He does not seek her out; she doesn't seek him out either.

A vital point of difference between a Beast type and a Charming type is the level of seeking: a Charming is actively looking for Cinderella, but a Beast didn't ask for Beauty. A Beast probably never even left his castle. A Beast might, perhaps, have *demanded* a Beauty (hired a nanny, for instance; or snatched her off the street in the mistaken and troubling belief she was a sex worker touting for trade[*]), but he certainly didn't go looking for her. Beasts don't want this and never wanted this. The Beast tends to be actually angry about Beauty's presence in his life, and especially in his home (and the wider territories of his sports club, his office, his private jet, his pirate ship). He is angry about a lot of things: angst is a key facet of the personality of the Beast!Billionaire. He is arrogant, inconsistent, sometimes violent, although too much violence tips him too far over to the Bluebeard side of things.

---

[*] *The Flame and the Flower*, Kathleen E. Woodiwiss, 1972.

Bluebeard, if you recall the (horrible) fairy tale, is the baron who marries a beautiful young girl, and gives her everything she wants, provided she asks no questions and does not attempt to open the locked door at the end of a certain passage. She opens the door: behind it are the bodies of his previous beautiful young wives. It is the most disturbing of all the fairy tales,[*] perhaps because there is no attempt to escape or sidestep the brutality of heterosexual relationships. It's a story, but it's a story with a meaning: men are dangerous. Men are mad. Men are violent and men are liars and men have secrets within them that may destroy you.

Bluebeards are Beasts without an explanation or any hope of expiation. They are Beasts without responsibility, who are driven by rage or the desire for revenge. He's a Heathcliff, of course. (There is an argument that RCB[†], with the trail of women behind him, is more of a BB[‡] than a B[§] – but let's give him, for now, the benefit of the doubt.) A Beast!Billionaire has a heart; a Bluebeard!Billionaire is fundamentally broken. A Beast!Billionaire will transform; a Bluebeard!Billionaire transforms only for Beauty. He will not heal, and it is not Beauty's job to heal him. Her job is simply to bear him as he is.

It is, in some ways, easy to see why this fantasy persists, why it gains ground: if we all understand men to be in some

---

[*] She finds a *room of corpses* in her own house. A room of corpses!
[†] Rupert Campbell-Black
[‡] Bluebeard
[§] Beast

way emotionally stunted (thank you, society!), there is a certain freedom in a story that does *not* seek to fix them. Perhaps there is a certain freedom in deciding – even at this extreme end of the spectrum – to accept the hero exactly as he is. If Mark Darcy famously loved Bridget Jones *just as she is*, then can we apply the same relief to the action of loving a broken man *just as he is* too? Can we find some deep satisfaction in being free from the work of mending him? If it's a step too far – too unbelievable – to conceive of a man in touch with his emotions and in charge of his reactions, is it then possibly more satisfying to imagine accepting that?

The story of Bluebeard is said, like the English folk tale *Mr Fox*, to have been inspired by the French medieval serial killer Gilles de Rais, although it feels likely that it's even older than that. There is a historic truth to this brutality.

Even now a woman is most likely to be murdered by her intimate partner out of everyone in the world: to marry a man is to dance with the possibility, the reality of marrying a violent man.

We understand that marriage is better, generally, for men than for women: for their happiness, for their mental health, for their physical health, for their longevity. Marriage is a trap, and yet the Hot Billionaire book – and, to be fair, many romance books – ends with wedding bells. We want it; we don't want it; we need it; we fear it; we love it; we hate it. We want our story to be the exception.

The Hot Billionaires Are Back

To take a Bluebeard!Billionaire story and give it a happy ending is an unlikely twist, but one that's very real in twenty-first-century romance writing. It is the purest fantasy: not that the heroine's essential goodness will reform him – if anything, the contrast between her innocence and his lack thereof drives him to new heights of depravity – but that the heroine's essential beauty will make her the exception. You, and only you, are not like other girls. For you, and only you, Bluebeard will learn to love – genuinely, deep, truly this time. You are now under Bluebeard's personal protection, and whatever price you pay will be just high enough that you are the only girl in the world who could ever be brave enough to pay it.

That price, of course, is sex. Bluebeards tend to require extravagant sexual tortures to overcome their personal trauma; it's vital for the Bluebeard!Billionaire that this girl is the first girl who has ever found real pleasure in his behaviour. She's both Madonna – literally the image of his mother, in some cases – and whore. This particular woman contains multitudes (and she's the only one, apparently): she's a lady in the street and a freak in the sheets. She is the only one to crave depraved sex *and* to deserve precious intimacy. She is permitted to be, to have, and to want *both* things. We live in a world where the dominant (sorry) social messaging is that women do have to choose one or the other: domestic bliss or sexual fulfilment.

But the one true lover of Bluebeard can have both.

Which makes her – bingo! – the perfect self-insert for the reader.

(Beast!Billionaires also require sex, often at least a little depraved in style, but their sexual appetites are not in the league of Bluebeard's. You know it's a Bluebeard book when something happens – sexually and otherwise – that makes you physically lean back from the page. It's for this reason – the lack of the what-the-fuck factor – that I'm not sure Christian Grey really cuts it as a true Bluebeard, despite being instrumental in the creation of the current crop of monsters. To quote the great Shirley Conran: "I don't want to slag another writer off, but basically, it took until page 100 for her to be whacked with a hairbrush and until page 400 for her to be hit with a belt.")

If we know there is no morally good way to be rich, really rich, then might it be that we lean towards the Bluebeard as a kind of implied permission: he's already bad, so we might as well enjoy his money while we're here. There's no pretence towards moral authority. There is, in fact, an abnegation of morality altogether.

A Bluebeard book is not just morally questionable: it's grotesque, in the most fundamental sense of the word. It's a medieval exaggeration of emotion and action. To take an example at random: someone gropes the heroine at a party, and the next day the hero is a little distant. He claims to be busy with work. Steadied up from a lifetime of romance, we smart readers know what *this* is: this is the misunderstanding! He thinks, perhaps, she invited the groping! He is jealous! He is possessive! Well, as it turns out, yes. But also no. He is busy tying up the groper and cutting his hand off to teach him a lesson. Then he shoots him in the head.

I cannot stress to you enough that this is merely *one scene*, and that this *one scene* has absolutely zero repercussions: not for the plot, and not for the hero's character. He remains the sexy and elusive billionaire, the hero. He still – and this is not a spoiler – gets the girl. (Name! That! Book!*)

What is fascinating here is the heroine's – and the reader's – proximity to revenge: we keep our hands clean, but anyone who touches us will die. This act of retribution is far from the machinery of the modern courts; it is violent and medieval. It is even courtly, albeit in a rather primitive way. And sex, of course, is always primitive. It is the primal instinct. It is the first instinct of all living things!

If the Hot Billionaire allows us power without economic responsibility, he also permits us pleasure without sexual responsibility. The Beast and the Bluebeard may do whatever they wish – and, again, they are written mostly by women, mostly for women – and their Cinderellas can do nothing but submit. Her pleasure comes as a consequence of his pleasure; and his pleasure has – sometimes literally, sometimes metaphorically – been bought and paid for.

There is a clear economic exchange at the heart of every Hot Billionaire book. And it is through that exchange that he will save you from yourself. He will save you from the life you have made yourself.

---

* *Twisted Love*, Ana Huang, 2021.

Perhaps the single sexiest Hot Billionaire is Vaughn, the hero of Sarra Manning's *Unsticky*. He earns this hard-fought title, I think, in one unbelievably powerful moment. Grace is chaos: a credit-card-addicted, high-spending low earner who keeps all her overdue bills, unopened, in a shoebox under the bed in her damp attic flat. Vaughn – a man who ran so Christian Grey could walk – goes through each one. He opens each envelope, one by one, and he *makes her watch*. He makes her look – really look – at the extent of the damage she has done to herself. Red letter by red letter; line by line; fine by fine and fee by fee. He strips her to the thing she is most ashamed of; he makes her beg for mercy; he is merciless. He is cold, clinical, methodical. She is seen entirely. Then he pays off all of her enormous debts. It is agonising. It is exquisite. It is a spanking with aftercare.

This is an escape from reality into reality: you're still in the real world, but this time, someone is coming to help you. There is something to be said for the idea that Bluebeards and Beasts, with their NDAs and oftentimes explicit contractual obligations, flourish in times of economic uncertainty. Perhaps the reality of our precarious finances is why the Charmings have been so quiet for a while?

Charmings were the original romance heroes – dashing, attractive, basically brusque and offhand in the beginning, then melting like ice cream on a sunny day – but you see them far more rarely these days.

The Hot Billionaires Are Back

In our current political landscapes, you have to be willing to dream *big* to imagine a modern Prince Charming. You have to be willing to leave the real world behind: for example, Casey McQuiston's *Red, White & Royal Blue*, an alternate universe in which the right-wing demagogue lost the 2016 presidential election to a Texan single mother with two Mexican American kids. In other worlds, and particularly in queer ones, there might be a place for Charmings after all.

Generally, though, Charmings belong to a softer, gentler era. They flourish in times of relative peace and prosperity (between the world wars, for instance), but I wonder whether – in times of very great uncertainty – we might not see a resurgence. The romcoms of the charmed 1990s – *You've Got Mail, While You Were Sleeping, My Best Friend's Wedding*, even *Friends* – are surfacing again, like cream on top of milk; it is possible, I think, that we might be so crushed by the world to come that the dream of the handsome man (very kind, lots of money, a lot less angst) might feel like a very nice place to hide.

Peter Wimsey, in Dorothy L. Sayers' detective romances, is a perfect Prince Charming. For the close-reading Sayers fan, I'm thinking particularly of the chess set – *I loved them, and you gave them to me* – and Lord Peter's secret charitable works – *Insurance against the Socialist Revolution—when it comes* – and above all, his constant patience. A Prince Charming must be willing to wait. He must be willing to look; and he must be willing, despite his great wealth, to *serve*. The Charming!Billionaire must be willing to bend his great wealth entirely to the heroine's needs, pretty much from the start; it's the heroine – or the loved one, as Charming!Billionaires are most common now in queer romance – who puts the brakes on. Cinderella is uncomfortable with so much money! Cinderella could not possibly accept this wine-coloured frock, this horse, this hound, this house, this library, this life. She will, though. Of course she will.

Henry de Tamble, of Audrey Niffenegger's *The Time Traveler's Wife*, is a Charming thinly disguised as a Beast. (*The Time Traveler's Wife* is a romance novel thinly disguised as a heavyweight literary proposition, which goes some way towards explaining why I love it so much.)

Despite Henry's (literal) curse, his entire function is to serve. When he uses his time-travel powers to go back and win the Lottery for his beloved Clare (in a scene that I promise is much more moving than this description makes it sound), Clare realises with an uncomfortable shock that he could have done this at any time for himself. He could have bent time to live in luxury for himself, but he chooses to abuse his power only for her – and for her need to make art. He will defraud the Lottery to buy her a house with a studio, and she will accept it. Clare's own wealthy background is the cause of much internal angst, but the time-travel element absolves all. She can and, indeed, must accept – even *already has* accepted – all things offered to her without guilt, shame or responsibility.

She must accept wealth; she must also accept sexual pleasure.

In, for example, Eva Ibbotson's 1980s romance novels meant mainly for "old ladies and people with flu", the Cinderella is swept away by the Charming!Billionaire into loving, creative, interesting sex, explicitly without shame. Harriet Morton, in Ibbotson's *A Company of Swans*, is brought up by an overbearing aunt and an overprotective father. The aunt believes it would be most suitable for Harriet to marry Edward Finch-Dutton, a man first seen dissecting a pickled dogfish. Harriet has other plans. Running away to Brazil to become a ballerina, Harriet meets the extraordinary Rom Verney, a *most un-English-looking Englishman*, rich beyond anyone's wildest dreams and obsessed with the wild creatures of the Brazilian rainforest. He is a true gentleman. "It seems to be *very* difficult to be ruined in this house," Harriet says, petulantly, before Rom sacrifices his principles and carries her upstairs. Sex with Rom is not just good, it's life changing. Only "the mystics … God himself … and Johann Sebastian Bach in places" could know how Harriet feels, "but they had not been ruined by Rom so they could not know it as Harriet knew it". Harriet has only one desire unmet: she wants to creep into Rom's presence as the "odalisques did for Suleiman the Great". Rom won't hear of this harem-style D/S foreplay, but, as Harriet argues, "They weren't abject, the odalisques … People have that wrong. They just worked very hard at love – it was all they had." These dynamics, these insights and longings are perhaps not what you might expect from books "for people with flu", and yet Ibbotson's Charmings are nothing if not a Heyer Mark 1.5: sexy and sweet at the same time.

Ibbotson's heroes are a perfect example, too, of another Hot Billionaire subtype: the Hot Billionaire with no billions, but a ramshackle country house and, metaphorically or otherwise, peacocks on the lawn. The Billion-Free!Hot Billionaire is delightful; he's grandfather's-silver-cigarette-case decadent, and part of an old-world order and charm that is absolutely irresistible to a certain kind of person. The aristocrat bringing nothing to the table but his class and his (stately) home is mostly, but not exclusively, a British-set phenomenon – think Eva Rice, Barbara Trapido, the whole real-life family of the Mountbatten-Windsors. (It's worth noting that at some point in these stories, usually near the end, there will turn out to be perhaps fourteen Turner watercolours in the attic: the magic of the Billion-Free!Hot Billionaire is that he is Schrödinger's billionaire, and with him all things are possible. But the point stands nonetheless.)

The Billion-Free!Hot Billionaire grants access to somewhere even money cannot buy entry: somewhere unfamiliar, bohemian, rough and refined at the same time. The rain comes through the roof; everybody is wearing tweedy or silky things they found in a vast, mothballed wardrobe; they belong to a place, and the place belongs to them. This kind of Hot Billionaire, unlike more modern Hot Billionaires, tends not to be quite so jet set. They tend to have somewhere to be, and they want to be in it. They belong somewhere. And Beauty, on seeing such a place, knows she belongs there too. Heather Simmons, on arriving at Brandon Birmingham's beloved plantation, feels as if she has always belonged among the live oaks and soft marshes of Louisiana.* Ruth Berger sees the north coast of England, where Quinton Somerville's family have lived for generations, and she "is lost".† Julia Wychwood falls for her husband not for himself – he is by turns very nice and very mean, *what could be going on?* – but for his rambling home and the trees in the orchard.‡ The standard-issue Hot Billionaire is fairly free floating (private jets and upscale city apartments, perhaps a ski chalet); the Billion-Free!Hot Billionaire lacks the funds to move through the world so easily.

The Billion-Free!Hot Billionaire highlights the fact, perhaps, that what is chiefly appealing about both Beast and Charming is their castle. We have been told that money does not buy happiness. This is, statistically, not true – but it's not true in a way that illuminates something vital about the Hot Billionaire trope.

A 2010 study showed that money does, in fact, buy happiness – up to £50,000 per person per annum. Money, roughly speaking, buys happiness up until about fifty grand a year, at which point it kind of levels off. This makes sense to me: money doesn't buy happiness, sure, but poverty is the quickest way to fast-track misery. Our heroines absolutely know this: they are always the Cinderella, slogging at endless,

---

* *The Flame and the Flower*, Kathleen Woodiwiss, 1972.
† *The Morning Gift*, Eva Ibbotson, 1993.
‡ *The Belle of Belgrave Square*, Mimi Matthews, 2022.

thankless work, never with a new dress or a pair of impractical party shoes, never with the freedom to pursue their creative dreams. What that £50,000 a year buys you, above all, is security.

When we seek to solve economic inequality, we are often talking about access to real estate. There are, obviously, other forms of poverty, but insecure housing is a key indicator of the failings of modern-day capitalism. If you scratch the surface of something like hunger, for example, you come very quickly to inadequate and insecure housing: if you don't have a kitchen, or at least somewhere to safely store and prepare meals, you're significantly more likely to struggle with eating something wholesome and delicious.

It's difficult to commit to any of the most vital acts of being a person without a secure and safe home: to make art, plant and tend a garden, have a baby, or to follow any of your dreams. It is, practically speaking, almost impossible to do these things in any way while falling through the cracks of inflated mortgage payments or wildly inadequate landlords.

And yet most Cinderellas, most Beauties, are women with dreams; dreams they can't fulfil because they are economically constrained by circumstance into working some lesser, shabbier version of their ideals. The doctor who seeks to open a clinic in a deprived mountain area, but instead must work long ER shifts for little pay; the calligrapher who dreams of building a greetings card empire, but instead must hand-letter planners for spoilt Manhattan housewives; the chef who slogs in the diner but secretly schemes either for her own restaurant or to run a Meals On Wheels service for the elderly. There are investigative journalists who are trapped writing mindless columns (when with a bit of backing they could bring down the corrupt cops); and bicycle couriers who can't even get a toehold in the mindless column market. There are fashion writers who dream of starting their own clothing line, influencers who ... dream of starting their own clothing line, and models who ... dream of starting their own clothing line. (A lot of women in romance novels dream of starting a clothing line.) These people – mostly but not exclusively women – want to make something of themselves, and what holds them back is two things: courage, and capital.

Capital brings courage: when you have a safety net, it's possible to take a leap of faith. And taking a leap of faith brings freedom.

The routine critical reading of the Hot Billionaire story is that it tells of a sacrifice of freedom for economic safety; that marriage, in these circumstances, is a trap – gilded, but still a trap. You trade your freedom to honour and obey a Hot Billionaire, and in exchange you fly on a private jet, or live in a castle, or buy whatever you want. This is the most conventional way of looking at it, certainly: a woman loses herself to marriage, loses her ambition to his ambition, subsumes herself along with her name into the rarified world of the Hot Billionaire Husband. And this, it is clear, is the traditional shape of a heterosexual marriage.

(This shape is, perhaps, why queer fantasies along these lines have an easier time of it: freed from the baggage of heterosexual relationships, we are able to more easily imagine an egalitarian approach to a financially unequal proposition.)

And yet, the Beauties and the Cinderellas in most modern-day romances are *not* subsumed. No matter how many baby-heavy epilogues may emerge, the salient fact is that the heroines of these books tend to *fulfil their dreams*. Sometimes the Billionaire helps; more often than not, it's simply his money which permits her to quit her minimum-wage job, spring an elderly relative (or former nanny) from a substandard care home, and open a pet shelter. The Billionaire himself, while sexually vital, is sort of irrelevant to the ending of Hot Billionaire books: their true ending is the heroine's ability to independently pursue her own dreams.

Furthermore, it transpires, it's *these very dreams* which have endeared her to the Billionaire in the first place. The Billionaire is not just happy to back her ideas, he's actively happy to be relegated to second place as her dreams come first. Even the Bluebeards, once in love, will grant their one singular lover anything their heart desires. The Billionaire's function is to cut the ropes of financial worries and allow the love interest to fly.

4

The Fox, the Hedgehog, and the Aliens

I would like to come back briefly to Eva Ibbotson's *The Morning Gift*. Actually, I could spend a whole book writing about Eva Ibbotson's *The Morning Gift*. It would, I think, be absolutely possible to write a whole book about romance novels without ever once leaving the subject of Eva Ibbotson's *The Morning Gift*.

(The main reason not to do this – the only reason not to do this? – is that I would hate to ruin it for anyone who has not read it. If you haven't read it, it is a perfect novel, and if you are reading this book, you will love it. In fact, go and buy *The Morning Gift* immediately. Put this book down, and come back when you've read it.)

One reason it would be good to do this is because it's impossible for even the most high-minded of people to dismiss Eva Ibbotson's literary credentials. Ibbotson is not just a bestseller, not just an award-winner, but the kind of writer most writers seek to be, writing the kind of books most readers seek to read – smart, careful, beautiful evocations of human relationships at times of great political and societal upheaval and trauma, located firmly in impeccably drawn landscapes as far-ranging as the Olduvai Gorge, rubber plantations outside Manaus, and war-torn Belsize Park.* Ibbotson fled Vienna following the Nazi invasion of her Austrian homeland, and her books are often about exiles, the lonely and the lost. Also, there are jokes. Also, there is kissing. They are, to me, the platonic ideal of "the romance novel"; they act as a complete rebuttal of the things some people like to say about romance novels; they are the kind of book I dare anyone, anywhere, to argue with. Whether she herself thought they were for "people with the flu" or not is sort of beside the point. They are perfect for people with flu. They are perfect for anybody who is tired; they are perfect for anybody who is a little lost. (And some, such as the spellbinding *Journey to the River Sea*, are even perfect for children.)

The story of *The Morning Gift* is this: Ruth Berger, the nineteen-year-old daughter of an archaeologist and his irrepressible wife Leonie, lives a charmed life in 1930s Vienna. Their world – an exquisite and gilded many-roomed apartment, high above a courtyard – is full of people and music and papers and furniture, operas and lectures and walks in the park, pigeons and heirlooms. It is a very tangible world, and the book is like an elegy. The first time I read this description I didn't know why I wanted to cry. I was only about eleven and I didn't know what was about to happen. It was a kissing book, not a history book! But it is 1930s

---

* *The Morning Gift, A Company of Swans* and *The Countess Below Stairs* respectively.

The Fox, the Hedgehog, and the Aliens

Vienna, and Leonie is ancestrally, though not culturally, Jewish. This distinction does not matter to the Nazis. Having got Ruth safely onto a Quaker transport to England, the Bergers make their own way to meet her in Belsize Park. But Ruth has been stopped at the border. Ruth has been sent back. The sixteen-room apartment has been ransacked. The heirlooms – including the cradle in which Ruth, and her mother before her, were rocked as infants – have been smashed. There is nowhere to go, and nobody left. And then there is Quinton Somerville: an old friend of the family, come to Vienna to be given an honorary degree by Professor Berger. Appalled to find Professor Berger replaced by an Aryan youth, Somerville arrives at the apartment to find Ruth there alone. With no papers, and no parents, there is only one way to get Ruth to safety: a British passport. And there is only one way to get Ruth a British passport. And that is marriage to a British citizen ... And so it unfurls from there. It is an impeccable premise, and one that unwinds through Goethe and bedbug eggs and sea-glass; striped pyjamas and Mozart and one-eyed puppies; science, wine and unbelievable emeralds. It ends, I need not tell you, happily for Ruth and Quinton.

It must be said that I once gave another Ibbotson book to a friend, who refused to read to the end: the third-act twist was too much for her. Ibbotson knows too much of the world for things to be completely perfect. Things are always lost along the way, though the people we find might, perhaps, make up for such losses. This balancing of loss is, undoubtedly, why I love her almost best of all the romances.

For now, what fascinates me most about this plot is the idea of the forced marriage – or, certainly, the marriage of convenience. Ruth marries Quinton because otherwise she will die. Quinton marries Ruth because he feels it is the least he can do under the circumstances. Falling in love, for either party, feels like a transgression of their relationship: marriage both keeps them apart, as it pulls them together.

Romance thrives on this kind of duality: a romance novel is really always an explanation and exploration of the ways we contradict ourselves. We all – not just the singular lovers of the terrifying Bluebeards – contain multitudes. Of course, opposites attract – grumpy and sunshine, city and country, rich and poor – but it's not only that: by the bonds of marriage and the binds of relationships, the romantic heroine is freed from her life of poverty and the romantic hero is freed from his life of trauma. Could it be that the bind makes us free, or is it that the promise of freedom is why we choose to be bound? A good romance novel is driven by the perpetual turning of the coin, first one side, then the other. What is freedom? What is connection? How tightly can we bear to be bound? In short, what do we want, and what do we need, and how do those two things interact with each other?

Desire, evidently, is not straightforward. Desire is complex and mysterious; it is basically impossible to explain. Why *that* guy? What *does* she see in him? She sees something; and he sees something in her.

The Fox, the Hedgehog, and the Aliens

Romance novels are about desire, and desire lives for contradiction: this is what I want; this is what I want to want; this is what I don't know that I want.

Another reason, then, for the decline of Prince Charming is that Prince Charming seeks to provide the heroine with everything she has ever wanted. This act of provision is, in many ways, his most vital role. An art studio? Takeaway noodles? Your elderly former nanny, now stricken with Alzheimer's, taken care of in the best nursing home there is? Your enemies fired? Jeans in four different sizes to follow the fluctuations of your female body week by week? (Name! That! Book!*)

If one of the functions of a romantic novel is to serve as a playground for women to work out their desires, it's difficult for the hero to *ask*, directly, how to fulfil those desires before the end of the book without demanding something that the heroine is not yet ready to give. (Maybe because she hasn't yet worked it out.)

There is this moment in *Gaudy Night*, Dorothy L. Sayers' great romance masterpiece (more commonly, and mistakenly, described as a Golden Age detective story), in which Harriet Vane finally permits Peter Wimsey to give her a present. This is after five books of prolonged suffering on both their parts (to say nothing of the reader's agonies), and

---

* Liz Tomforde in *Mile High* is responsible for the jeans in multiple sizes to accommodate hormonal fluctuations. A thoughtful and unusual gift, which I respect, but don't know how well I would respond to myself.

she eventually capitulates to him almost on a whim. All he wants is to give her everything, and yet *[f]or a moment her mind was a blank. Whatever she asked him for, it must be something adequate. The trivial, the commonplace or the merely expensive would all be equally insulting. And he would know in a moment if she was inventing a want to please him.* Her first response, to being offered the world, and accepting it, is to have no conception of what that world might consist.

(This quotation, and the book it belongs in, is seared so deeply into my heart that just typing it out makes me want to cry with longing. A strong recommend, if you like clever people and yearning, and can skim over the worst of the 1930s mindset.)

Harriet, happily for Peter and for the desperate reader (five books!), thinks of an adequate present shortly thereafter. But the fact of her initial response, I think, is telling. It is, naturally, romantic to be offered everything you have ever wanted; but if you have never known what it is you want, then the offer itself becomes a demand and an obligation.

Listen: do you remember that scene in *Fleabag*? You know which scene I mean. There's a decent argument for Phoebe Waller-Bridge's *Fleabag* being one of the most important cultural artefacts of the 2010s: it's the kind of TV show that changed the way TV shows are made, the kind of TV shows where everyone writing anything with a young woman in it would be asked to measure both creation and success against the *Fleabag* standard. It is also, according to itself, a "love

The Fox, the Hedgehog, and the Aliens

story". Fleabag tells us this repeatedly. The words were printed on the bound scripts, which were sold as books in their own right: *This is a love story.*

So you know, I think, the scene I mean. You can watch it online very easily if you search "fleabag scene", which tells you something about the way this scene sticks in people's minds.

Fleabag is crying in the confession booth, divided by the little screen from the Hot Priest, the only person who truly understands her. It's dark; Fleabag is crying. He is invisible. I want— says Fleabag, desperately. I don't—

It's ok not to know what you want, says the Hot Priest, through the screen. I know exactly what I want, says Fleabag, clutching her whiskey in the confession booth. I want, she says in essence, someone to tell me what I want. *Tell me what to do, Father,* she says.

And then, in the words of Amazon Prime Video, "*Fleabag's Heartbreaking Confession To The Hot Priest Turns Into A Steamy Moment*". This title made me laugh quite a lot – it's so at odds with everything about the scene, except the actual facts of the scene – but it's also worth noting, I think, that whether or not *Fleabag* is a romance,* the language of romance has been used to sell it. It calls itself "a love story", which is true, for sure, it's a story about love – but what gives it the texture of romance is both the yearn (oh, how Fleabag

---

* *Fleabag* would like the cultural pulling power of romantic fiction but without any of the humiliating, cloying, historical connotations of romantic fiction, and for that reason I will never truly love it.

yearns!) and the fact that this, too, is an exploration of female desire that has no simple, no tidy, no one-size-fits-all answer. It is about how hard it is to know what you want. It is about how hard it is to take what you want when it's offered to you, and how hard it is to distinguish what you want in the moment from what you want for all time.

"I saw my life branching out before me like the green fig tree in the story," says Esther Greenwood, the heroine of Sylvia Plath's *The Bell Jar* (not a romance! very much not a romance!). Futures, like figs, hang before her: marriage, children, poetry, journalism, academia, even an Olympic rowing career or a string of exotic lovers, and beyond them even more and more she can't begin to imagine. "I saw myself sitting in the crotch of this fig tree," she says, "starving to death. I wanted each and every one of them, but choosing one meant losing all the rest."

The thing that has defined our era, perhaps, is *choice*.

For the first time in human history, it seems as if we have a choice about almost everything.

Humans are small animals in a big universe: we have designed ourselves to live in little huddles, little live-wire groups of connection and interconnection. We evolved to live in communities where we knew everyone, and everyone knew our place; we learned to love our friends, mistrust strangers, and to take what we could get from the hard world – not just for ourselves, but for our people, for those close to us. We ate what we found or grew or made; we loved the people who were near us; we bloomed, as the fridge magnet says, where we were planted. We were happy there, and we flourished there, and we died there, too! And we were unhappy, and we were lonely, and we died in places that weren't right for us among people who never understood us; and as a culture we have fought our way out of that to where we are now. We have fought our way to a culture of ever-expanding choice.

When we eat, we can, if we have even a little spare money, choose from things that ripen at all different times and in all different places: we can eat strawberries from Japan and apples from New Zealand and pineapples from Spain in the dead, dark depths of winter; we can have things flown in and shipped in and brought to us at far less immediate expense than our ancestors would assume for such princely behaviour. We can wash in endless hot water, in our own homes, at the flip of a switch, and the scent of our soap is not lamb fat and ashes, but roses or lemons or coconuts. We can wear what we like; live where we like; work as we like. We are not weavers because our mothers were weavers, or farriers because our fathers were farriers. We are not domestic servants because we were born to be domestic servants; we are not slaves because we were born to be slaves. We leave our villages and go where we please. We can go anywhere in the world, pretty much, and often people do; and we can do things with our lives that our ancestors could never have imagined. We can choose to do something with our days that pleases us. We are, in fact, encouraged to do so. We can be anything, or so we tell our children. We can do anything we want in this life. Which is, for a small animal, quite a lot of an ask.

We are told that if we find the right work – and we must find the right work, the right place, the right life – we will find real happiness. And we have become, in some ways, happiness fetishists. Actually, it's worse than that: happiness is – in my opinion – a fairly noble goal. I would love it if we were happiness fetishists, for real actual ordinary low-key happiness. I love happiness, which is why I love romance novels.

The dark side of romance novels – and the dark side of our happiness fetish – is that we have become a people hell-bent on perfection. Or, at least, hell-bent on the idea of perfection.

Physical perfection – whatever that means – can be attained by suitable quantities of cash, exercise, surgery and drugs, obtained legally or otherwise. Domestic perfection can be attained by a constant, daily struggle, and the application of money; financial perfection can be attained by any number of pyramid schemes or perhaps by documenting all other perfections. Clothes can, and must, be bought new for every occasion; homewares, ditto; everything else, ditto. Aesthetics can be changed at the drop of a hat to match the current mood. Perfection can be purchased, and it is your duty to purchase it. However perfection might look, the quest for it is contagious.

And marital perfection – again, whatever *that* means – can surely be purchased on the apps. Or so the apps – *designed to be deleted* – would tell you.

The Fox, the Hedgehog, and the Aliens

Like any good mobile game, you can pay to play with your money or your time. Either way, you need to keep looking. You need to keep tapping. You need to keep flicking through person after person until you match with the perfect person to spend your life with – because the perfect person, the truly perfect person, the one who will make your life feel like a romance novel? That person is out there. Maybe they are no more than a single swipe away.

The first time I ever went to a big supermarket by myself – I was eighteen and had just left home – I was staggered to the point of panic by the loo roll aisle in the big Sainsbury's. There was a *whole aisle* to navigate. How could anyone choose? How could anyone possibly know which was the *perfect* loo roll to buy? There were forty-six different kinds of toilet paper and I could not fathom how there could be forty-six different kinds of ass on one standard-type human being. I left without buying anything. At the corner shop I bought the only loo roll they had, plus some Tangfastics for dinner (I was eighteen), and I went home.

The day I first downloaded a dating app, I thought about the loo roll aisle in the big supermarket, and I felt like the world might be too big after all.

We are made to be near people, and to be afraid of the dark: that's it. To look up at the whole universe and try to make it bend to your will – whatever it is that you don't yet know you want, and don't yet know you need – is the action of a mad professor in a movie. Who knows what the consequences will be, Professor? Who knows what will happen if you wipe out mosquitoes or reanimate the dinosaurs?

The truly terrifying thing, in all of this, is that every choice begets another choice. Everything is linked. If we make one wrong move on one thing we might inadvertently be shutting doors to ourselves later on. How to know? How to know what to do, who to choose, where to live? Have a baby, don't have a baby; fall for him or fall for her; this life or that life? Everything is overwhelming.

"We have a proverb in Russia," explains a character in Ibbotson's *The Secret Countess*. "It goes 'The fox knows many things, but the hedgehog knows one big thing.'"

He claims it as a Russian proverb, but you can trace that precise phrasing back to the Greek lyric poet Archilochus, writing three thousand years ago, and there are dozens of similar fables everywhere else remarking on the knowledge of fish, frogs, cranes, cats, squirrels, owls, doves. The fox is fairly constant, and so too is his boast that he knows many things. The fox has many tricks, many ideas, many choices. When the hunters come, the hedgehog rolls immediately into a ball. The fox stops to decide – what to do? what would be best? – and is eaten at once by the dogs. The moral of the story – to quote a seventeenth-century retelling – *too many expedients may spoil the business*. Have one, and be done with it.

To know what you want enough to choose from a whole vast universe is the kind of self-knowledge that takes a lifetime; and then it's over. You are a mote of dust in an infinite

The Fox, the Hedgehog, and the Aliens

cosmiverse. Our sun is one star among hundreds of billions of stars that are suns, and we are only one galaxy in trillions of galaxies. How can anyone look up at the stars and know what they are supposed to do?

Fortunately for you, then, you have been kidnapped by aliens, and you no longer have a choice about anything.

Hooray! The aliens are incredibly sexy, and as well as sexy, they are incredibly horny.

This alien is your alien, and you are now his human. Don't bother trying to argue. A seven-foot-tall alien, covered in blue suedette armour plating, and boasting two penises (well, one penis and a spur, the latter designed purely for clitoral stimulation), has chosen you to be his lifelong bride. Or, no, that's not entirely accurate: some higher power has chosen you both for one another as the perfect genetic match. This is surprising, since you're a human and he's a seven-foot-tall blue alien; yet the higher power – something in your chest *resonating* with something in his chest – has decreed that the only thing, now, that will ever make you happy again is having pretty much endless sex and making endless babies together. There is no longer any choice in the matter. From now on, you will have one relentless urge that renders all other instincts moot. You are an alien bride. You are the mother of alien babies. Every day you will have wild sex with a tall, blue, two-pronged alien who cares about nothing so much as your sexual pleasure; and you will no longer care about life on Earth in any meaningful way whatsoever. You will no longer yearn for anything you don't have; and this lack of yearning, in a way, is a subversion of the classic romance novel.

A good romance novel typically hangs on the quality of the yearn: the intensity with which the key characters long for what they don't have, and the intensity with which they long for one another. These kind of books – the alien books – are yearning's natural endpoint.*

This is the premise of the thirty-nine novels and novellas in Ruby Dixon's *Ice Planet Barbarians* series. In the interests of full disclosure, I have read seventeen of them, and will probably read more. It is very easy, I think, to dismiss books like these: it's easy to go to bat for the big almost-literaries, like Eva Ibbotson or Audrey Niffenegger, and even reasonably easy to stick your neck out for Jilly Cooper or Jill Mansell or Emily Henry, but to write about *Ice Planet Barbarians* with any degree of analysis or detachment is to almost immediately invite mockery. Not for myself, I mean, which I could survive – but for the books. When writing about a romance series about seven-foot-tall sexy aliens, in which the plot of every book is almost identical to the extent that it's perfectly plausible for the author to simply forget which character she's currently writing about, it feels important to come (as it were) in good faith.

As all space invaders say: I come in peace.

---

* This is also the central idea of all "fated mates" type books – prominent in faerie novels – and also, I think, the Omegaverse. If you are unfamiliar with the Omegaverse, *please do not google it on my account.*

The Fox, the Hedgehog, and the Aliens

The aliens live on a planet that is like ours, in that it's possible for humans to breathe and exist there, but not like ours, in that it is covered with ice. (The clue is in the title.) It is also not like ours in that the inhabitants – the hot aliens – are barbarians. (Ditto.) Much like "Dude! *Forbes* just named you World's Hottest Billionaire!", *Ice Planet Barbarians* has no pretence to being anything but what it is. It does what it says on the tin. I respect this very much, as an approach to literature. Dixon asks her readers at the end of each book which alien-human couple they would like to read about next. Then she writes it. Sometimes she serialises it. Sometimes she goes back and edits a book she has previously written to make the next book in the series make more sense. It is an entirely new, or very old, approach to literature: it exists somewhere between fanfiction of itself, and stories told round the campfire. Characters are mostly delivered in bold strokes – more like folk heroes than literary devices – and the plots kept similarly simple.

The barbarian aliens live in a small community, but they are running out of women. Happily, it is perfectly possible – even desirable – for the aliens to mate with humans. They are blue; the human women are pink. The alien barbarians are hard; the human women are soft. Sometimes the human does not want to be the mate of a particular alien; sometimes the human doesn't want to be the mate of any alien at all. In these cases, the humans are always proved wrong. Consent is – well, listen, the humans *will* consent.

Consent culture, as the theorist Katherine Angel writes in *Tomorrow Sex Will Be Good Again*, is more complex than it at first might appear. While we can all agree, I hope, that two consenting adults are the bare minimum needed for successful sexual intercourse, from there on it tends to get tricky. Is it hoping for too much that the two adults aren't merely consenting, but enthusiastically consenting? Do people have the right to consent unenthusiastically or for reasons other than enthusiasm? Plus, what, exactly, counts as consent? How does consent cope with changing minds, or changing contexts, or changing expectations? How can we consent without knowing exactly what something entails, and how can we preserve the mystery and magic of sex if we know exactly what is going to happen? These are the questions of the ethics of consent, but also, again, of romantic fiction.

Romantic fiction does not answer these questions – how could it? What it does instead, I suppose, is allow us to play, over and over again, with the ideas of desire and discovery and danger that are embedded – sometimes even glossed over – in the conversations of consent culture which now dominate discussions of *doing it*.*

---

* The best romance novels to handle consent, I think, are in the Jasmine Guillory mould: each act of consent, each seeking of consent for each individual act, is in and of itself a kind of erotic foreplay. But then, that's just me. I suspect there are plenty of people for whom this feels strange and unintuitive; like the characters are talking too much, and kissing too little. YMMV. I recommend.

Consent culture is "suspicious of tentativeness". As Angel puts it, women "must speak out – and they must speak out about what they want. They must, then, also know what it is that they want".

Consent culture is symptomatic, then, of *choice culture*. By eliminating the need for choice, the aliens essentially also eliminate the need for consent, and above all the need to think carefully, with your big-girl brain, about every one of those complex questions raised by new articulations of the concept of consent and consensuality.

Chosen by an alien, you don't have a choice in the matter! The higher power has chosen you for each other! The higher power knows that this will make you happier than anything else, and so – fight it if you must – you will, in the end, be content with the hand you've been dealt.

This is also true, by the way, for the alien pregnancies. No human woman, in *Ice Planet Barbarians*, is unhappy to be alien pregnant. While a human woman may have fears, they are swiftly dealt with – did I mention that the higher power also makes them practically immortal? It's true. The alien higher power can heal almost all wounds.

The half-alien, half-human babies want to be in their community; their mothers want to be in community. Ruth, in Ibbotson's *The Morning Gift*, finds herself pregnant and abandoned (temporarily, and through misunderstanding alone). She has one impulse: she runs away, in a storm, to the family seat of her estranged and lordly husband. She is compelled to do this, she thinks, by the foetus itself: *half-Somerville*, she rationalises, *the baby wants his home.*

Ruth's experience of pregnancy is no less a fantasy than those of the alien brides; the choice to have a baby is fraught with difficulty every step along the way. Practically, financially, morally: the whole thing is basically a minefield. Whether to have a baby at all! When to have a baby! Where to have a baby! How to have a baby, and who with! Why would anyone have a baby in a world like this; and what to do with it once you've done it?

There is something very soothing about every single one of these choices being removed from the equation. Also, it's soothing to imagine that if you're having a baby, everyone you know is also having a baby, and you're all living in the same enormous cave, where nobody is ever left alone. If you *want* to be alone, someone else can hold your baby for you. There are many other hands to help. You are not being left out of anything; everything is going just as it is supposed to. You are fulfilling your one purpose on this icy planet, and you don't need to worry about buying the right kind of high chair or feeding it the right kind of baby food. You don't need to worry about failing your child, or failing yourself, or failing the planet: you can simply exist. Existing is enough. Existing is all you have to do.

The half-alien, half-human babies are born; grow up; and I am sure, in time, that Ruby Dixon will write *Ice Planet Barbarian* erotic romances about their lives, too. The barbarian colony thrives amid the ice. They hunt, they kill, they feast, they hibernate against deep winter and they rejoice in the spring.

"I'm overcome," muses Maddie, in *Ice Planet Barbarians: Barbarian's Taming*. Her alien, a hunter named Hassen, is checking their cave for terrible space-monkeys that could tear them limb from limb. "Any single hunter could survive on [his] own, but they choose to work tirelessly to bring home for the tribe. In turn, the tribe cares for them when they are sick, gives them a place to sleep, and people to socialise with. It's all very 'circle of life', and I'm fascinated by how different it feels from my old life back on Earth."

There is no subtext here. If you need subtext, go back to civilisation. This is a simple place: much like the past, they do things differently here.

The aliens are as much the past as the characters in any historical romance. More, perhaps, as most historical romances tend to carry with them a flavour of the time in which they were written – although, I suppose, the Ice Planet's bizarre caveman-socialism speaks profoundly to our own century. We are in an era of startling progression and sweeping conservatism: everything might change, and so people either cling tightly to the ideas of what came before, or seek to sweep away every truth we used to know. It's like how the ideas behind feminism are so widely acknowledged to be true that it's almost embarrassing to talk about them – remember the teeth-achingly trite *This Is What A Feminist Looks Like* t-shirts? – and yet the tradwives bloom. Queer people are more a part of mainstream culture than ever, and yet equal human rights for those queer people are under constant attack. The internet has connected us all together, all over the world, and yet global borders are being reinforced and policed on an extraordinary scale. It's the future; it's the past; here we are, open to the universe, and suddenly we need to make that universe very small as quickly as possible.

Ice Planet Barbarians is evidently the past in that it's a story more about cavemen than modern humanity, but it's equally and more pertinently the past insofar as it's simply a *Clan of the Cave Bear* reboot, complete with erotically depicted interspecies rape.

The Clan of the Cave Bear, by Jean M. Auel, is book one in a multi-book narrative about a Cro-Magnon woman, Ayla, raised and integrated in a Neanderthal society. While not precisely a romance, the most memorable part – as in, literally, the part people remember – is the sex. "Mention *The Clan of the Cave Bear* and the *Earth's Children* books to anyone who read it as a kid, and they'll immediately start talking to you about the novel's sex," noted the journalist Tammy Oler in a piece about the series. "Not just any sex, mind you. Hot Cro-Magnon 'Pleasures.' Neanderthal doggy-style, initiated by special hand signals. 'Nodules,' 'warm folds,' and 'throbbing manhood.'" Oler also notes that all this hot sex occurs after more than nine hundred pages of harrowing depictions of Neanderthal society: brutal, patriarchal, unfair. Ayla suffers abuse, torture and rape before setting off into what feels like a dystopian landscape to look for something better – and she succeeds. Ayla eventually marries, has a child, settles down, becomes a medicine woman; she finds not just hot sex, but all of the future. She meets a shaman, and sees our world unfold. Auel wrote the book as a response to the "glass ceiling" she experienced in her career: if *The Clan of the Cave Bear* is a response to the invisible barriers that halt women in their professional development, to what might *Ice Planet Barbarians* be a response?

There are echoes here, too, of *The Flame and the Flower*: a 600-page epic, set at the turn of the nineteenth century, about a woman kidnapped, raped, then married off to Captain Brandon Birmingham. He happily (!) turns out to be the love of her life. "His possession of her was complete," notes the narrator, cheerily, as Heather settles into life with Birmingham. She gives him the heir he desires; he turns away from a life of the sea, and settles down to a good ol' boy lifestyle of hunting, fishing and shooting. Pre-*Flame* romance novels tended towards the chaste; Kathleen Woodiwiss could not be any further from chaste if she tried.

This is not a coincidence.

The Flame and the Flower was published in 1972: a significant year for American romance. A change in the law permitted the reprint, after many decades, of John Cleland's *Fanny Hill*, originally published in 1749. This is, I suppose, akin to the *Lady Chatterley's Lover* case in the UK.

Fanny Hill, or The Memoirs of a Woman of Pleasure is early erotica that conforms in some ways to modern romance novels; it is, even by today's standards, absolutely filthy. Imagine an old-timey man, in old-timey language, magically transported to the modern day, writing a series of free Kindle Singles about what he thinks life might be like for a teenage girl tricked into sex work, complete with lesbian interludes. *Fanny Hill* is *exactly like you are imagining*. I found a copy at a car boot sale when I was about eleven, read two pages – I liked history books! There was a teenage girl in it! – and promptly threw it back into the stranger's car boot. It was very clearly an adult book, but what kind of depraved adults would read such filth? I was horrified.

It was, I guess, this kind of reaction – but among adults with legislative power – that led to the ban. While never out of print in the UK, the US refused the reprinting of the text until a landmark case in 1972 redefined obscenity – and did so in such a way as to make it clear that novels with erotic content might also escape legal action. Erotic novels were permitted to be commercially printed.

Thus, Kathleen Woodiwiss.

Whether Woodiwiss ever directly encountered *Fanny Hill*, I don't know, but the fact that both books, much like the many volumes of *Ice Planet Barbarians*, detail the eroticised rape and abduction of a young woman is hard to ignore. That all of these texts turn the rape and abduction into domestic bliss is certainly notable: Fanny ends up wealthy in her own right (thanks to an elderly punter who leaves her all his fortune), married to her one true love (who had, of course, been the first to buy her charms), and the mother of his children. Heather marries Brandon Birmingham, is settled with diamonds and acres of land, and becomes the mother of his children. The wives of the Ice Planet Barbarians bear, quite literally, endless children for their alien husbands.

These books become, I think, a vehicle for a unification of the two great male-gaze female archetypes: if the patriarchy insists on an artificial division of Madonna and whore, perhaps modern romance makes a space for their reunification. For the female reader – and perhaps the writer – it might grant the reimagining of a more complete self.

5

Cowboys and Horses

About four times a second – every second – someone, somewhere, buys a Harlequin romance book.

This means that in the time it takes you to finish reading this sentence, roughly another twenty-four will be in the hands of readers, just like that.

And in the time it takes to you to finish reading this chapter, assuming you read about a chapter a day – around twenty-five brand-new Harlequin books will have been *published*. You could come across them in 107 countries, and twenty-nine languages. You could, if you're in the US, grab one simply by stretching out your hand in a bookshop: one in every six paperback books printed in America is a Harlequin book. A Canadian company, originally specialising in reprinting British Mills & Boon paperbacks, Harlequin is now the largest publisher of romantic fiction in the world.

It publishes chiefly what are called "category romances": shortish novels and novellas (topping out at about two hundred pages) published with clockwork regularity. Harlequin is divided into imprints, and each imprint will produce a certain number of books a month, always on that imprint's particular theme.

Harlequin Historical, for instance, releases a dozen books a month, all with titles like *Compromised into Marrying the Duke*, *His Unlikely Countess* and *The Lord's Maddening Miss*. There are Vikings (*Wedding Night with Her Viking Enemy*) and Napoleonic battles (*A Naval Surgeon to Fight For*), and many more: *Wedded to His Enemy Debutante*, *Becoming the Earl's Convenient Wife*, *Their Inconvenient Yuletide Wedding*, *Snowed In with the Viking*, and *Snowbound with the Brooding Lord*.

(I, myself, succumbed instantly to Lotte R. James' *A Liaison with Her Leading Lady*: an 1830s theatrical romance, for which James has written her acknowledgements in a startlingly accurate pastiche of early Victorian poetry. "Ruth Connell's beloved theater is under threat!" begins the blurb. "In desperation, she approaches reclusive playwright Artemis Goode. If Artemis can write a hit, Ruth can save her troupe from financial ruin. Yet it's not just Ruth's livelihood in need of saving, but Artemis's shattered heart, too . . .")

There is Harlequin Presents ("the glamorous lives of royals and billionaires, where passion knows no bounds") with such enticing titles as *Crowned for His Son* and *Expecting the Greek's Heir* and *Billion Dollar Ring Ruse*; there is Harlequin Medical, "where life and love play out against a high-pressured medical backdrop". Illustrated by stock images of models in sage-green scrubs, the reader may choose between *The Surgeon's Relationship Ruse*, *Flirting with the Florida Heart Doctor* and *Surgeon in a Tux* – or subscribe to receive the full monthly package. Harlequin

Afterglow, by contrast, tends to look a little more like a standard-issue romance novel. Titles like *Much Ado About Hating You* and *Unlikely Neighbours* feature soft, modern, cartoon-y covers: men in glasses, apartment blocks, bright blocky colours. These focus chiefly on characters "on the path from showing up to glowing up" – and, of course, "finding sizzling romance along the way".

It's hard to know where to start. What exactly is the difference between Harlequin Medical's *City Doc for the Single Mom* or *Finding a Family Next Door*, and Harlequin Heartwarming's *Reunion with the Single Mom* or *The Teacher's Forever Family*? Is it merely the profession of one or both characters? (And if so, what is *The Firefighter and the Single Mum* doing in Medical?)

Harlequin Heartwarming promises to "connect [the reader] with uplifting stories where the bonds of friendship, family and community unite" – a *lot* of Amish stuff going on here – but *The Cowboy's Rodeo Redemption* by Susan Breeden could surely just as easily belong to Harlequin Montana Mavericks. "Discover love in big sky country": *The Maverick's Promise, Sweet Talkin' Maverick, All In with the Maverick*. The Montana Mavericks are a new venture for Harlequin: the earliest Maverick for sale on their website dates back to March 2025.

Hot cowboys, it seems, are hot property right now. Ranch romance is the talk of the town: Elsie Silver and Lyla Sage have both shimmied seamlessly to the top of the bestseller charts (and, not incidentally, from self-pub ebook to prominent Waterstones shelves). TikTok is full of shirtless men in large hats with a horse in one hand and a beer in the other – and if it's hot on TikTok, you know it's hot in the world of romantic fiction.

But the hot cowboy isn't a flash in the pan: he's been here a while. The Western has deep roots; the Western love story goes back almost as far.[*]

According to a 2009 analysis, "Western themes" – including words such as "cowboy, Texas, Montana, Wyoming, cattleman, horseman, lawman, horse, rodeo, western, wrangler, shotgun, sheriff, outlaw, and ranch" – appeared in 1,015 titles in the surveyed range of Harlequins: the third most

---

[*] The history of "Indian romance", i.e. cowboy-type romances featuring Native Americans, as distinct from romances written *by* Native American authors, is as fraught and unhappy as you would imagine. While created initially as a tool for social justice – Helen Hunt Jackson's troubling-but-well-intentioned *Ramona* – as a genre it quickly and obviously descended into exploitation, grim stereotypes, and liberal use of the word "savage". While they operate in the same theoretical world as cowboy romance – wildness, horses, etc. – the "Indian romance", as it historically stood, had much more in common with the Hot Alien romances of today: they offered readers, I think, a similar freedom from choice. Unlike Hot Aliens, however, Hot Native Americans are real. Using race as shorthand for personality and action sits badly with me. For this reason, and for many other obvious reasons, I have never read any and don't especially want to. It's a subgenre that is, I think, dying out – Cassie Edwards, maybe the most famous author of this kind, was caught in a plagiarism scandal in the noughties and the "Indian romance" never really came back. Stripped of his original purpose (and traditional enemy), what then becomes of the cowboy? And why has the cowboy romance not only survived, but thrived?

popular of all the title topics. (We can, I think, take industry-leading Harlequin to be a fairly accurate measure of the trend picture as a whole.)

This study is not a perfect yardstick. To separate out "millionaire, billionaire, tycoon, fortune, wealth, money, diamond, dollar, inheritance, heir, gift, treasure, rich, and gold" (796 titles) from "professional, consultant, executive, boss, secretary, corporate, CEO, office, business, company, boardroom, and assistant" (302 titles) betrays a small misunderstanding about the nature of the Hot Billionaire (to say nothing of the idea of dividing gold, diamonds and treasures from the 489 titles mentioning "king, prince, royal, castle, knight, queen, duke, duchess, and palace"). To me, this triple threat probably places the Hot Billionaire, in all his guises, at 1,587 mentions and thus up on top. But only just. Even with all Hot Billionaires combined, the Hot Cowboy still places easily above, for instance, "medical themed romances".

(Still, we must concede that the most popular job for a romantic hero – even outwith Harlequin Medical – probably remains "doctor". Even as someone who avoids almost all medical romance like the plague – pun not intended – this makes perfect sense to me. Medical romance carries some uneasy connotations, but a medical career is basically a perfect fit for a romantic hero: reasonably wealthy, basically caring, and far too busy to pay us too much attention. He's elusive! He's untameable! The chase stays exciting. Thus: doctors!)

The only two titular themes, according to this study, which beat out Hot Cowboy (and Combined Hot Billionaire) were "commitment" – "marriage, wedding, bride, groom, husband, wife, honeymoon, engagement, fiancé, altar, and bachelor" (2,793) – and "reproduction" – "baby, child, mommy, daddy, mother, father, daughter, son, pregnant, paternity, and maternity" (1,830). It's hard to see how these themes *exclude* the Hot Cowboy: it's hard to see, actually, how they exclude Hot Billionaires, Hot Doctors, or anyone else when most romance novels end with wedding bells and all that those bells conventionally promise. These categories, then, don't seem to pose significant competition to the Hot Cowboy's market dominance.

The enduring popularity of commitment and reproduction does, however, explain the fact that – much like with alien romances – cowboy romances love to end with a barefoot pregnant woman, and a man in a large hat. The woman and the man are somewhere very beautiful, often on a porch swing. They can either hear their loud, loving family – mostly his family into which she has been adopted, but occasionally the other way round – or nobody: in which case, they sit in tranquil, perfect peace, hearing only the birds and the wind through the tall grasses. Their house, which usually he has built and she has made homely, is an island of human contentment in the wilderness. There is at least one dog. There is at least one horse. Usually, there are many horses. Such is the way of the cowboy. If aliens are "hard" lack of choice, cowboys are "soft" lack of choice. Nobody *has* to date anybody: the choice is clear from the off. Wear the hat; ride the cowboy.

Perhaps, then, one purpose of this kind of romance is the reconciliation of the domestic and the erotic. We return to Perel's Paradox! Is it – can it be – possible to be both? Is it possible to be wild and tamed?

Perhaps we can trace the current success of the cowboy romance to the fact the Wild West sits at the precise point where the exterior meets the interior: if the "Little House on the Prairie" is simultaneously very small (little house) and very big (prairie), it is also inside and outside, familiar and strange. The cowboy romance is an old ranch house, lived in and loved for generations, surrounded by mountains and forests and wolves. It is the smallness of safety, and the largeness of the world, and the men who can walk with ease between both.

Zane Grey's 1912 novel *Riders of the Purple Sage* is *the* ranch romance: the book that defined a genre. It falls, I suppose, somewhere between romance in the modern sense, and romance in the Edwardian sense of "novel": certainly, the characters are easily recognisable to the modern romance aficionado.

Our heroine is Jane Withersteen, of Withersteen House. She is twenty-eight years old, with "dreamy, troubled eyes" and seven thousand head of cattle all of her own; and, much to the community's dismay, she has "not yet come to see the place of Mormon women". She will not be told; she will not be married. She will not be a third wife to Elder Tull; and if she chooses to adopt a Gentile (non-Mormon) orphan, she shall do it. She does as she pleases, "asking only the divine right of all women—freedom; to love and to live as her heart willed" – and she suffers for it.

Enter, then, the outcast: "black-leather-garbed Lassiter, looking like a man in a dream". He lives in exile; he is hated by Jane's whole community; he is, she thinks, a "gentle-voiced, sad-faced man who was a hater and a killer of Mormons". (Gosh.) He has "lived as a black fox, driven from his kind". He needs nothing from anyone – except, perhaps, could Jane give him a little water for his exhausted horse?

The horse is not just exhausted; he is also blind. Jane's people "roped an' tied him, an' then held white-iron close to his eyes". "Lassiter, the men of my creed are unnaturally cruel. To my everlasting sorrow I confess it," Jane tells him, and then she takes the horse's bridle, leading Lassiter and the pony to her "soft-hued" home.

(Jane's house is, it must be said, an interiors-addict's dream: "a flat, long, red-stone structure with a covered court in the center through which flowed a lively stream of amber-colored water ... flowers, stone, the bright colors of rugs and blankets on the court floor, [with] hammock and books and the clean-linened table".)

She gentles both man and beast, before both reject her offer to sleep in her home in favour of their wild bed in the sage under the stars. The Hot Cowboy moves between both worlds, but he cannot abide to be imprisoned. The natural world is as key to him as his horse – or his woman. "Love of man for woman – love of woman for man. That's the nature, the meaning, the best of life itself," declares Lassiter, later: man, nature, beast and woman form the four corners of the ranch romance, and without one of those corners the whole thing falls apart.

Ranch romance is profoundly heterosexual. Even modern ranch romance tends towards a world of big strong men – and their tender, often pregnant, women.

It's a Wild West, almost: the kind of world in which *men were men and women were women*, whatever that means. It's not that queer ranch romance doesn't exist; it's that it becomes a metatextual experiment on what's already there. Queerness is a porous categorisation by definition: it has to be flexible, capacious, fluid, acting in opposition to something. Queerness is, I suppose, everything that is not straightness; and so queer ranch romance is difficult to call because so much of ranch life is already *so gay*.

Brokeback Mountain is a cultural phenomenon and also a punchline rebuttal to toxic masculinity and middle-American homophobia: we understand that you simply cannot get away from the campness of cowboy camping.

It's not just the inherent queerness of leather, whips, and strong men sharing a sleeping bag under the stars. It's also the ways that classic Westerns tend towards an immutable division of gender: women over here, men over there. If women only or mostly spend time with women, and men only or mostly spend time with men, those relationships will unavoidably have elements of homoeroticism, in its most practical sense – we love the people we know.

Rigid gender boundaries beg to be pushed against: what makes a man a man, and a woman a woman? What is gender, and what is sex? Even in the straightest of Westerns, one of the heroine's features will usually be the push-pull of her relationship to femininity: "a rancher's daughter, at ease on a cow pony's back or on a ballroom floor," writes Mark Boardman, describing the tropes of the genre. "Folks said she had a will of her own, and most thought she'd never be tamed."

It is, for Boardman – editor of *True West* magazine, and a historian of the Old West – one of the *defining* traits of a ranch romance heroine that she should push against gender stereotypes: it's the job of the hero – a "strong, silent type, with more than a hint of danger in the way he carried himself ... his past a mystery; his future unknown" – to break that spell and return his bride to type, *without* losing any of the characteristics that drew him to her in the first place. She must be made into a wife and mother, but she must retain herself, and her freedoms, in the process. The wild mustang must be broken without losing her spirit!

If these character tropes can be found in most early Western writing, Boardman nonetheless traces their undying popularity to one key source: a woman named Fanny Ellsworth, also known by her initials when she wished to go gender-incognito. Ellsworth has been called "one of the great fiction editors of all time", and yet, like many extraordinary women of the twentieth century, she is now largely unknown.

This obscurity might be because of her determination to leave publishing and become a scholar of female life in the Ottoman Empire. But is also pretty typical of the way we talk about – or rather, don't talk about – the kind of women who make the kind of stories that women enjoy.

"It's true that the number of basic plots is limited, but the number of ways they can be varied is endless," Ellsworth wrote; clearly, she understood how we are working, at all times, with a palette that can make many pictures. She knew what it was to work in tropes: she understood, above all things, how tropes can be manipulated, created and reimagined to make something new for even the most knowing reader. She loved "strong emotion" and "humour". She loved to see something real even in the stock photo: "how a ranch house looks when you first glimpse it from a distance; from what kind of wood the corral poles are made; what happens to a man's face when he's lived out of doors in all kinds of weather". Ellsworth was, in short, a romance editor.

"When people ask us how much action we must have in 'Ranch Romances,' we say as much or as little as the plot demands, if by action you mean fighting," Ellsworth wrote. "If by action however, you mean the impact of people on each other, of incident on people ... we want plenty."

Ellsworth was the first editor, and creative powerhouse, of one of America's most successful "romance pulps", *Ranch Romances*. *Ranch Romances* ran for 860 issues, most of which were overseen by Ellsworth, and all of which followed her detailed editorial feedback.

"Make your hero first a person and then a cowboy, your villain a good ordinary everyday heel before you dub him rustler," she instructed, in *The Ogden Standard-Examiner* in March 1941. "Cowboys and prospectors and ranchers' daughters surely love and hate and fear and dare much as any other people."

Essentially: you may take your trope, but paint him human. Don't be afraid of the tension between the idea of the person, and the person; let that tension drive your work. Let the tension between what we want, and what we want to want, play out.

It's not quite a ranch romance, or maybe even a romance novel, but when we talk about longing and landscape and horses it's hard not to think of D. H. Lawrence's 1925 novella *St. Mawr*: an American heiress in a failing marriage in London falls in love, or something, with a stallion.

(Perhaps we should call these books, more generally, *horse romances*; because are not horses often signifiers of great sexiness and romance in books? And *St. Mawr*, if not a *romance* romance, definitely counts as a *horse romance*.)

It's a remarkable story in lots of ways, but there is this one moment in which the heiress realises she must become a rider. Her mother, Mrs. Witt, has taken her horse to Hyde Park, and is riding down Rotten Row with her steely judgement fixed on every person she passes:

Mrs. Witt seemed to be pointing a pistol at the bosom of every other horseman or horsewoman and announcing: "*Your virility or your life! Your femininity or your life!*" She didn't know herself what she really wanted them to be: but it was something as democratic as Abraham Lincoln and as aristocratic as a Russian czar, as highbrow as Arthur Balfour, and as taciturn and unideal as Phoenix. Everything at once.

The size of Mrs. Witt's desire, astride her enormous American horse, forces her daughter to act as chaperone; which means that Lou must buy a horse; which means that Lou must buy her husband a horse; which is how Lou comes to meet the titular stallion. He is, she thinks, "slippery with vivid, hot life". (Gosh.) When there are other horses, or other men, about, St. Mawr seems to Lou to "loom like a bonfire in the dark".

"When I speak to him," says Lou's mother of her groom (equine, not marital), "I'm not sure whether I'm speaking to a man or to a horse." The man who loves the horse becomes part horse, almost animal. The cowboys in the ranch novels are somehow more alive than other kinds of men the heroine has known; they are closer to something real. They make the heroine understand, as St. Mawr teaches Lou, that the "nice clean boys" have "no wild animal left in them. They're all tame dogs, even when they're brave and well-bred. There's no mystery in them." Lou dreams of a "human animal": a "dangerous commodity". "I want the wonder back again," she says, "or I shall die."

This is the wonder of the wild: this is the thrill of the hunt. The hunt is a chase; and the chase is for sport; and, as a contemporary publication wrote, "no sport is worthy of the name that cannot in some measure be traced back to this primitive necessity for chasing a wild animal in its native haunts, incurring woodcraft, long initiation, toil, patience, courage and quickness of mind and soundness of body — a failure in any one of which may mean disaster, shame, or even death." This is taken from *To Whom the Goddess*, published in 1932: not a romance novel, but a manual for riding, specifically hunting, specifically for women hunters. Lady Diana Shedden and Lady Viola Apsley, two great equestrians of the time, give detailed advice to the reader – but it's something more than that, too. Apsley, at the time of writing, would never ride again: broken in a terrible hunting accident, she was unable even to walk. The book is a eulogy, and a defence, and a refusal to admit defeat. It's a tribute to the wonder: to the wild. The upshot is that the book reads like a love letter both to horses and to the people who ride them. It reads like a horse romance.

It is the kind of book that invokes not just a character, but author *as* character: there is something irresistibly of Dame Jilly Cooper, queen of the bonkbuster, about *To Whom the Goddess*. The advice given, and the brisk, forthright, conspiratorial tone in which it's dispensed, evokes the whole county of Rutshire and the world within it. The understanding, in *To Whom the Goddess*, that a horse is pretty much the most important thing on the planet is shared, of course, by most of Cooper's enlightened characters. The people who don't care for horses either learn to care; or are entirely without hope. (Women who don't care for horses are beneath our contempt – possibly they are even intellectuals – and men who don't care for horses are not worth the paper on which Jilly has written them.)

There are, *To Whom the Goddess* tells us, eight elements of riding to be considered: *understanding, harmony, anticipation, confidence, grip, balance, resolution and correct use of aids*. They offer, in short, a fairly clear parallel to the comparable elements in a romance. Riding is romantic; horses are romantic. The people who ride horses are romantic people because riding, in practice, is dangerous and expensive and physically taxing. There is no reason to take up riding except that you can't resist.

This is, incidentally, the plot of perhaps the best decaying-manor horse book of all time: *Flambards*, by K. M. Peyton. Twelve-year-old Christina is sent to live at the titular Flambards with her alcoholic uncle and two older cousins. Having spent her whole life with maiden aunts, this world is all new to her: booze, dogs, horses and blood. The novel opens with her frailer, nicer cousin being half-killed in a riding accident, while Christina, far off, sips tea with an aunt. There is blood; there is bone china. The power of the horse could not be clearer. Horses can hurt; horses can maim; and the aim of the horse, in any case, is to ride to hounds. It takes Christina less than three chapters to know that she will never resist riding. It takes her less than three chapters to fall in love.

It is, basically, *The Secret Garden* aged up a little: the same love triangle, the same setting, the same unsettling, overpowering sexiness throughout. (If *The Secret Garden* wasn't any kind of sexual awakening for you, have the decency to reread it as an adult.) *Flambards* is, of course, much darker than *The Secret Garden*. It is *The Secret Garden* if you knew Colin would never recover, and Dickon slaughtered the fox cub to rub blood across Mary's face. *Flambards* is, at face value, a book for children. *Flambards* disturbed me so much when I first read it, aged about eight, that I had to keep it under my bed: as close to me as physically possible, with no chance of it being removed from me for unsuitability, but also completely invisible. I felt the pull of something adult and powerful and dangerous in its pages. I knew, absolutely, that if a grown-up person found out what I was reading they would be appalled.

When I came back to it as a grown-up myself, I was staggered to find that there was no sex in it at all. Of course there isn't: it's a book about a twelve-year-old who takes up horse riding. And yet, and yet. It is agonisingly sexy, agonisingly dangerous. It is no less powerful to me now than it was twenty years ago. It leaves me sort of breathless: hopeful and horrified and powerless to resist. It's not a ranch romance, it is a horse romance.

Sigmund Freud famously had a lot to say about horse romances. From the case of Little Hans – boy sees terrible horse accident, is afraid of horses, which must mean he's afraid of his father's penis – to the idea that girls see horses as a kind of portable, possessable penis, the undeniable link between horses and sex was conclusively created in the psychological record. Anna Freud, his daughter, agreed, and she took it even further. There were four reasons, she said, for "a little girl's horse-craze": it might be her "primitive autoerotic desires (if her enjoyment is confined to the rhythmic movement of the horse)"; her "identification with the care-taking mother (if she enjoys above all looking after the horse, grooming it, etc.)"; her "penis envy (if she identifies with the big, powerful animal and treats it as an addition to her body)"; or her "phallic sublimations (if it is her ambition to master the horse, to perform on it, etc.)".

The author Susanna Forrest, in her excellent book *If Wishes Were Horses: A Memoir of Equine Obsession*, writes about meeting the evolutionary psychologist Harald Euler. He could not disagree more with Freud *père* and Freud *fille*: "It's bullshit," he tells Forrest. "The girls really love the horse but it's not a sexual love, not at all, far from it." He tells her that men have always loved horses because men love to travel, to explore, to see the boundaries of the world; but that little girls love horses because it's like "caring for babies". They love "to make their horse really pretty". The horse "is the last doll a girl has".

Jilly Cooper, in conversation with the journalist Tanya Gold, might have disagreed: as a child, she said, "I threw all my dolls away. I smashed my dolls. Is that Freudian?"

Forrest, a keen rider, who spends three hundred pages talking to many other keen female riders, definitely does disagree. She tentatively ventures to suggest to Euler that women like horses "not just because they were like great, pettable dolls, but also because they offered a channel for all those princely virtues otherwise forbidden to them: physical bravery, risk taking, courage". Euler ignores her. (As, probably, he would have ignored Cooper.)

The Hot Billionaire and the horse fulfil the same fictional function: a means by which to travel further, go faster, be braver. A means by which to move. Then again, if sometimes the self-insert might be not the Beauty but the Hot Billionaire, why shouldn't the self-insert be not the heroine, but the horse?

Why shouldn't the self-insert be something like that "human animal" which Lou Carrington seeks in *St. Mawr*: something with all the clarity and drive and beauty of a well-cared-for horse, still just a little pleasingly wild?

A horse is a wild thing, and a kept thing. A horse is unpredictable and beautiful, sexy and safe, totally familiar yet never knowable. And a horse is always loved. We can, perhaps, more easily accept that an animal should always be taken care of than that a person should always be taken care of.

The Hot Cowboy always takes care of his horse, no matter how hard he rides it. The Hot Cowboy runs his hands over his horse, brushes the mane, plaits the tail, fits new horseshoes with a bucket of water and a blazing fire.* The Hot

---

* Related: I think the sexiest job it's possible to have is a farrier. I would like quite a lot more romance novels about farriers doing their sexy work of shoeing horses, and judging by the number of internet-famous farriers, this would go down well with a lot of people. Horse girls who are also writers: get on it.

Cowboy might push the horse to the limits of what it can take – but the Hot Cowboy will stay up all night if the horse is hurt. The Hot Cowboy treats his horse – in all versions of the story – with such tender physical and mental care. As Ladies Diana and Viola might say, he treats his horse with "*soft hands, and a firm seat*".

Rupert Campbell-Black may sit somewhere between the Beast and Bluebeard Billionaires – but he is, at heart a Hot Cowboy. Consider the gentling and racing of his horse! Consider the landscape in which he lives: the Rutshire countryside, the beauty of it, the shapes and shadows within it. He belongs to the people (almost like an aristocrat of the old school); he is known in a community. He belongs to a place, and his horse belongs to him.

He is never indecisive. A good rider can't be. "The spineless sort of rider who does not know her own mind, has no idea of her own, or has two minds about everything, invariably communicates her indecisions to her horse, till the pair are a danger to themselves and a nuisance to other people," the Ladies Shedden and Apsley tell us. "It is better to make your mind up wrong than to have no mind at all or try to do several things at the same moment."

A good rider has to know exactly what he wants, and then make it happen.

A good rider has to know exactly what *she* wants, and then make it happen.

Having spent many books refusing to countenance her own clear interest in the Hot Billionaire Genius who adores her – in spite of his charm, generosity, thoughtful help with her work, nice notes, nicer dinners, and the fact that they are obviously meant for one another – what tips Harriet Vane over the edge is something she never expected: *"She realised that there was, after all, something god-like about him. He could control a horse."*

The Hot Cowboy – and the horse romance as a whole – is always about control.*

Whether a Silver bull rider, a Sage blacksmith, or a Cooper racehorse trainer, there is a trifecta of control, competence and care.

If a man can ride a wild bull, tend to a horse, and drive stick, what else might he be able to do?† *Tame the beast and now tame me*, my sister texted, succinctly.

But if he can also teach her how to drive stick, so much the better. This skillset falls under the same category as teaching her to ride – or to ride again, in the case of Violet in Elsie

---

* I sometimes wonder if control is also behind the rise in STEM romances: impeccable control over every element of an experiment; precise and eagle-eyed observation of every new atom; and God-like decision-making skills when it comes to the pipette and the Petri dish. Are Ali Hazelwood's Hot Scientists, most of them easily as brusque as a Jilly Cooper hero, tapping into the same need for handsome-handed control as an Elsie Silver horse tamer?
† We cannot underestimate the importance of "driving stick" in contemporary ranch romance: an indicator of both competence, and erotic control, given the obvious phallic symbolism. If you were raised in a country where most people don't have automatic cars, and therefore most people who can drive "drive stick", this is extremely charming and adds an extra frisson of eroticism and power to a trip down the M1.

Silver's *A Photo Finish*. It is an explicit demonstration that the gates are open, an implicit invitation to dash forward into freedom whatever the cost.

To ride a horse is both to be master and mastered: it is to be vulnerable to the wild world, and to charge through it with violence. Modern sex, Katherine Angel writes, both "acknowledges vulnerability and disavows it: you are vulnerable, therefore you must harden yourself; you are violable, therefore you must cast yourself as inviolable". The dance between vulnerability and inviolability carries the same weight either side of the equation, riding or ridden; and this is the dance which underpins *all* horse romances.

"That's the consequence of letting a girl follow the hounds," says Mr Audley, in the classic Victorian romance *Lady Audley's Secret*. "She learns to look at everything in life as she does at six feet of timber or a sunk fence; she goes through the world as she goes across country – straight ahead, and over everything."

Harriet Vane, investigating a murder and in great danger, receives a letter of advice from the man she loves. He does not tell her to stop investigating. He does not tell her to be safe. He tells her that "disagreeableness and danger" should never turn her back from what she believes to be right, and Harriet is staggered. "If he conceived of marriage along those lines," Sayers writes, "then the whole problem would have to be reviewed in that new light; but that seemed scarcely possible. To take such a line and stick to it, he would have to be, not a man but a miracle."

"Proof of love," writes the journalist Tanya Gold, on the novels of Jilly Cooper "—is buying someone a horse." Proof of love is letting someone go boldly into danger, into excitement, into exhilaration – into a place where small domestic cares intersect with, and indeed permit, adventure into the wild unknown.

For the ranch romance is not just a cowboy romance, but a horse romance, and a landscape romance too. We can't divorce any horse romanticist from the landscape in which the horse moves: like the Billion-Free!Hot Billionaire, with which there is a clear horse-based overlap, the romance novelist who specialises in anything horsey also specialises in creating an emotional and practical landscape of escapism. There are very few city-based horse romances (would read!): the whole genre is about openness, about spaces for freedom, about the world that exists beneath our own. It is, in fact, about something more primal and vital than the world most of us live in now.

When St. Mawr throws Lou's husband from his back, the pathetic husband demands that he be either killed, or castrated. Lou refuses. "I'll preserve one last male thing in the museum of this world, if I can," she says (extraordinary sentence!): she takes the horse, ungelded, to a ranch in the West "like a Zane Grey book-jacket". The spell of the ranch romance runs deep; the ranch romance is capturing something real and potent and true. The horse, here, is explicitly and metaphorically playing the role of Hot Cowboy. The Hot Cowboy becomes the Hot Horse, which becomes the Hot Wild.

"The wild other of an animal is something strange and thrilling," Clover Stroud writes in her memoir *The Wild Other*, "when a child ... can escape altogether into a landscape that [she] and pony create together." Later, Stroud runs away to Texas to ride fast horses, chase a girlhood fantasy of cowboys, and look for something lost. "I knew my life there had to be as real as possible," she writes. "I wanted to feel and inhabit every part of myself."

I'm sure the readers of ranch romance are looking for something that feels real: for something that feels like a place where they might, without the confines of modern life, find out who they are. They might find something that makes more sense than the endless whirl of late-stage capitalism and forty-six kinds of toilet paper.

"People realized they didn't have to stay locked into the hustle if they didn't want to," Elsie Silver told an interviewer in May 2025. "[The pandemic] shifted priorities for a lot of us ... [I think] people are craving that sense of community and simplicity."

As the bride of one Ice Planet alien muses, cheerfully: "Survival feels like a never-ending job. You take, you give back. It just makes sense." It's simple; it's real; it's everything.

"*There's something else for me, mother,*" Lou says, looking out at her wild horse and her wild land. "*There's*

In Love with Love

something else even that loves me and wants me ... [H]ere, on this ranch ... in this landscape. It's something more real to me than men are, and it soothes me, and it holds me up. I don't know what it is, definitely. It's something wild, that will hurt me sometimes and will wear me down sometimes. I know it. But it's something big..."

    The cowboy gives us entry to a world that we thought might have been lost. The horse is the landscape is the relationship. And the cowboy holds the door open to the wild.

6

Daisy Bacon and the Fifty-Fifty Girls

Daisy Bacon, Queen of the Pulps, was born in 1898, and the next thirty years are all conjecture. Either a proficient liar, or a natural-born storyteller, she shaped her early life depending on her listener. She might have come from anywhere. She might have been anyone. She might have been entirely self-taught; maybe not. A media darling, a kind of literary It Girl – pictures show impeccable curls, polka-dot shirt dress, feet up on her desk, surrounded by swoons and clinches and stacks of stories and dozens of ceramic cats – she was called the best-dressed woman in America. She wrote an advice column, in which she argued that the answer – just sometimes, and shockingly – might be divorce.

At thirty, she was made editor of *Love Story Magazine*: "a magazine larger than *Harper's Magazine*, *The American Mercury*, and *The Atlantic Monthly* rolled together".

"And so we have taken love for the theme of all our stories—the love of the One Man for the One Woman, the kind of love that ends in happiness and the warm human joys of home," ran the first ever editorial. "To be happy you must learn the difference between True Love and False, between the baser feelings which end in suffering, and the right and noble ones which bring real joy." As a starting place for the next century of romance novels – the restrictions of "Man" and "Woman" notwithstanding – it's not a bad one; although it may be argued that the romance novels of the last hundred years have striven fairly tirelessly to reconcile the base instincts and noble joys in one attractive package.

Love Story contained serials, complete stories, poetry, advice, astrology, and more. The March 30, 1935 edition, for example, features the regular column 'Your Stars And You', by Kai ("Mr. C. F. W., born January 18, 1912, Ohio, about 4:00 a. m.: There is no doubt about your having artistic talent but I am sorry that you spent your money on a correspondence course"); and a lively pen pal exchange ("Boys, cheer up Lonely Ben!") that clearly indicates the breadth of *Love Story*'s readership. The youngest pen pal is a fifteen-year-old boy, hoping to exchange "snap-shots"; the oldest in her mid-forties, hoping to find some other "older readers fond of camping". It's hard not to detect queer undertones to these unabashed longings – or, indeed, overtones. Under the headline "This Pal enjoys gay pleasures!", Miss Morris urges her readers to befriend "a young man of twenty-four, very broadminded, interested in everything and everyone. My main hobbies are dancing and singing, and I always enjoy a good show."

In addition, the reader can find an advice column ("Dear Mrs. Brown, Before I married my husband's mother seemed to like me . . ."), Elfrida Norden's poem "Love", the fourth part of Joan King's *Midnight Madness* (one more to come!); and the final instalment of Cordelia Snow's *Primitive Love* (Anne L. Kimball's *Too Reckless!* will take the slot next week). These various features are plainly recognisable as romances in the most modern sense. Previously, as Daisy Bacon herself noted, romances – while "very good reading" – had told "not of girls and men but of heroes and heroines personified and of Fate". Daisy, like modern-day editors and writers, wanted stories about real people meeting in real and interesting ways. Which is why the stories she published still feel so fresh. There are, obviously, things that don't play now – but the all-important shape, and the shape of the characters, is the same.

To take a random example: the first story in that March 1935 edition is Gerry Ann Hale's *Two in a Fog*. Here is Melina, who has just had her heart broken; here is Rod, who broke it; here is Erin (boy Erin, tragically) here to mend it. Here is the scheming and exquisite Jada to stand in their way. Here is the fog that keeps them all trapped. But Rod has left Melina because he can't stand that she has a successful career – he hoped that travelling business class meant she had rich parents, not that she was travelling on business – and Jada's scheme for stealing back Erin is to strip naked and slip into his bed. Erin and Melina make each other laugh – really laugh. He toasts to her career, and makes sure – after their first, off-page but presumably passionate, night together – that she gets to the office for 9 a. m. It's all surreally modern – not least for the metatextual commentary on *other* romance writing. "I've just discovered that romance and the working girl doesn't mix, despite the Cinderella myth," Melina tells Erin, drily. "The movies are all wrong, so are magazines, and novels. It's all wrong."

For something so vital in literary history, *Love Story* has been given surprisingly little attention. Mostly, now, the critical attention – and it would be remiss to suggest it is anything less than real literary criticism – given to *Love Story* survives in fragments on early internet blogs, the kind typed in Times New Roman, with one picture per page, and a Next button. For a magazine with a weekly circulation of 600,000 readers, it's an astonishing vanishing act.

Love Story published fifty-two issues a year, for more than twenty-five years. It was the single most successful pulp magazine of all time – which, given that the word "pulp" has become synonymous with horror, fantasy and sci-fi, says something about just how little consideration was and has ever been given to the world of women's fiction. Almost all of the writers of romances of this era are completely unknown today – not so much as a Wikipedia page – which is a marked contrast to the figures who wrote for the darker, "manlier" pulps, and also perhaps a consequence of how many of Daisy's beloved readers wrote for the magazine themselves. These were not career writers, but amateurs in the best sense of the word: people who wrote for the love of it.

Daisy's only book, written well into her descent into alcoholism and following a failed attempt to write the definitive romance novel of the romance pulp era – set *in* the world of romance pulp publishing, and thus making it my most-longed-for of never-written novels – was *Love Story Editor* (1954). As the name suggests, *Love Story Editor* is an intimate, scolding, all-knowing guide to successfully publishing romantic fiction. It remains remarkably solid as a primer. It also shows a profound faith in the genre itself.

"If you will just send me the formula for writing for your magazine, I will send on some stories," she remembers one (many) hopefuls writing to her. Not just fans of the magazine, but "actresses playing romantic roles in summer theatres or bits in the movies", "men [who] worked in department stores or in businesses which cater to women", and "superior and sophisticated" "writers established in other fields of writing"; they all thought they might have a go at a romance. Everyone thought they could write a romance; few, Daisy thought, could do it right. "More than any other story type, the love story is looked upon as a freak, which can be turned out without much thought or preparation," Daisy writes, sternly, and romance lovers everywhere understand that they are in the hands of someone who truly *gets it*.

(Again, the modern-day parallels are obvious. Many writers I have met have suggested that they could write a romance novel, since there's *so much money in it*. Almost all of those writers, unless they truly love romance novels, have failed in this ambition.)

Some elements, of course, were traditional: as Daisy's biographer, Laurie Powers, notes, she felt strongly that "all heroines ... should be looking for a change ... restless, unhappy, be at risk of losing their livelihood, or be hiding a secret". The question of money, too, remained central to *Love Story*'s mission: "obtaining it, the lack of it, the imbalance of who had how much of it, or whether the hero and heroine could live without it". Furthermore, having to pretend to be a handsome stranger's wife or girlfriend never went out of style. Nor did mysterious happenings. These tropes ran the whole length of *Love Story*'s tenure as reigning queen of the romance world, and – it must be said – are hardly unknown today. (Who knew fake dating had such a long and varied history?)

Daisy made clear the tropes that worked – and what she wanted to see more of on submission. She hoped for stories about, for instance, "the way men and women stand by each other when one of them is accused of a crime" (specifically, she thought, it would be "especially dramatic in a murder trial when a man believes a woman innocent and is able to help, more dramatic still if that man is attached to the prosecutor's office". Had she read *Strong Poison*, by Dorothy L. Sayers? It's possible.)

She is very brisk: one chapter is called "Delaying Tactics" and even seventy years later it hits this writer directly in the solar plexus; and "Authors Address A Parade, Not A Convention" remains startlingly good advice. She is also very funny and very inviting: you can't help but want to get on with it. The magazine itself actually carried adverts requesting contributions and offering correspondence courses in writing. One opens: "How do you know you can't WRITE?

Have you ever tried?" The unfortunate (or fortunate) reader is instructed to send away for an aptitude test, which will be critiqued, "corrected and constructively criticized" by a "group of men, whose combined newspaper experience totals more than 200 years". (Rather you than me.)

Further adverts propose a "book on social graces", an exhortation to "be your own music teacher" (pamphlets available on request), plus offers to buy pennies. There are treatments for piles, prostate troubles, and "ruptures"; a home gym (just $2.99!) to grow "big husky muscles", or, if you don't fancy that, a "free trial treatment" to "GET RID OF YOUR FAT" without "starvation diet or burdensome exercise". There are also what seems to be an implausible number of job placements for "detectives", who will "earn big money". Experience unnecessary. (But "Literature will NOT be sent to boys under 17 years of age".)

There are, in fact, a great deal of employment advertisements in the editions of *Love Story Magazine* – or, rather, advertisements for *opportunities* for employment. There is not, necessarily, a *job* available in this brand-new "big pay field" of electricity – but you can certainly send away for a free, fully illustrated book about the "sensational new plan", and get started. There is no specific advertisement for a job in radio, but J. E. Smith, President of the National Radio Institute, is so sure that "its future is certain" that in exchange for the attached coupon, he will send you his 64-page book to "learn at home to get a good job in radio". "Get Ready Now For Jobs Like These", he says, in the obligatory bold type. An advert, on first glance for "New Deal government jobs – men and women aged 18–50" transpires to be a "32-page book describing salaries, hours, work, and giving full particulars telling how to get a position". It is 1935: the combination of a dismal economy, brand-new technology and global instability speaks, I think, directly to our present moment.

While most pulp magazines of the era carry adverts of this kind, we can't ignore that their presence here means it must have been worth advertising to the readers of *Love Story*. The (mostly) female readers of romance are being clearly and explicitly targeted by the makers of radio and producers of electricity: for the advert to be worth running, they must have been reasonably likely to embrace the newest technologies and biggest ideas. This is not surprising to me. Romantic fiction, seen by many as a backwards-looking genre, has always been on the cutting edge of what's technologically possible.

Jane Austen is writing, for instance, at a time before the publishing industry has even really settled on a model (subscription? Single sale of copyright? Commission? Profit-sharing?); Daisy Bacon's *Love Story* exists *because* the technology to produce cheap paper has suddenly come into being, and has created with it a space for almost a million new manuscripts every year (only counting those delivered to the *Love Story* offices). The technology to mass-print is only, in Bacon's time, forty years old: before that, type had to be set by hand. Academic Janice Radway, writing mostly about Harlequins and Mills & Boons in the late 1980s, makes clear that the unbelievable proliferation in romance at the time is directly related to the ways that the "modern mass-market paperback was made possible by such technological innovations as the rotary magazine press and synthetic glue as well as by organizational changes in the publishing and bookselling industries". Christine Larson, in her excellent study *Love in the Time of Self-Publishing*, convincingly attributes our current kissing boom to 2007's "digital disruption" in publishing "with the introduction of the Kindle".

The things we read are products not just of our social and political culture, but also of our material culture; or perhaps it's more accurate to say that our social and political cultures are a product of our material culture, and vice versa. Romance fiction is a product, always, of new technology. And it is, as Larson says, "a unique site of feminized labor". Are these two things connected?

New technology is, I suppose, often the preserve of women and other people pushed to the margins: people pushed out of mainstream spaces will seek work, fulfilment and room for dreaming in the new untested places. The first mainstream "computers" were not machines, but women: it was a descriptive job title for someone who made computations to run what we would now consider to be code. The work was dull and low status: institutions like Harvard hired women because they were cheap, and easy to fire. Hardware was for men; software, as the binary implies, was for women. It was clerical. ("It's just like planning a dinner!") Today, the vast majority of computers – "coders", as we call them – are men. And they are no longer quite so cheap.

When technology becomes mainstream, the keys are handed over to, or snatched by, the people with greater power. In very blunt terms: men take the established technology and give it gates, and establish themselves as the gatekeepers. When something new comes to light, women are often the early innovators. I am thinking, especially and most recently, of the emergence of various social media platforms – Instagram, TikTok, Substack – and the ingenious, creative uses through which they have been charged to create capital, mostly by young women. I am thinking of the many ways those platforms have been initially dismissed, before being consumed and subsumed by the loud ideologies and inanities of men.

It is, perhaps, pertinent that those platforms are themselves often a kind of romantic fiction. A beautiful young woman finds herself. There is often some private trauma made public: anxiety, anorexia, acne, hyper-mobility, grief. This is part of the journey: the reason, or ostensible reason, for the documenting of the journey. There are coffees in cafés, and out-of-focus friends; and sunlight through glass jars. There are green smoothies and high, swishy, athletic ponytails. Then an out-of-focus man across a table; a masculine hand holding a masculine beer; the hard launch of the Boyfriend. An engagement ring showcased on slender, manicured fingers. Keys to a house. Paint swatches, wallpaper samples, scalloped edges, a baby. There are endless variations on this theme: I've done them myself. I've been the romantic fiction in question, and it's hard to stop. It's hard to stop looking at your own life through this lens: you take the pictures, curate the order, write the captions, and suddenly that's what your life is. It's like a memoir, but like all memoirs, it's fiction. The truth is always more complicated than that, no matter what *that* is. And the truth is always harder to swallow.

The queen of these real and unreal romantic fictions is, of course, the *tradwife*.

A tradwife, if you have been lucky enough not to engage with this concept, is a kind of internet influencer famous for behaving like a *traditional wife*, which is to say, a housewife ... but more. An impossible creature, trapped somewhere in the last half of the nineteenth and first half of the twentieth century: the hundred-year span between the invention of modern femininity and the invention of mass feminism. She exists in the twenty-first century on the internet: in earlier eras, she lived between the pages of advice guides, cookbooks, women's magazines and the happy endings of some – not all – pulp love stories.

Not all tradwives are millionaires, or indeed married to millionaires. It's just that once you know the most famous tradwife – Hannah Neeleman of Ballerina Farm – is married to a man whose father founded five airlines, big ones, everything both makes a lot more sense and grows a lot more murky. The lovers of the Hot Billionaire and the Hot Cowboy come together to create this singular tradwife. Neeleman is a beauty queen and onetime dancer, like many internet influencers of the tradwife school. She is also a Mormon, which is, if not compulsory, certainly helpful: the shimmy from "ballet in college" to "Mormon mommy blogger" is, at this point, a well-worn career path. The shimmy, in fact, from "New York dancer" to "cherished wife and mother" is *such* a straightforward romance plot.

The tradwife makes toothpaste out of powders, and bakes bread from scratch. She keeps a cow, perhaps. She puts lipstick on before her husband comes home. She is almost constantly pregnant. Her "job", as far as the cameras are concerned, is to raise children on wholesome nourishing foodstuffs, teach them to live as she lives, and keep herself and her home beautiful. Of course, her real job is to make interesting and compelling photographs, essays and short films *on the subject* of these activities. Her real job is to run a very successful business, while pretending that her only sphere is the domestic. She is the writer, star and producer of these artefacts – art works? – and this career choice is, in many cases, extremely lucrative. The farm itself – the work of rearing so many children and animals – is not the point; the point is the content created *about* the work. That's where the money is.

Do we have a duty to practise what we preach? And are we in dereliction of that duty if practising what we preach creates a result that takes us further than ever from the subject of our preaching? If the tradwife preaches female subservience to a wealthy husband, does it matter that she

Daisy Bacon and the Fifty-Fifty Girls

is, in truth, a substantial contributor to the household finances?

Daisy Bacon called her readers, her women – who are, in essence, our women, *us*, the readers and writers and heroines of romance novels – "fifty-fifty girls". It took me quite a long time to understand what this meant: it's a lost bit of slang.

The best-known use of the phrase is from a movie of the 1920s. We have a poster, we have a summary, we have one photo of the stars on set. That's it.*

The Fifty-Fifty Girl was – of course – a romcom. I surmise this from the brief summaries available, and the only

---

* We assume everything will continue to exist forever; it's startling, sometimes, to realise that most things – most media – will vanish even as we look at it. A whole culture that feels so solid and obvious – this word, that truth – can be gone almost entirely in twenty or even ten years, and fifty years later a term Daisy Bacon uses with cheerful frequency is almost impossible to trace. One thing I love about Daisy Bacon is that she knew this absolutely; one reason Daisy Bacon became so phenomenally successful was her ability to move with the times. "Modern Miss Doesn't Want the Old Hokum", blared a headline of 1931, above an article about Daisy in the *Boston Sunday Globe*. There is a whole chapter in her book solely dedicated to trying to explain why some of the most successful writers of the early days of her tenure at the magazine were unheard of in its pages by the last, some thirty years later: the answer is always that they failed to understand that what people want from romance is constantly changing. She understood, I think, that romance is always and absolutely a product of the socioeconomic time and place, while simultaneously tapping into something universal and unchanging in the human condition. The "human animal" Lou yearns for in *St. Mawr* needs satisfaction on both counts: wild sex and economic relief (and vice versa). Romantic fiction, like all fiction I suppose, must always respond to the eternal and the temporary.

remaining still from the film, in which James Hall, as Jim, looks vacant in an enormous hat, while next to him in the car, Kathleen O'Hara – played by the exquisite Bebe Daniels – in a huge fur coat, perfect Clara Bow lips, has both hands firmly on the steering wheel. Kathleen and Jim are engaged, and have both just separately inherited separate halves of the same gold mine. (What a set-up.)

But Kathleen is the titular "fifty-fifty girl". She believes firmly in equality of the sexes, and so – on jointly inheriting the mine – they agree that they'll trade traditional roles. Jim will run the house; Kathleen will run the mine. Who will crack first?

This is feminism pre-feminism; this is proto-feminism, pre-Code.

(The Hays Code, a 1930s directive for the film industry, forbade among other things "suggestive nudity" and "any instance of sex perversion". It also strongly limited the inclusion of "first-night scenes", "Man and Woman in bed together", "deliberate seduction of girls" and "excessive or lustful kissing, particularly when one character or the other is a 'heavy'". If one rules out kissing, sex and seduction – especially of a known bad man – it's remarkably impressive that any romantic films at all got made between 1934 and 1968, when the Hays Code regulation ceased. The "institution of marriage" was also a "maybe". Which rules out even some of the tamest of heterosexual romances, no?)

But Daisy's fifty-fifty girl is an update: "the fifty-fifty girl of today," she says, "is the girl who knows how to be a business woman in business hours and an alluring feminine thing after 5 o'clock."

The tension here, then, is not so much between the domestic and the erotic, as the personal and the professional. It isn't the uncomplicated shoulder-pad power of Shirley Conran's *Lace* as a phenomenon, but the complex interplay between family and career, softness and hardness, of Conran's individual characters.

Sex is, as Katherine Angel notes, always a question of "play with power and relinquishing". When many women are as powerful as many men, and all of us know it, where does the power dynamic that drives heterosexual sex come from? This question might sound flippant, but I mean it: in a world in which the gender dynamic is fixed, it's easy to know what sex is supposed to be. The rules are already in place. You either go with the rules – big man, little lady, he's on top and she says thank you – or you turn that on its head and everyone gets to play nicely with gender. You either follow the rules, or break them. It's easy.

If you are starting from a point where the power dynamic has to be figured out first, that's a whole new level of complexity and emotion. That is, in some ways, sex on hard mode – and we are all having sex on hard mode. It is also the only kind of sex that's ever going to be mutually satisfying. The thing about romantic fiction is that because it can simplify all these choices, all these worlds, right down, we are permitted to have all of them at once. We can try things out without danger; we can learn how we want it; we can learn what dynamics look and feel like without having to engage in the risky business of asking someone to surrender with no sense of where we're taking them. We can practise; we can play; we can run all our different lives at once without losing anything. We can find out who we are. We can become. We can *be*.

And we can, for once in our lives, have it all.

7

The Hometown Hero

"Having It All" was invented, pretty much, in the 1980s. (Before that, maybe, we just took what we could get?)

Helen Gurley Brown's book *Having It All: Love, Success, Sex, Money—Even If You're Starting with Nothing*, now seems, as the *New York Times* put it, "a charming artifact from a more hopeful time".

Gurley Brown was the editor of – and, really, the founder of the modern – *Cosmopolitan* magazine; Daisy Bacon's nearest inheritor. (While they overlapped in time, I don't know if they ever met. I hope so. I hope there was a secret club for troublesome and exhilarating editors.) She is about as controversial a figure as publishing has: deeply beloved, deeply worrying, part feminist icon (a strong advocate for the Equal Rights Amendment; passionate about women's ability to dazzle in the workplace), and part the opposite ("you may have a tiny touch of anorexia nervosa to maintain an ideal weight ... not a heavy case, just a little one"). She was troublesome, elitist, rude, funny, delightful and blunt. Her writing remains all of these things. Despite the fact that Gurley Brown had no children herself, and never wanted any, her "having it all" phrase has become synonymous with the desire to balance both career and motherhood.

Even Gurley Brown is forced to admit the existence of the problem. In her book *Sex and the Single Girl*, which is in many ways a manual for attracting and securing the attention of a potential husband, she tells her readers that "when a man thinks of a married woman, no matter how lovely she is, he must inevitably picture her greeting her husband at the door with a martini or warmer welcome, fixing little children's lunches". By contrast, she says, when the man pictures the single woman, he pictures her lounging in dozens of cushions, clad only in pink silk capri pants. (Extraordinary.)

To be respected in the boardroom; and made to beg in the bedroom, *but also* to be adored everywhere else by your charming husband and precious small children – all while staying thin, toned, beautifully turned out. This is an impossibly high standard of discipline and self-presentation to maintain. It *might* be possible if you either come from vast amounts of money, or marry rich. (Hello, Hot Billionaire, we meet again.) Even then, though, you've still got to find a way to be happy, and that's the real kicker.

And yet, in we all go, thinking we will be the one to win this game of having it all. Trap? What trap? The handsome man sits on the picnic rug holding out a bottle of champagne and a diamond; the net comes down the second you step towards him. And yet we are still not stupid. We know it's not real. We know there's a tension there.

The Hometown Hero

And it's the tension, in fact, which drove the entire women's magazine movement of the 1970s, '80s, '90s and even noughties: those glossy magazines which spun effortlessly between twenty ways to drive him wild, and ten ways to ask for that pay rise you deserve. It's *Sex and the City*'s ongoing self-interrogation: if the women of *Sex and the City* are, like Gurley Brown's single girl, "self-made, sexual and supremely ambitious", they are also very determined to fall in love.

The original Fifty-Fifty Girl, Kathleen O'Hara, is, of course, brought low in the end. She is humbled by bandits in her ambition to run a gold mine; she calls for help from her fiancé – as one might – and while her life is saved, her stake in the mine is handed to him under the terms of the bet. They kiss, they marry; and the mine becomes, in a much lesser way, hers once more.

It's dated, it's jarring, and yet – did this story-shape ever really go away? Did we ever really *believe* we could have it all? How many romances are there where the woman ends up *more* powerful than she was at the beginning, and why does writing that sentence feel tantamount to revolution? She might end up richer; she might end up happier. But does she ever end up more powerful?*

---

* Jasmine Guillory, one of the best writers we have, romance-wise, is about the only exception I can think of, and I strongly recommend all her books, in order, without stopping. You will love *The Wedding Date* if you have ever thought about being trapped in a lift with a handsome man and a plate of cheese and crackers. You will also love it if you have ever wondered why only teeny-tiny heroines get to eat.

Consider Sandra Bullock at the start of *The Proposal* – who cannot show an inch of vulnerability – versus Sandra Bullock at the end of *The Proposal*: publicly voluble, and handing herself over into the custody of a man. She keeps her job. She, maybe, has it all. Except, she has been thoroughly humbled, learned a good lesson and lost, perhaps, the respect of her in-laws, who presumably spend the next twenty years saying, wait, *what*?

Just as Kathleen O'Hara is humbled by bandits, so too are the powerful businesswomen of today humbled for love. The made-for-TV movie (once Hallmark, now Netflix, soon no doubt somewhere else) has always loved the story of the city girl and the hometown hero: the girl who flew too close to the sun, who now must transfigure into an earth mother. Her big-city life was no good! Now she swaps her top job as a surgeon to run the clinic in the small town; she quits her lawyering to raise cute babies on the ranch; she takes over the finances for his business, and together they transform it into a sensation. (It's his business first and foremost, though, even if he puts her name on the door.)

The Hometown Hero is, essentially, the opposite of the Hot Billionaire. (The Billion-Free!Hot Billionaire is kind of a Hometown Hero, but not a humble one.)

The Hometown Hero has a lot in common with the Hot Cowboy, and indeed may well be – if not exactly a Hot Cowboy himself – ranch-romance adjacent. Elsie Silver's *Flawless*, for instance – the first in her extremely delicious

Chestnut Springs series – is the story of a troubled bull-rider and the lawyer sent by his management to keep him on the straight and narrow. *Heartless* – the second in the series – is the story of ranch manager Cade, and Willa, the city-girl nanny he reluctantly hires to care for his precious little boy. *Powerless* – well, look, people find a niche. (I could perform strongly in a *Mastermind* chair on the works of Elsie Silver.)

Daisy Bacon was a big believer in the Hometown Hero. "Cities do not furnish any more glamorous backgrounds than the country," she explains, firmly, "and besides glamour depends upon the author and not upon the background." Commissioning mostly in the Great Depression, Bacon's in tray was swamped with stories set in big-bucks New York, the last true home of real money. (It's very tempting to draw a parallel between the current Hot Billionaire boom and Bacon's boom, isn't it?) But mostly, she did not like these stories. She felt that they missed something vital about the human experience, about romance as a whole.

"I once corresponded with a woman living in Winslow, Arizona, who sent us highly artificial stories about New York night club life," Bacon writes, scathingly. The Winslow woman had a sister who had once won a tour of New York; her stories were set in her sister's stories of the tour guide's stories. Bacon replied, in anguish: "The Painted Desert is in your front yard!" Not just the Painted Desert; Winslow, Bacon happened to know, is where the Pullman train cars stopped for the night. There were dust storms that raged through, and hotels "like an oasis", and things "so remote and so close". The Winslow woman tried again. "When she wrote the story of a night telephone operator and a young deputy sheriff who pitched in and worked together during a freak tornado, she sold it."

What Bacon is looking for, then, is the universal hiding inside the specific: the thing, in short, that all fiction editors are looking for in the stories they publish.

She also, in this example, clearly understands that small-town romance often depends on being trapped: a dust storm, a freak tornado, a blizzard, a landslide, a broken car where the needed part just won't arrive in time. The city person must be held there before her worst instincts can carry her away from what she most needs – and what she most needs is people.

I once saw someone complaining on the internet that what people didn't understand about the small-town romance was that it's not just *set* in a small town: the small town has to be one of the main characters. I am usually sceptical of "the setting is a character in itself" conversations – I often think it's just a mistaken way of saying "the setting is really good" – but this person, in this context, might have been onto something. In so many romances, of so many kinds, the heroine falls in love not just with a person but with a place. In the small-town romance, what she really falls for is the *community*.

It's tempting to connect this with Margaret Thatcher, Ronald Reagan and the decline of society: perhaps we seek in fiction what has been destroyed in real life. We fantasise about a pre-Thatcher time where everyone knew everyone, and there was a village to raise your children with you. We mourn the death of community every day. We long for the simple life. This feels to us like a modern problem, and in some ways it is.

In other ways, this longing for the simple life – the tradwife's urge to milk a cow, or the human urge to turn a patch of earth in company with a friend – is the same urge that drove the pioneers down the Oregon Trail: there is a better life, more in communion with the things that matter, somewhere else. Somewhere where each job will have a purpose, where we will all have purpose. There, away from everything that plagues us now, will we find fulfilment.

Obviously, there are books where both hero and heroine hail from the same small town. Much like books where both parties are hot billionaires from the get-go, these books don't quite click as small-town romances for me. I want to see a small town through the eyes of someone new: that is, someone to whom all of this is absurd, tiny, almost baroque in the insular patterns and routines of life somewhere where everyone knows everyone. I want to be allowed to live in this small town too, at least for a book (okay, ideally for several books), and I want to meet it on my own terms as a newcomer.

"There once was a town, and I was so certain that it would feel like home if I ever made it there," begins Ashley Poston's *A Novel Love Story*. "There was once a town, and it didn't exist." *A Novel Love Story* is a love letter to small-town romances, but all small-town romances are love letters to small towns and the people who live in them.

Sophie Kinsella's *The Undomestic Goddess* is, to me, the landmark Hometown Hero book. It also has a very funny premise. A trainee lawyer accidentally loses a £50 million deal, then loses her head, gets on a train to the middle of nowhere, and through a series of unfortunate events, accidentally lands a job as housekeeper to a fancy couple. She has, of course, never done a stroke of housework in her life: she can't cook, can't clean, can't do laundry. Hijinks – all of the "decanting a fancy takeaway into spotless Le Creusets" variety – ensue. Luckily, there is a handsome gardener. And his mum, who can cook – but won't. Instead, she teaches our heroine how to cook, and our heroine – against her will – finds herself falling in love ... Her growing affections for our handsome hero are, I think, a little by the by. Really, she falls for his mum. She also falls for his mum's cooking, the local pub, the landscape and the people in the village. She stops being a snob. She stops being anxious. She starts to like things again: the transformation is not so much of her romantic life, but of her whole self.

These, then, are the questions asked by so much modern romance: how can we live our fullest lives? How can we be our best selves?

The Hot Billionaire gives you something; the Hot Alien takes it away. The Hometown Hero is a combination of both: the city girl, drained and pale with the stress of her big city job, arrives in the charming location, is stripped of her previously held beliefs, and is given a whole new town's worth of people. It's important to note that the heroine has, up until this point, usually enjoyed a pretty successful life. She's no bike courier; no nanny with a dream. She doesn't need rescuing by a Hot Billionaire, and she doesn't want to give everything up to be a wife and mother as per the Hot Aliens. The heroine has worked very hard to get where she is, and it's everything she's ever wanted, and it's killing her. Achieving her dreams is *killing* her.

She either comes to this town because it has all fallen apart – she didn't get the promotion, was harassed at work, lost fifty million bucks, etc. – or she comes to this town and it all falls apart as a consequence: she misses an important phone call, for instance, or she can't bring herself to finish the draft.

This falling apart is vital, because the small town often gives the heroine a new job. It is preferably the kind of job that people who work at computers all day can only dream of. It's a job where she never looks at a screen at all. Something with good smells (surrounded by fields of lavender, she becomes a perfumier!), and beautiful things to see, and plenty of human connection. People, people, always people: the city girl has been lonely for a long time. The city girl did not know how, before now, to find this kind of connection: not just with her one best friend, or her gay roommate, but with all the spiky, funny, ordinary, extraordinary people around her.

The job must be one where she meets the people in the place, and ideally one where she can perform them a service, understanding their needs, their lives, their small dreams. Florist, say. Bookseller. Baker.

There are so many books like this, and they all have titles that do exactly what they say on the tin: a Quirky Little Job in a Charming Little Location. These are the cosiest of romances, and I want to write about these books with the immense love I feel for them, even as I wonder whether at this point it might be worth making one of those spinning wheels you get on game shows: the outer ring to decide the quirky occupation, the middle ring to decide the location, and the centre ring to decide the season. Florist in the Mountains in Spring! Chocolatier at the Coast in Summer! Painter in the Saltmarshes in Autumn! Although that last one might be a little bleak. Still, we could redeem it with a Christmas tree book. (I love to read about Christmas tree farms, even though I have never been to one.) We could spin the wheel, and choose the romance. It would – I guarantee you – already exist.

The author Sarah Maria Griffin once said that the best advice a debut author can be given is to remember that books are sold on tables, not pedestals: when people love a book, they want to read another one like it. Romance is a generous genre. It's interested in meeting people where they are, not where you wish they were: it's interested in giving people what they want, and plenty of it.

Should you wish, for instance, to read about a barista by the sea, I can offer you not only *The Café at Beach End*, *The Beach Café* or *The Little Beach Café*, but also *Summer at the Ice Cream Café*, *Summer at the Cornish Café* and *The Little Ice Cream Shop by the Sea*. If what you enjoy about these cafés by the sea is easy access to baked goods, there is always *Little Beach Street Bakery*, or *The Little Bakery on* either *Rosemary Lane* or *Wishing Well Lane*. There are bakeries on *Little Bicycle*s and *Canal Boat*s; there is *The Little Village Bakery*, *The Little Italian Bakery*, *The Little Brooklyn Bakery*, and both summer and Christmas at *The Little French Café*. There is *Rosie's Little Café on the Riviera*. There are *Secrets at the Little Music Shop* and *Christmas Promises at the Little Wedding Shop by the Sea*. There is *The Vintage Dress Shop in Primrose Hill*. Beth Good has gone one better, and written *The Oddest Little [Insert Shop Here] Shop* series: not just tea shops and bread shops but flower shops, Cornish Christmas shops, and even Christmas tree farms (hurrah for me!). Kellie Hailes has *The Little Bakery of Hopes and Dreams*; Jodi Thomas has *The Little Teashop on Main*; Saskia Hart has *The Little Shop Next Door*.

What I like about this last one is that it lets us see quite plainly the lineage of this kind of book, or at least this kind of title, all the way back to *The Shop Around the Corner*. These books are, in fact, a reverse *Shop Around the Corner*; as if the *Shop* were the lino and all the Quirky Employment in the Charming Location books were the lino prints, with all the dark and light places reversed.

In Love with Love

If this rings only the faintest of bells, the 1940 film *The Shop Around the Corner* is both the source material for, and the shop name in, the frequently misunderstood 1990s romcom classic *You've Got Mail*. *You've Got Mail* is the story of Kathleen, who runs a bookshop called The Little Shop Around The Corner. The Little Shop Around The Corner is about to be put out of business by Fox Books ("F-O-X Fox"), and this would be bad enough, but Kathleen is, of course, unknowingly in love with her enemy. I suppose you might call this the ultimate *bad* Hot Billionaire move, but it is also, in my opinion, the best Nora Ephron movie. I think this because it is about books, chatting on the internet and, above all, giving up on stuff, three things I absolutely love. People love to hate *You've Got Mail* because the big bookshop tycoon a) lies to her and b) puts her bookshop out of business. It is my contention that she wanted the bookshop to go out of business, so she could go and be the Daisy Bacon of children's books: the Ursula Nordstrom of the 1990s, the Kaye Webb of New York. (I appreciate this is a very specific set of references, but to someone out there, this means everything. To that person, please get in touch. We are probably soulmates.)

Kathleen, like all the city girl heroines of the Quirky Employment books, has to have her life crumble away so that her real life – the life of her own choosing – can begin. The little shop – her mother's shop – must be shuttered, so her own career can blossom.

The Hometown Hero

This is unusual, in Quirky Employment terms: Quirky Employment usually means leaving the big city job for the cute little bookshop job. Only Nora Ephron could flip it – and even then, it only works because both the fancy city job and the cute little bookshop are in the same city. If Kathleen Kelly's mother had set up The Little Shop Around The Corner in her adorable upstate hometown, and Joe Fox had come in from New York to crush it? Not even Nora could have saved him then. Kathleen would have been tied to that store for life.

It would be, pretty much, the plot of *Bohemian* by Kathryn Nolan: Calvin inherits his grandfather's bookstore in Big Sur, intending to sell it. He can't afford to keep it open! Nobody buys books anymore! He agrees, reluctantly, to go ahead with a high-fashion photoshoot, agreed to by his grandfather, in order to afford the legal fees of selling. Enter Lucia, a supermodel with the soul of a poet. Hijinks, up to and including a landslide, ensue. Lucia and Calvin wind up – and I'm sorry for the spoiler – married and running the bookstore together. If Calvin and Lucia had wound up back in LA, with the bookshop sold, there would be no story, no book *even if they were perfectly happy*. The happy ending has to be a happy ending for the community, too.

A gender-swapped Quirky Employment novel works fine; it may, in fact, be the only truly gender-neutral trope in romantic fiction. A big city girl and the guy she left behind follows the exact same patterns as a big city boy and the girl next door: it exists in the same shapes, and in the same stories. A big city boy has further to fall, while a big city girl has bigger lessons to learn. Both hometown girls and boys are likely to be furious with the intruder, especially if they have come home after a long time away.

A location-flipped Quirky Employment is, however, hard to swallow. It's almost impossible to pull off successfully, perhaps because it feels unsettlingly like punching down.

I can think of only one that truly works: Jill Mansell's debut, *Fast Friends*, is almost like a low-key, sweeter *Lace* (this is a compliment). Written in the early nineties (perhaps before the true horror of Reaganomics and Thatcherite community destruction had really sunk in, and still sparkily fresh from the Tina-Brown-glossy eighties?),* *Fast Friends* starts with three girls in their last year of boarding school: sexy Roz, funny Lou and dumpy Camilla.

Roz becomes a TV star; Lou an It Girl; and Camilla marries and has two children. When Camilla discovers her husband is having an affair (with Roz!), she hurls a bowl of chrysanthemums at his head, and runs away to London to live with Lou. I read this book far too young, and it seared itself into my mind as the epitome of glamorous adult life. Her tumbling gold and silver curls! The fur rug in front of

---

* *The Vanity Fair Diaries*, by Tina Brown, is the perfect audiobook. It is not really romantic fiction except that she loves her husband, her job, her husband, New York, her husband, her children, her job and her husband *so much* that you can't help being swept along with it.

the fire! Nico's leather trousers! The betrayal of the photography exhibition! The buttery-soft tan leather jacket that becomes Camilla's symbol of her new life!

Standing in front of a buttery-soft tan leather jacket in a shop window, a good twenty years after the book was published, I tried to explain to Mansell – via email, I think – what her books had meant to me. I was having a very difficult time, and it felt important, suddenly, to tell the person who had shaped my ideas of adulthood that they had done that. I attached a picture of the jacket, as a sort of explanation of why I was writing to her.

"I'm sorry to say," Mansell told me, "that I barely remember it. It was so long ago!" I was gently devastated.

The next day, the buttery leather jacket arrived at my editor's offices. "You sounded like you needed something nice," she wrote. We had never spoken before, and I was a nobody who loved her books.

Mansell wrote the novel in an attempt to "write the kind of book I would love to read, which was basically *Riders*, minus all the horsey bits because I knew nothing about horses". This is, in some ways, a great way of thinking about Mansell as a writer: she is always writing the kind of book she is reading, which makes her both one of the most consistently delightful of romantic fiction writers – and a useful barometer for changing fashions in romantic fiction. Mansell's novels have sold more than fifteen million copies: her covers, titles and even her general themes demonstrate clearly what it takes to be a consistent bestseller. *Fast*

Friends taps into the Jilly/Shirley shoulder-pads power era; *Millie's Fling*, ten years later, perfectly encapsulates the early noughties Bridget Jones-inspired chick-lit craze for relatable, scatty heroines who love snacks and losing their shoes; *Three Amazing Things About You* is a love story about a lung transplant for the 2010s *Me Without You* and *The Fault in Our Stars* era. *Meet Me at Beachcomber Bay* emerges in 2017 to meet the trend of specifically named seaside locations.

Before the novel's publication, Mansell was at a literary party when she found that snow had stopped the trains. Jilly – magnificent Jilly – immediately invited Mansell to come back in her chauffeur-driven car, and stay with her in her gorgeous Georgian pile. "She was every bit as wonderful as her books," Mansell told a journalist. Which was how I felt too: it was as if I had stepped, briefly, out of my own difficult life and into one of her books. Something generous and magical had happened to me, and I was lifted up. The romantic fiction had become, in some ways, a romantic fact: an author, a real author, had been briefly and supremely generously my fairy godmother. (I still, of course, have the jacket.)

It's in this way, maybe, that romantic fiction most closely resembles a fairy tale: the idea that, just for a moment, at any moment, something magical might occur. It might be literal – Abby Jimenez's shifting stained-glass window![*] – or metaphorical – Jill Mansell's fleeting encounters that change both

---

[*] *Part of Your World*, Abby Jimenez, 2022.

The Hometown Hero

lives – but there is, always, a moment of chance. There is, always, a moment where things line up just right, and without such a moment, everything would have been different.

We are all, I think, given such moments in our own lives – if we are prepared to notice them. We who read romance novels are prepared. Perhaps we can't have it all, but we can have a moment – a single sunlit moment – when it all feels right.

8

Sex and Text

Writing is an attempt, against the odds, to preserve a moment that should already have been lost to time. It's an attempt to make something tangible out of something brief and almost gone: an idea, a feeling, a split-second sensation of how things were or are or might have been.

All writing is like this, I think, but writing about love is an attempt to preserve something that has to be – must be – alive to matter. The people don't have to be alive, I don't think, but the love itself has to *live*: you can't love someone just because you used to love them, or because you hope to love them later. (You can't really make yourself love someone, either.)

Love is so extraordinary and unlikely – us two? meeting here and now? alive at the same time? in *this* economy? – that it has to belong to the moment it's in; and to preserve that sense of belonging to the moment in writing in a way that lets you keep it, return to it, refresh yourself in it is probably the most difficult task in all of art. It's like keeping a fly in amber, but the fly is still alive; it's like a fossil that breathes; it's like time travel with something precious and immensely fragile.

In Love with Love

I remember once being in the pub watching someone I know introducing his very new girlfriend to a group of friends, and thinking he looked exactly like a man holding a very big and very fragile and very expensive Ming vase – also in the *pub* – and trying very, very hard not to drop it. You could see that he genuinely believed this relationship was the best thing that had ever happened to him. You could also see that he needed, really needed, everyone there to see that this was a *real Ming vase*, which with the slightest knock could shatter into a thousand pieces. Writing about love is trying to time travel with a priceless Ming vase.

Which is why, maybe, when writing about love works, it's the most precious thing in the world to me. I only ever really want to read about love. I only ever want to read something that feels like a love letter.

Romantic fiction is a genre made up, in one form or another, of love letters. Readers of romantic fiction are readers of love letters; writers of romantic fiction are writers of love letters. It's a genre of, and about, the written word: texts, emails, actual in-an-envelope mail. Books written in Post-it form, or books about romantic fiction writers who have forgotten what love feels like. It's a genre full of the written word, because, at least in part, *romance itself* is full of the written word. Written artefacts are, to most romances, a vital talisman: a Valentine's Day card, a wedding speech, what Clary Cazalet would call "pieces of love sent".

Sex and Text

While the Cazalet Chronicles, a series of five books by Elizabeth Jane Howard, are not really romance novels, they are certainly love stories – and there is something about their general vibe that undoubtedly hits many of the same textural sweet spots. Detailed observations of possessions, clothes and domestic interplay; loves and betrayals of all kinds; relationships to tear your heart out and mend it again. And Clary Cazalet – the awkward teen who will grow up to become a novelist – who treasures two things above all others: the scraps of paper on which her parents (one dead, one missing) wrote simply "love to Clary". This written ephemera is a tangible representation of an intangible sensation. Might we, one way or another, love romance novels the way Clary Cazalet loves her scraps of paper: as tokens of an indefinable feeling made, even briefly, real?

Romantic fiction *loves* words; it loves the texture of a letter or the heart-stop buzz of a text. This is why romantic fiction, more than any other genre, lends itself so willingly to the epistolary format – and, actually, any format that circles around the existence of text. Think of Ana Steele and Christian Grey's texts in *Fifty Shades*, or the almost entirely epistolary *Dear Aaron*, by Mariana Zapata, or the Post-it exchanges in Beth O'Leary's *The Flat Share*. Think of romances about romance writers like Lizzie Vereker in Jilly Cooper's *Rivals*, or pretty much any heroine Emily Henry has ever written. Think of the sheer number of diaries we're permitted to peek inside.

There is, in romantic fiction, an explicit awareness of the power of words. We understand that, through words, we build communion and community. We understand that we are writing love letters in a grand tradition of love letters; we understand that through words we can get to the core of somebody, or at least we hope we can.

Partly, of course, romance novels lend themselves to epistolary and diary formats because romance novels invite the crossing of a boundary: they invite you to peek inside the most personal parts of a life, even a fictional one. But I think there's more to it than that.

The novelist and lecturer Rebecca Makkai says that, when she is teaching creative writing, 95 per cent of the problems she sees in her students' work "can be traced back to point of view": "who exactly is narrating the story and what their deal is"; "when, in relation to the story's events, the story is being narrated"; "to whom, theoretically or literally, the story is being addressed"; and "for what purpose the story is being narrated". The beauty of an epistolary, or diary, novel is that these questions of perspective are answered immediately.

I write this sitting in the kitchen sink may be the greatest opening of all time because it announces, with alacrity, the narrator's location, state of mind, and – shortly afterwards – purpose. A new notebook has been bought; this writing is to fill it. *I Capture the Castle* is the kind of book I don't want to talk about too much because it's just too precious to me. What could I say about Dodie Smith that hasn't either already been said – or won't give away too much about me? I will say, though, that it is the kind of romance novel that sets you up for a lifetime of romance reading.

Cassandra Mortmain is seventeen years old, and she lives in the ruins of a castle. Her father is a novelist who has written one (1) book, many years ago; her stepmother, Topaz, is an artist's model. Her sister Rose is impractical; her brother Thomas is a child. Stephen, their "man of all work", keeps bringing Cassandra poems he has copied out of books, while saying he has written them himself. Nobody has any money. Into this scene, then, arrive two handsome American brothers – who are the real owners of the Mortmain castle.

I Capture the Castle is the ultimate diary novel. Could there be any Bridget Jones without Cassandra Mortmain? That confessional, self-interrogatory tone – with occasional forays into vital statistics – that Bridget is so famous for can be traced, I think, directly back to Cassandra.

My friend Rachel says that she knows one of her main personality flaws is that if she saw a diary lying around – in someone's house, say, or sticking out of the top of their bag – she would be compelled to read it. She gets ahead of this flaw by telling everyone about it in advance. Lock up your journals! "But that's dreadful!" I say, a lifelong diary keeper. "God, I know," she says, genuinely rueful. "But what can I do? It's irresistible to me. Irresistible!"

Then she adds: "Everyone wants to, though, don't they? I mean, on some level. At least I'm honest."

People who read diaries love to tell you that everyone wants to read diaries.

My own diary keeping was almost derailed aged nine, when a friend of mine fell in a ditch outside my house on the way to school. We rescued her; she came in to borrow some uniform that wasn't covered in mud, then while she was getting changed she read her way through the battered exercise book in which I had been, mere moments before, writing my diary. I cannot remember what secrets I had at nine, but I think they were very profound. It was a clear and absolute violation. "You would have read mine!" she said, outraged. "If you didn't think I'd find out! And I never thought you'd find out!"

And I have to concede that she – and Rachel – might be right. If we feared absolutely no repercussions, not even the prick of conscience, would we all go around reading any private scrawlings we happened to stumble upon? Diaries, letters, emails, texts, Post-its, even wills and legal documents: there's something compelling about the things we set down in black and white.

Writing in fiction feels real because it is as real to us as it is to the characters. There is no other place where we can interact with a fictional artefact in the same way as a fictional character: we can't taste sexy spaghetti Bolognese or slip into cool cotton bedsheets; we can't experience the physical sensations or the practical realities of the imaginary life. But we can read the same letter. The emotion is mediated in precisely the same way between the writer and the intended reader as between the writer and ourselves.

Sex and Text

There's something, for instance, very moving and spooky about finding an old postcard in a charity shop: my personal favourite find was a *box* of postcards, dated to the late Victorian era, sent between sisters on the Isle of Wight and in the New Forest. Nothing much happened to them, over the course of the decade they exchanged postcards; they sent multiple postcards a week, sometimes even a day (that Victorian postal service, my God!), with nothing more exciting than what they bought for dinner or who said what to Mother and what Mother said in return. They had, I think, very dull lives. And yet there was something magical about reading their correspondence: their fleeting thoughts and shopping lists, snippets of gossip and small-town minor scandals – the price of cod, the holes in the church roof! – preserved somehow for more than a hundred years. The act of writing had transformed the ephemeral into the permanent, or at least the more permanent. It felt like the imprint in the sand of an emotion, an idea. It was like they were briefly alive again, and real to me. I could see the shape of them. I loved those postcards; they made me want to reread, as many things do, *84 Charing Cross Road*, by Helene Hanff.

Published in 1970 and never out of print, *84 Charing Cross Road* is not a romance novel.

Or rather, it took me ten years to realise that *84 Charing Cross Road* was not a romance novel. Then, another ten years to realise that I was wrong.

Helene Hanff is a writer in New York City; Frank Doel works in a bookshop on Charing Cross Road in London.

In Love with Love

(I should, I suppose, use the past tense for Helene Hanff; I find I am completely unable to do so. I thought there must have been a mistake when I found out she was born in 1916, and died, aged eighty, in 1997. How could that be? Helene and I are surely contemporaries. To me, Helene and I are more than contemporaries; we are friends. I can hear her voice in my head whenever I want to! I know what she would think about things! This is the power of writing. Helene Hanff is forever, to me, magically preserved in her mid-thirties, a single woman living in a loft apartment with orange-crate bookshelves and a tablecloth too nice for her cheap table.)

Helene, in New York, seeks the kind of old books she can't get in the States; Frank is the person who answers her ad in immediately post-war London. She orders books; he sends the books. She writes as if they already know each other; it takes him twelve years of regular correspondence to sign "love, Frank" instead of "yours sincerely, F. Doel". He addresses her as "madam"; she replies that she hopes "madam doesn't mean over there what it does over here", and signs herself, merely, "HH". She never met a capital letter she thought was worth it; he treats the rules of grammar like a holy text. He dedicates himself to the antiquarian books of Marks & Co.; she does scripts for TV murders. "maybe i'll do one about the rare book business in your honor," she writes. "do you want to be the murderer or the corpse?"

He explains how to make a Yorkshire pudding ("like a high, curved, smooth, empty waffle"). She sends food parcels to a heavily rationed London – not just for Frank, but for Frank's elderly neighbour, and everyone in the bookshop. She tries, and fails, to get to London in person – dental bills keep her trapped – but they write, back and forth, for twenty years. And these are their real letters! These are their real, true letters!

To read them is to know them both; to be allowed to be on the inside of their relationship – tentative and reserved on his part, sarcastic and exuberant on hers – is an intimacy unparalleled.

People love to read other people's letters. And perhaps this is why Janet and Allan Ahlberg's unbelievably perfect picture book, *The Jolly Postman (or, Other People's Letters)*, has sold more than *six million copies* since 1986. It has not been out of print for forty years. If you were a small child obsessed with nosing your way into Cinderella's press releases, the Wicked Witch's spooky catalogues, or Goldilocks's humbling apology letter, you almost certainly grew up to be a person interested in the things other people are doing with their lives when they think nobody is looking. I just want to know! I just want to know. While, unlike my friends, I have never read someone else's diary, I can't really swear it's not because I don't want to. Personally, I think it's because once I broke that seal I'd never be able to stop. I'd have to know everything! I'd have to see the story through until the end.

So, in one sense, *84 Charing Cross Road* is not a love story. Frank was (is, in our continual presence?) married to Nora, and Helene never, in any of her writing, mentions a single lover of any kind. And yet a relationship that develops slowly, letter by letter, towards a perfect harmony of mind and mind is *always* a love story. How could it be otherwise? When I realised, the first time I read it, that they were *never, ever* going to kiss – they never even met in person! – I was stunned. More than stunned. I was furious. I was betrayed.

Frank's death – sudden, obviously off-stage, anti-climactic in every way – felt (and feels!) inconceivable to me even now. But why? I knew it was a true story. I knew, because Frank had mentioned his wife and Helene seemed so thoroughly disinterested in romance, that they couldn't or wouldn't or shouldn't end up together. I knew that they didn't end up together. But the intimacy of the epistolary format was so entwined for me with the structure and shape of a romance novel that the sudden departure from it felt, frankly, obscene.

This switch from the soothing rails of predictability is also – sort of, and in reverse – what happens with Jean Webster's *Daddy-Long-Legs* (1912). Inexplicably billed as a children's book, *Daddy-Long-Legs* is a one-way correspondence between Jerusha "Judy" Abbott – romance novel nicknaming coming into play – and her mysterious benefactor, an anonymous millionaire who has sent her to college. She has seen only his silhouette – long-legged and stark – and doesn't know his name. He will pay her tuition, expenses, allowance and wardrobe (which she details with total glee).

Sex and Text

In exchange, Judy will "write a letter once a month. He will never answer [her] letters, nor in the slightest particular take any notice of them". He believes she will turn out to be an author.

The original subtitle, *A College Girl's Letters to a Man She Didn't Know*, has a kind of *Penthouse*-quality which somewhat undercuts (correctly) the Puffin Classics cover. The Puffin Classics cover is pink, featuring a little girl in a frilly pink dress and hat sitting up a tree writing in a notebook, while a Victorian silhouette, complete with cane and top hat, paces at a distance. This design seems rather misleading for a book in which the "little girl" – who, in canon, is living alone with friends and furnishing her own flat and feeling inadequate about her previous education – will inevitably, must inevitably, fall for Daddy-Long-Legs himself. Is it problematic? Perhaps it's problematic. It's significantly less problematic, I think, than much modern romance (Boyfriend's Dad trope, anyone?), but it's certainly an unusual vibe for a children's book.

He calls himself John Smith; she says it's impossible to imagine a John Smith well enough to write letters to him. "I suppose I might call you ... Dear Mr. Rich Man, but that's rather insulting to you," she writes, exuberantly, in her first letter. "Besides, being rich is such a very external quality. Maybe you won't stay rich all your life; lots of very clever men get smashed up in Wall Street." (It's almost impossible to believe this book was written well over a hundred years ago. Like Helene Hanff, Judy loves Samuel Pepys, exclamation marks, and bowling over silent men with her sheer force of living.) She writes every month, every week, sometimes more. "I must love somebody, so you'll HAVE to put up with it," she scrawls as a PS to her eleven-page missive. He never writes. He never replies. And Judy finds herself instead inexplicably charmed by her shallow roommate's "real human being" of an uncle: the tall, dark, "companionable", "unusually rich and desirable", "youngish and good-looking" uncle.

The mysterious benefactor sends her to stay in the countryside for the summer – which turns out to be at the childhood home of the desirable uncle. "Did you ever hear of such a funny coincidence?" Judy writes, to Daddy-Long-Legs. He does not reply, but the uncle – let's call him Jervis Pendleton, because Jean Webster did not bless him with the name of a romantic hero for us to ignore it – Jervis Pendleton turns up after his car breaks down. Judy's letters become Jervis central. "Master Jervie" is beloved by everyone who has ever met him. Including Judy.

Years pass. Judy writes her letters. And her letters are, quite frankly, perfect: "Dear Comrade, Hooray! I'm a Fabian. That's a Socialist who's willing to wait. We don't want the social revolution to come tomorrow morning, it would be too upsetting. We want it in the distant future when we shall all be able to sustain the shock." It is impossible not to love Judy. And yet Daddy-Long-Legs does not reply ... But Jervis does.

Listen: I have read this book one hundred times. Typing out the start of the last letter – "My Very Dearest Master

Jervie Daddy Long Legs" – makes me burst into tears. I never expect it, even now, to be a romance novel – but perhaps I should have done. That's what epistolary novels do: they feel real. And romance – however silly, however escapist, however many aliens or billionaires it may feature – has to *feel* emotionally real. It gets under your skin, and into your heart. And this is why, surely, so many romance novels have exactly that kind of private correspondence – diaries, letters, emails, texts, the actual act of writing – at their core.

The magical thing about Beth O'Leary's *The Flatshare* (I loved it) is not really the truly bonkers premise – There Was Only One Bed taken to its logical conclusion – but the fact that the romance is conducted entirely by Post-it note. When two people meet and form their relationship mostly via correspondence, it means that the reader gets to experience the romance exactly as they experience it: the written word *is* the written word. We get to fall in love too; we miss nothing. We belong from the start.

And when Ruby writes *Dear Aaron* at the top of an email to a soldier she's never met, we're in. When there's no corresponding *Dear Ruby* coming back, it hits deep: we've been here too. We've been wanting so much to make this person, this stranger, feel better, and the truth that he doesn't seem to care feels unbearable. We've been abandoned just as much as Ruby has. When he does reply – "All your emails have come through. Sorry for taking so long to reach out. A." – it's hard to know whether to be angry or exhilarated. We experience his words as Ruby does. We are *right there.*

And we are right there, too – held cleverly, strangely, guiltily, deliciously in the middle of things – when, in Rainbow Rowell's *Attachments*, Lincoln falls for Beth by reading her emails to other people.

The year is 1999. Lincoln O'Neill's job, to quote his mother, is to "read other people's mail. At night. In an empty building. *That* shouldn't be someone's job". The ad, Lincoln reminds himself, had said "Internet security officer". The Internet is a new experiment at *The Courier*, the "last newspaper in America to give its reporters Internet access". All employees have just been given email addresses, and it's Lincoln's job to monitor them. He is mainly employed to read every email that is flagged for banned words. The banned words register is fairly comprehensive.

"Am I worried someone is reading our e-mail?" movie critic Beth writes, to her best friend Jennifer. "Uh, no. All this security stuff isn't aimed at people like us. They're trying to catch the pervs. The online porn addicts, the Internet blackjack players, the corporate spies."

"Those," copy editor Jennifer replies, instantly, "are probably all red-flag words. *Pervs. Porn. Spies.* I bet *red flag* is a red flag." She's right. They all are. Lincoln starts reading their correspondence, and he can't stop. They keep getting flagged, but he doesn't send a warning. He just … keeps reading. Their emails make the nights go quicker. "And also … Also, he kind of liked Beth and Jennifer, as much as you can like people from reading their e-mail, only some of their e-mail." Reading Beth and Jennifer's emails feels to the reader most like being quietly on the sofa while your two favourite people talk, and you know immediately that Lincoln feels the same. Lincoln wants Beth, especially, to never stop talking. Lincoln wants to know everything Beth thinks. Especially about the Cute Guy she sees sometimes in the break room. The Cute Guy who sounds a lot like Lincoln. Lincoln's moral quandary – *should I keep reading?* – is the reader's moral quandary; when he takes a break, or when Beth and Jennifer briefly devise a code to get around the flagging system, the reader is as desperate as Lincoln to know what's going on with these people we have come to love.

Attachments is Rainbow Rowell's first novel and it is perfect, I think: weird, spiky, real, full of great kissing. (Rainbow Rowell is a total master of the "desperate kisses all over the face" scene.) But it is worth thinking about not merely for its perfection as a romance novel, but for what it reveals about the genre more widely.

Rainbow Rowell may always be writing about desperate kisses, but underneath that she is *also* always writing about the power of words. Literally, in her YA romances, where the more a phrase is spoken by the Normals the more powerful a spell it becomes for the magicians;[*] but also in the real world, too. The things we say, but, above all, the things we read and

---

[*] The Simon Snow series, Rainbow Rowell, 2015–21.

the things we write have power. Neal wins Georgie McCool with the comic strips he draws for her;* Cath falls in love with Levi by reading *The Outsiders* to him in full.† (When neither of them laughs at "Stay gold, Ponyboy"! When she sees his bedroom with the turquoise love seat!) And Beth wins Lincoln with the person he sees in her words. (Lincoln wins Beth, by the way, with complete emotional honesty, unfailing kindness, and being very large.)

This Is How You Lose the Time War by Amal El-Mohtar and Max Gladstone, is a time travel epistolary romance novel about the end of the world in which the two characters – and there are only two, Blue and Red – are soldiers on opposite sides of an intergalactic battle. They are also trying to kill each other. They are equals, evenly matched. There is nobody else in the galaxy for either of them. "I'd been growing complacent," Blue writes, in her first letter, written in flame and Red's own *rainbow blood*. "But then you turned up." Neither can live while the other survives. Nor can they bear to live without each other. They leave each other letters through time and space, each letter destroyed forever as they read it. It was, one of them notes, "the kind of letter meant to be read once, and then destroyed. She read it again." *This Is How You Lose the Time War* is a romance novel disguised as an apocalypse novel, but then, perhaps there is an element of the apocalypse in all romantic fiction. After all, the reason

---

* *Landline*, Rainbow Rowell, 2014.
† *Fangirl*, Rainbow Rowell, 2013.

we turn to love stories is not because we think the world is as simple as a happy ending makes it seem, but because we know the opposite is true.

Love is complicated; love is uneasy; love is terrifying. If you don't love me, I will fall apart, and my world will fall apart with me. And yet, of course, if I love you I will lose myself as I have always known myself. If I love you, I will become someone else, and then what if you don't love me anymore? Life is change. And love changes everything it touches.

"Albert Camus wrote that the only serious question is whether to kill yourself or not," muses the offbeat novelist Tom Robbins in his "post-modern fairy tale" *Still Life with Woodpecker*. "There is only one serious question. And that is: Who knows how to make love stay? Answer me that and I will tell you whether or not to kill yourself." The book is, I would say, an unsettling, somewhat-dated read: the kind of book that clumsy teenage boys with dyed-black hair give to teenage girls they have crushes on, hoping this will convey all their feelings.

But the line has stuck with me for a long time. (Since I was, in fact, that teenage girl.)

Who knows how to make love stay?

How can love be made to stay, unchanging, in an ever-changing world? How can love be unchanging between two changing beings? How can we keep this thing alive? How can we remember something without condemning it to the preserve of the past? How can we let life be as big as it needs to be, without losing the love we most want to keep? Perhaps romance novels, of the kind we return to again and again, are one answer; and letters are another.

Epistolary novels are so frequently love stories – and romance novels sit so well in the epistolary form – because they are in essence the same thing. So many precursors to the novel are epistolary; and so many of these ancestors of the novel are romances: Aphra Behn's *Love Letters Between a Nobleman and His Sister*, for instance, or Diego de San Pedro's *The Prison of Love*. *The Prison of Love* might have a title that feels like a 1970s Mills & Boon, but it dates, in fact, from five hundred years before that. Before Columbus had ever crossed the Atlantic, San Pedro was writing "courtly romances" in letter form; featuring one of the earliest appearances of a self-aware narrator, *The Prison of Love* tells the story, interspersed with "real" letters, of a love triangle gone awry. "El autor" (as the narrator calls himself) sits like a spider within the triangle, managing and wrangling; middleman and profiteer, he passes letters, keeps secrets, and spins his tale. He sees all. He reads every letter. And so do we.

Reading someone's diary – or letters – is not *exactly* voyeurism, but it's not *not* voyeurism; it's certainly more than mere nosiness. It's driven by something like a desire to know people as they see themselves, to see inside their minds, to see with their eyes. It's a desire for intimacy without any input: it offers an immediate shortcut to understanding. It is also, of course, often a false shortcut.

Sex and Text

The ill-fated and infamous Donner Party, making their way to the Gold Rush of California, were led astray by the promise of the Hastings Cutoff: a path that looked, on the map, to be much shorter and easier than the more traditional routes to fortune. Reading someone's diary to circumvent the more traditional routes to connection can be an emotional Hastings Cut-Off: full of potential for mishaps, misunderstandings and becoming lost forever in the cold. Diaries are both true and untrue: an accurate account of what has passed and an entirely rule-free zone for figuring out your own emotions, ambivalences and dreams. Diaries read like facts, but are essentially – like all memoirs – fictitious. "There is, indeed, no transaction which offers stronger temptations to fallacy ... than epistolary intercourse," wrote Samuel Johnson.

The first romance novel I was truly aware of was *The Notebook*. I hadn't read *The Notebook* then, but *The Notebook* cropped up in books I *had* read and loved. People were always crying about *The Notebook*. A million-dollar debut, and one that stayed on the *New York Times* hardback bestseller charts for more than a year, *The Notebook* was the kind of cultural romantic phenomenon that comes along every once in a while to remind people that this genre is the true powerhouse of publishing. (See also: *Twilight*.) *The Notebook* is a romance novel about writing your own romance novel: an old man reads from the notebook (titular) to an old woman, telling her the story of two young people, separated by class, falling in love before (and after) the Second World War. Wealthy Allie, and returning soldier Noah, first met seven years ago – pre-war – and fell for one another instantly. Noah writes to Allie every day for a year, but Allie's mother hides the letters. And Noah goes off to war.

Letters are tricky! Letters go unsent; letters go astray; letters are hidden or stolen or lost. Letters are both less and *more* prone to misinterpretation than a face-to-face conversation: while, in some ways, the act of writing is an act of commitment, of committing thoughts to paper, it also exchanges the invulnerability of unformed thought for the obvious pitfalls of becoming a real, tangible, permanent object. A thought can be mutable; it can be expressed differently, depending on context, can be kept private or shared as necessary. That thought set down in black and white becomes an object to be misplaced and misunderstood: now, it is something to be criticised, in the most academic sense of the word. A letter can be read by many people outside the intended recipient, and read in many different ways. (Romeo and Juliet! Tess and Angel! Prince Henry and Alex Claremont-Diaz!)

"In a man's letters, you know, Madam, his soul lies naked," wrote Samuel Johnson – even as he was perfectly happy to say, in other letters, that they were the site of false belief. Writing can be the truth; it can be a double bluff. Writing is both clothing and uncovering: the more words we add, the more we show the shape of the thing underneath. Fiction is often more revealing about an author than a memoir; there is certainly no more truth in one than the other. To write is to be exposed; to write is to be hidden in a sea of words. Where speech dissipates into thin air, writing lasts: it becomes a real-life location of the complexities of being alive.

We fall in love to be understood. We fall in love to be seen completely and correctly. Maybe we are always misguided in this: maybe people are always too complicated to be seen absolutely. And yet that moment of being seen – of feeling yourself perceived entirely – is at the heart of every romance novel, because it's at the heart of every romance. We two see each other clearly. Alone in the dark, to us we are alight. To us, we are the only things that are visible: bright stars with no secrets. Only you can see me, only you know the truth – and even then you don't want to stop looking. (Please don't stop wanting to look, even if there's nothing new to see.)

If to write is to risk being misperceived, then to love is to risk being misunderstood.

And yet we do it anyway. We write. We exchange letters. We fall in love. We seek connection, despite everything that might go wrong, because there is nothing else for it.

The world is very dark, and growing ever darker. All we have is each other.

The poet W. H. Auden, days before the Second World War broke out, sat in a dive bar on 52nd Street in New York. The world was about to burn. The worst atrocities of humanity were unfolding five thousand miles away. He was a queer immigrant man with a Jewish partner who would never truly go home again. *We must love one another or die*, he wrote, desperately.

To write about romantic fiction in an age of horrors is to grapple constantly with what matters. There can, as Adorno never said, be no poetry after Auschwitz, but can there be romance novels in a time of Gaza, Yemen, Myanmar, Sudan, Ukraine and so many others? Can writing about pleasure – can reading for pleasure – really be worth our time, when such darkness seems so close to overwhelming all?

I was thinking a lot about this question, as I wrote this book. I was thinking, and reading, and trying to understand whether there could be any real relevance to what I was doing. I was on a train, thinking about this. The news was growing worse and worse every time I refreshed the page on my phone. I put my phone in my bag and pulled out my book instead. The book was Shelly Jay Shore's (wonderful) *Rules for Ghosting*: a queer romance novel about a Jewish funeral home, family, and an awful lot of spooks.

A woman next to me saw the cover, and struck up a conversation. She was on her way back from a Jewish funeral, and it felt like a sign to her, to see a Jewish grave on a book cover. She taught writing in a besieged Palestinian city. She asked about the book, and I told her it was a romance novel.

That's so funny, she said. *All my students in Palestine are writing romance novels. All they want to write is love.*

This was a true thing that happened. I didn't know then what to make of her; I didn't really know what to make of the story. I don't think there is necessarily a moral here, but it's true and it happened, and I think, always, of Auden after the war – after everything, after Auschwitz – refusing to allow that poem to be reprinted without one single, small amendment that somehow means everything.

We must love one another and *die.*

That's all there is. That's all we have. We have each other, and then the end. It's dark – of course it's dark – but our love for each other, our connections with each other, are the necessary light.

9

Two Tickets for the Love Train

"A community without romance," Maya Angelou told an audience, in 1998, "risks being brutish and crass, superficial and brittle, cruel and even murderous ... I don't just mean romantic romance, I don't just mean erotic romance ... I mean the romance that allows us to soften our voices when we see each other."

What, then, does a community built on romance look like? What does that kind of deep, intimate connection look like? What would a community of softened voices feel like?

It feels to me like a woman named Chelley Kitzmiller. The year is 1983, and Chelley Kitzmiller is carefully cutting out construction paper hearts alongside her teenage daughter and two chihuahuas. (One assumes the chihuahuas are not being *that* helpful.) She has already made a sign – perfectly round, with thick lettering a decade out of date – to hang over the train door. It reads "The Love Train". She has organised with Amtrak that the pancakes served on the Love Train will be heart-shaped also. She has, in fact, organised with Amtrak the *entire train journey*: where it will start, where it will stop, and who will board. It will start in LA, where Kitzmiller lives. It will end in New York, at the Romantic

In Love with Love

Times Booklovers Convention. Along the way it will pick up more than a hundred romance readers and romance writers, among them – *hello!* – Barbara Cartland. (These construction paper hearts will be name tags.)

Filmmaker George Csicsery cuts to Chelley's husband: leather jacket, armchair, his gun hanging over the fireplace behind him. "I think it's just like fishing, you know?" he says. "I believe that ten percent of the fishermen catch ninety percent of the big fish. And of course the other people — just you know, too bad. And it's the same in the romance industry. Ten percent of the people are published and write romance novels and the other ninety percent of them are people that tag along as followers. That's where Chelley probably picks up."

Csicsery is remembered mostly, now, for his contributions to mathematics: he has made thirty-five films, and most of them are about maths. *N Is a Number*, for instance, is a biographical documentary about the mathematician Paul Erdős; Csicsery has made documentaries about many mathematicians. His funding, often, has come from the Mathematical Association of America.

And yet *Where the Heart Roams*, from 1987, is all about romance readers. Not a mathematical equation in sight.

"I am interested," Csicsery told a journalist, "in people who can find happiness in creating their own world. That is true of mathematicians and romance writers. These people are creating universes different from where they live."

Or, perhaps, they are making the universe different *where*

they live. Chelley Kitzmiller is making the universe different for herself and for the women who think like she does. She is making a community, and a community in which she matters. She is lit up with meaning; she is surrounded by people who love the things she loves, and who make the things she loves.

To the *New York Times* of 1987, however, it is all too "sad and ineffable". The books are "paperback junk"; the women the film features have "barren lives", despite their friends, families, partners, passions and projects being quite literally the subject of the documentary.

The director, says the *New York Times*, "doesn't make fun of the women – he doesn't have to. That's the sad part ... The sight of so many people devoting themselves so earnestly to such easily parodied wish-fulfillment leaves one nearly speechless."

Chelley Kitzmiller is criticised not just for neglecting her housework, but mostly for daring to dream that she might herself be able one day to write one of the books she loves.

The *Times* doesn't explicitly say that Kitzmiller is pathetic for dreaming; it doesn't have to. The mere suggestion that she might want to write anything at all is dismissed, neatly, as "desperate". And yet the Love Train is, in fact, full of people who write. People who read are often people who write. The train carries her passengers through seminars and writing sessions; they talk about why it's vital to know where your characters have both their hands in a kissing scene and why it's less sexy to write a full-frontal nude than a shirt just slipping off a shoulder. Communally, they co-write a romance. Writers become readers, readers are writers, and everyone is a fan.

Riding the train in all of these capacities was Elsie Washington, also known as Rosalind Welles. As Washington, she was a journalist for *Newsweek*; as Welles, she was a widely beloved romance novelist. (She was, in fact, the first Black romance writer to write a mainstream romance novel about Black characters. *Entwined Destinies* tells the story of Hot Billionaire Lloyd and journalist Kathy. It sold 60,000 copies, almost all of which have disappeared, but the cover alone – Lloyd in blue pinstripes, Kathy in an incredible frothy salmon and white blouse, Houses of Parliament and sleek black car in the foreground – feels like it belongs in a gilt frame.) Washington is reporting on the trip for *Newsweek*, but she's also taking notes for the communal romance-write.

This sounds, per Christine Larson's retelling of the story, electric. In a kind of call-and-response that gives the early lie to the idea that romance readers are too stupid to understand what they are reading, Chelley and the crowd write a romance story on the train about two (fictional) journalists, on a (similar but fictional) train. Washington, there technically to report on the trip, is right at the heart of it, writing the collective story in her own notebook. Washington calls out, "He was tall, dark and—" The crowd screams, "Handsome!" Then, Washington: "Cynical, but with a heart of—" Crowd: "Gold!"

Elsie Washington, journalist, blurs into Elsie Washington, fan, who blurs inevitably into Rosalind Welles, author. The boundaries are porous. The community is all.

Chelley Kitzmiller is now, aged almost eighty, the author of many romance novels. ("Despite his embarrassing comments, [I am] still married," she notes in her biography.) Many of her companions on the Love Train have also written romance novels, some published, some unpublished. The community built around the thing has become a machine for making more of the thing: a near-perfect reproduction engine for joy.

And not just joy. Concealed within it, like a knife in a sock, is the possibility for change.

This is the power, for instance, of Casey McQuiston's *Red, White & Royal Blue*. While a classic romance in some senses – it's a classic Prince Charming story, quite literally – in other ways it is more sensibly classed as a political alternative universe. If, instead of Donald Trump, the 2016 US Presidential election had been won by a Texan woman with Latino kids, what might the world look like? The space created by romance is here a space for a creative reimagining of the politics, and the future, of America: one that is, as time goes by and timelines diverge still further, increasingly difficult to read. McQuiston's AU is not a perfect world, but it is one filled with people mostly looking to do better. The world McQuiston's work creates, then, is one in which all their readers are people interested – actively interested – in making a better world. The book acts as a community space within itself.

It is interesting, however, to wonder how the mainstreaming of romance will affect this kind of sense of community.

If everyone reads romance, what happens to the pleasure shibboleth? What happens to the people for whom romance was a home, a place of safety and acceptance? It would be nice to think that everywhere might become a home, but can that possibly be true? It's interesting, also, to wonder if this mainstreaming of romance is behind the rise in ever more specific sub-genres: if everyone is reading romance, but you are reading Hot Billionaire Alien Only One Bed, you can form an instant connection with other Hot Billionaire Alien Only One Bed readers in a way that would be impossible with, say, everyone who has ever read an Emily Henry bestseller.

I read Curtis Sittenfeld's 2023 novel *Romantic Comedy* with gritted teeth: I loved it, I loved it completely, but I was so afraid the whole time that she was going to perform a literary trick and crush me. Sittenfeld felt too famous to be allowed into my genre; she knew too much. She wrote *American Wife*!

(Which should have been my first clue, because *American Wife* is – somehow! – an extremely romantic and sexy novel. "Did you get to the part where you want to shag George Bush yet?" my friend said, wisely, when she saw it in my bag. "Oh yes," I said. We nodded our heads sombrely. A dreadful state of affairs, but there you go.)

And yet something about the title – something about the way that Sally, a producer at what is obviously *SNL*, and Noah, a rock star, fall in love with genre-specific precision – something about the way every beat hits – something about their beautiful funny perfect emails, if you will forgive me bringing it back to correspondence again – it was all too much. It was too good! Why would that be the title if you weren't going to do something dreadful to it?

Romantic Comedy was in every shop window and serious people I knew were reading it. I was afraid that it would be too romantic for them, and they would make fun of me; or it would be not romantic enough for me, and I would know that Sittenfeld was making fun of me. It felt like my own personal world was under a spotlight, a literary sort of spotlight, and I wasn't sure what people would see in it.

And yet – if you have not read *Romantic Comedy* – it was ok in the end. It was more than ok! People who had never read any romantic novels kept telling me, surprised, how much they had loved it. How exciting it had been, how thrilling; how they had cried. Are there more books like this? someone asked me, and I saw my world open up to include her too. I saw all the people who had come in, and thought perhaps we might all be on the same page after all.

Then I felt foolish. Of course it would always have been ok. How could it be otherwise? Because Curtis Sittenfeld is (of course) the author of *Eligible*, the modern-day, alternative-universe retelling of *Pride and Prejudice*. Or, as we would usually call it, if it wasn't by a famous literary author – fanfiction.

A person who loves fanfiction – who writes fanfiction – is not a person who is going to pull the rug out from under a romance reader's feet, for fanfiction is a community built on romance. It is a community built explicitly for and about love: not love for one another, necessarily, but a shared love for something higher, greater, all-encompassing. *Star Trek*, perhaps, in the early days; or the BBC *Sherlock*; or, always, eternally, Harry Potter.

It is sort of humiliating, but absolutely necessary, to admit that probably in my top ten romances of all time is a piece of Harry Potter fanfiction.

This fanfiction has been read almost a million times, and maybe only half of those times by me. It has been translated into Russian and Chinese, among other languages. It is illustrated in full colour. At 131,000 words long, it is about twice as long as *Harry Potter and the Philosopher's Stone*, but not nearly as hefty as *Harry Potter and the Deathly Hallows*.

It is, in other words, a book. A book without a cover, a publisher, original characters or an original world – but a book nonetheless. Nobody has made any money – not the author, illustrator, editor or translators – from this book, yet it can't be denied: it feels like a real book. It reads like a real book. It reads, remarkably, like a real book for adult readers.

It is set seven years after the events of the existing Harry Potter books, and it is an extremely gay and extremely tender, thoughtful meditation on trauma.

It is also, as the author puts it, a sustained attempt to "dismiss the words of J. K. Rowling". Which speaks, I think, to an elemental tension at the heart of all fanfiction, even ones without the complication of Rowling's personal views. Fanfiction is both a love letter to something, and a project to break the love object down into its constituent parts and reassemble it into something else, brand new, the same, but different. (Is this the elemental tension at the heart of all romantic relationships? I love you, just as you are, so become something new, something different, with me.)

In fanfiction, characters can be plucked from their roles as background extras and given a whole life; in reverse, a hero can be relegated to villain or even total obscurity. They might share motivations, or just appearance, or nothing but name with their officially sanctioned counterparts; they might be faithful replicas, painted stroke by stroke to mimic the original author's work, or shadow-selves living lives the original never could have dreamed. The setting might be the same; it might be completely different. There might be magic, where there was none before, or vice versa. How would these characters fare in an utterly different kind of world? At an ice hockey rink? A university? A coffee shop? How would wizards survive with no magic, if they were forced to rely solely on the contents of their character – and their personal skills – to sell lattes and pastries to strangers? How would any of us function, stripped of our contexts? Writing fanfiction – even reading fanfiction – is simultaneously both an intellectual exercise and a romantic engagement with the text, and the history of the text. To do so is to understand both the primacy of the author and the author's death. It is to understand that there are, for all of us, a million possible lives, like and unlike our own: fanfiction shows us the multiplicity of possibilities in all the vastness of being alive.

In the case of this particular fic, the possibilities are mostly queer. (They are also about food and trauma, and so, it must be said, this was always going to be a slam-dunk for me.) Seven years post-Hogwarts, and therefore seven years post-war, the dust has settled; the scars remain. Museum curator Draco Malfoy is attacked in his home; Harry Potter, a man who loves only to cook, is the inept protection agent assigned to his case. This is, of course, the perfect set-up for a romance novel.

And how could it be otherwise? Fanfiction is to romance novels what the MFA programme is to slim literary volumes. It is a kind of factory, or a training ground: an MFA for people with too many feelings and not enough money.

It is the machine that makes *Fifty Shades of Grey*; it is Ali Hazelwood; it is Christina Lauren. Fanfiction, of all genres, tends to the romantic, which means that fanfiction, of all genres, lends itself to translation into a traditional, commercial, romantic fiction.*

Much has been made of the Twilit origins of not just *Fifty Shades*, but also books like Mafia romance *Sempre*, and

---

* It also leaves its telltale fingerprints on other more literary successes. If you've spent enough time in the fanfic mines, it's unmistakeable. Think you've seen examples in the wild? Chances are, you're right. Which smash-hit literary sensations began as fanfic? Answers on a postcard, please.

Two Tickets for the Love Train

business romance *Beautiful Bastard*. (Hot Billionaires all, Edward Cullen included.)

Whether *Twilight* itself counts as *Wuthering Heights* fanfiction I am unable to say definitively. Maybe? Where's the line? *Twilight* certainly references *Wuthering Heights*, and was clearly written with *Wuthering Heights* in mind: readers of a very specific age may also remember the truly astounding black and red Emily Brontë rebrand of 2009. ("Love the *Twilight* books? Then you'll adore *Wuthering Heights*, one of the greatest love stories ever told. Nothing can come between Cathy and Heathcliff. Even death.")

It might seem a little anachronistic to consider *Wuthering Heights* as inspiring fanfiction, but we have had fanfiction as long as we have had novels. Literally. There is, I am happy to say, just under a year between the invention of the novel and the invention of the novel-length fanfiction.

The first novel – arguably, I know; there's competition for this title – is published in 1740. It is called *Pamela*. The first piece of fanfiction is published in 1741. It is called ... *Shamela*. *Shamela* is like *Pamela*, except that instead of being about a shy and righteous virgin, it is about a sexy and scheming minx who is only *pretending* to be shy and righteous in order to have more sex. *Gulliver's Travels*, a fairly sexless if startlingly physical tome, inspires immediate poems about the sex Gulliver might have been having with those tiny and enormous women of other lands who he meets on his adventures (Hot Giants are, I must admit, something outside of my wheelhouse), and the sex he either was, or was not, having with his wife upon his return. ("*Never neighbour call'd me slut!/ Was Flimnap's dame more sweet in Lilliput?*")

There are those, I suspect, who would bristle at the idea that Fielding or Pope might ever be considered fanfiction. These are serious men! These are authors of note! Call it pastiche, call it critique, call it satire: it might well be all of those things. Fanfic usually is, isn't it?

Pastiche, critique and satire are three key functions of fanfiction, not forgetting, of course, pleasure. How are Pope's attempts to undermine Swift, in a funny and sexy way, any different from the explicit attempt by Tumblr user *gyzym*,* with his trans-masculine queerness, to deconstruct the "biggest issues in the Harry Potter series – its overwhelming whiteness, the whole 'Albus Dumbledore is gay but only when you're not looking directly at him,' thing, etcetera"? The function of *What We Pretend We Can't See (M/M, Draco Malfoy/Harry Potter, trigger warnings for unhealthy drinking; verbal abuse, anxiety, panic attacks, depression, and PTSD; ableist language; light-ish stabbing)* is to act as both a critique and, I suppose, a territorial marker: *you wrote it, but I read it. And I can imagine what I want.* Who is the reader, and who is the writer? Who has the power in this dynamic? The reader and writer are as close as lovers.

If romance novels are a playground for our emotions, fanfiction is that playground without a single safety feature.

---

* Who also writes under the pen name Dylan Morrison.

No fences, no guard rails, no supervisor. Total freedom, like childhoods in the past, or a Famous Five novel: you may go where you like, roam wild and free, build things, break things, sail across the lake, camp out on the island, so long as you take the consequences. And the consequences are, generally, fairly comprehensible: if people like it, they will read it. If they don't, they won't. (Sometimes, it's true, there is yelling. Or full caps, which amounts to the same thing.) Everything else is fair game. You can find fanfiction of pretty much anything, transposed into pretty much any scenario – consider the many *Pride and Prejudice*s – and, obviously, endowed with pretty much any sexual predilection you care to name.

Fanfiction's erotic and sexual nature is famous: it's why people laugh at it.

It's also why people laugh at romance novels. People love to make fun of women's sexuality, mostly because it's very frightening to certain ways of thinking, of operating in the world. Female sexuality is about as dangerously destabilising as it gets to the nuclear family, to say nothing of the patriarchal transfer of wealth: if women have the right to choose, what if they choose the wrong thing? The wrong man?

The sexual nature of fanfiction, as we see from *Mary Gulliver* and *Shamela*, is a feature, not a bug: it's nothing new to take a standard text and rewrite it, remix it, to make the dark parts light and the light parts dark and the whole thing generally more erotic. Can we put this down to basic human lusts? Maybe.

But what if, perhaps, the sex in fanfic was not *just* sex? (What if the cigar was not just a cigar?)

What if the sexually unbridled nature of fanfiction was the outward and most graspable sign of a more inward, more general, more widespread unbridling?

What if, to take it one step further, the sexual nature of much fanfiction is, in fact, what allows us to see it as a space for the testing of social norms, established rules and customary facts?

Spaces for explicit sexual content are often, also, sites of radical thought. Radical, here, I mean in its most basic form: radical as the opposite of established, radical in the sense of extreme.

Sex is a space for the unknown, which makes sex a space for reinvention. In sex we have the possibility of being something other than what we are in our ordinary lives: or, perhaps, sex offers us the possibility to shed that which we aren't in our most secret hearts. Sex is often the only place adults play: the only place adults are encouraged to dress up, buy toys, pretend to be a doctor or a chef or a fireman. Sex is play; play can be change; play lets us work out our fears and hopes and desires.

Sex is the only place in a relationship where you can be a stranger to each other. Sex is perhaps the only place where you can be a stranger to yourself. (See also: jumping in very cold water.)

"To be met in one's desire, and to be surprised in one's desire," Katherine Angel says, "is an exercise in mutual trust and negotiation of fear." For good sex, we have to be willing to forgo the usual social rules; we have to create a new universe of two. Relationships are always a subculture of two,* and sex is the peak, the pinnacle, of that subculture. Sex is where that subculture shrugs off, or should shrug off, the clothes it wears to pass in public. Sex is where we can set down our normcore drag.

Maybe we could consider that the sexual content of fanfiction and romance novels acts like a "KEEP OUT" marker for the establishment, but as a "WELCOME" mat for everybody else: come in, we do things differently here. Pleasure is not usually part of the political system. Pleasure is not usually important. If pleasure matters here – if we are writing for pleasure and reading for pleasure *about* pleasure – what else might matter here that matters less elsewhere? What might we be able to establish in this place?

Founded in 1998, Literotica.com is one of the internet's oldest porn sites. Intended to "bring together those who enjoy reading original erotic fiction and those who like to write it," it is worth looking at in the development of fanfiction and romantic fiction because it is, in some ways, the rawest and purest form of both.

---

* "Relationships are a subculture of two" is a Sarah Maria Griffin phrase that everyone who hears it has to write down immediately. I'm attributing it because it's definitely hers, although I think she has not written it anywhere herself. Find it in books by Caroline O'Donoghue, Dolly Alderton and, now, me.

It is a collection of writing that exists purely in service of pleasure. It is also remarkably – for a site with categories like Non-Consent, Non-Human, Incest and Androids – sort of bizarrely sweet. It feels like what it is: something from the olden days. It feels like finding an old issue of *Playboy* in a barn, full of soft, unwaxed women and troubling, unquestioned preconceptions. It is also, of course, depraved and deranged. It's an erotic literature website. What else would you expect?

Which makes the "Non-Erotic Literature" section of Literotica.com one of the most obviously baffling, oddly compelling corners of the internet. Why does it exist? Who is writing there, and why do they do it?

"This is a non-sexual story about a man's complex relationship with his late mother," warns a note before one such story. "It is NOT sexual in any way." Another gives, in painstaking detail and heavy prose, a complete list of the weights of everything a woman might want to take on the Oregon Trail. "I like to respect my readers and let them know up front that this does not contain sex – sorry about that, but that just didn't fit in with my story," announces one writer. "On the other hand, there are ninja spies with millions of dollars, and wizards!"

I am told that Pornhub now boasts multiple coding tutorials: clicks, maybe, are clicks, and a captive audience is a crossover audience. And yet surely there must be more commercial places, easier places, to publish your stories about ninja spies and wizards. There must be, if not more commercial, then less *stigmatised* places. (Are there? Is Literotica.com the last place available online to write freely?) There must be places you could tell your friends about; places you could share; places to show off your hard work and good hobby. There *must* be places to write online which are less closely associated with busty wives and tentacle anal! There must be!

And yet they write here.

But if we think more about what these spaces might possess, instead of what they lack – a great rule for life, generally – what is truly remarkable about these stories is the number of comments they receive, almost every single one supportive, thoughtful and clearly committed. "Another great read! Thanks so much!", swiftly followed by ten police car emojis. ("Ten police cars to honor your great story!" the commenter explains, in case the writer didn't understand.)

"Just read this again after I heard the news," one anonymous commenter writes soberly, on another story about a knight and his pregnant wife slowly falling in love. (Sex, when it happens, happens off-stage.) "This website is a poorer place without you. RIP dude, and thanks. You have helped so many, including me, with their work here."

It's as if the proximity to sex grants permission to play but also that the explicit expectation of intimacy demands permission to be vulnerable. Everyone involved in the erotic writing community has broken several social rules to be there. Everyone reading is running a risk; just as everyone writing is running a risk. If it's embarrassing to admit you read romance/fanfiction/erotica, it's still more embarrassing to admit that you write it. The "stigmatised social position" of reader and writer creates a community which sits just a little outwith the law; just a little on the other side of the things we all know to be true. Thus a space for possibility is created, and within that there is a possibility of community, even communion.

If it's fair to say that the rise of fanfiction over the last quarter-century goes hand in hand with the normalisation of the more extreme reaches of pornography – we're no longer content with topless top-shelf babes – and the explicit eroticisation of romantic fiction, it also goes hand in hand with the corresponding rise in romantic fiction itself. (Consider the chilli emoji.)

We have now a generation of authors trained within, and readers brought up on, the traditions of fanfiction. Even those writers and readers who have never sought out a single piece of fanfiction are vicariously grandfathered in – look at the way new romantic fiction is almost always promoted with a list of tropes, à la AO3.[*]

We have a generation of authors trained not just in writing, but in community building. Yes, it's true that romantic

---

[*] AO3, or Archive of Our Own for the uninitiated, is probably the most reputable fanfiction site on the internet. They have lawyers, and an academic journal, and they take the whole silly business of joy incredibly seriously. They have a tagging system for fanfiction which is, quite genuinely, the envy of data analysts everywhere. I love them very much.

fiction is a generous genre, but it's also greedy: it gives readers what they want, but it relies on reader feedback – on interaction – to thrive. It relies, in fact, more profoundly on the connections between author and audience than perhaps any other modern genre. It is not remotely uncommon for a romance author to ask her readers, at the end of the book, what they would like to see happen next; it is not unusual for readers to write in and suggest not just tropes, but *applied* tropes, requesting stories and sequels about characters who already exist. *Ice Planet Barbarians*, for instance, carries a nice little note from the author at the end of each volume – thanking readers for their feedback, and highlighting the next characters to be paired off. The first books were written as short six-part serials – with feedback and subscriptions solicited in between each episode. It is a very old form of storytelling and publishing – think Dickens, think Thackeray – and also something very new: once again, romantic fiction lives at the cutting edge of technology, of what we can do with words and the sharing of ideas.

Christine Larson believes that one reason romantic fiction has been so preternaturally successful, above and beyond other similar genres, is the "uniquely close bond between readers and writers". The fact that both parties are committed to the "relational labour" of creating the dynamic is, she thinks, unique to romantic fiction. (We might even link the recent boom in romance – an ever-popular genre, but rocketing once more to the top of the charts above thrillers and crime – to the relational labour of predominantly female online spaces: parasocial relationships between content creators and viewers might make this particular dynamic feel more real, relatable and comforting than ever.)

Samuel Richardson's 1748 novel *Clarissa* (or, to give it its full title *Clarissa; or, The History of a Young Lady: Comprehending the Most Important Concerns of Private Life. And Particularly Shewing, the Distresses that May Attend the Misconduct Both of Parents and Children, In Relation to Marriage*) is one of the earliest, best-known novels in English. It is also, of course, a romance novel – by the man whose *Pamela* (1740) we've encountered earlier.

Clarissa was released in serial format, obviously, and the ending was seen as a brutal blow. *It has no HEA! There is no happy ending!* The distress of eighteenth-century readers was no less than you would expect. I imagine they felt how I felt when I first read *One Day*, but worse, because I had not been reading *One Day* in serial form over many months.

And it is, therefore, immediately rewritten. It is rewritten by fans pretty much as soon as it comes out (were some the same fans who responded to *Pamela*?): fans who write to Richardson, and whose rewritten endings are circulated widely by other Richardson fans, and indeed Richardson himself permits them to be printed among collections of his correspondence. A famous rape scene is removed, or doctored to become loving, tender sex; bad men are reformed and sinners forgiven. Happy endings are supplied. And Richardson's response? Richardson hopes, above all, that his book can make of his readers "if not Authors,

Carvers". And this, above all, lets me know Richardson was one of ours.

He might have meant it, and probably did, pedagogically and patronisingly; he might have meant it, as Richardson scholars mostly surmise, as part of a wider project to educate the eighteenth-century reader. And yet, to wish your reader might have more agency – that is, to hope your reader will pick apart your text and make of it something new – while knowing that your reader *can* and will carve different meaning from your text and at the same time replying to letters, getting into conversations (and arguments) about characters with fans, printing fan theories alongside your own letters – the porous boundary, created by eighteenth-century advances in the postal system, is the same porous boundary created by pulp magazines and cheap paperbacks and e-readers and online forums and fax machines and Twitter and Goodreads. It is the same porous boundary that has always existed between readers and writers (and rewriters) of a certain kind of book.

The readers and writers of romance exist on the cutting edge; they move with the times and ensure nobody is left behind. They have always been – *we* have always been – people who make something out of nothing.

For this is the secret of community: when you make a collective, you can make things anew, change them.

And, yes, the writers of romance novels are doubly vulnerable: doubly exposed, they seek love on two counts at once. Love my characters, and also love me. Understand their need for understanding, and in doing so, understand me. But exposure, and vulnerability, create intimacy – without it, true intimacy is impossible. And, as intimacy invites intimacy, in shared intimacies we create community.

Community is power; intimacy is power.

If sex is always at least a little about power – who wields it, who takes it, who surrenders it – then romantic fiction, or the making of romantic fiction, can be read as a means of taking some of that power back. When we forge a community in these ways, we become more than ourselves.

We become, as Samuel Richardson hoped of his readers, "if not Authors, Carvers": we slice the text together, we put it back into new ways. We slice the world apart, we put it back new.

We step on the Love Train, and ride.

10

Gay Boys, Straight Girls, Queer Awakenings

It's hard to imagine now, in the era of media-on-demand, but we had four DVDs when I was a teenager and they all came off the front of newspapers, which was a thing newspapers did twenty years ago: they gave away DVDs of popular movies in cardboard sleeves. I can remember three of them: *Love Actually*, which needs no explanation; a weird little movie called *Love and Sex* with Jon Favreau, about a magazine journalist with an unsuccessful romantic history who has to write an article about love in twenty-four hours; and *Bridget Jones: The Edge of Reason*. (No Bridget Jones classic, unfortunately.)

The plot of *Bridget Jones: The Edge of Reason* is that Bridget and Mark Darcy are in love, but Mark's beautiful genius assistant, Rebecca, keeps getting in their way. Also, Bridget ends up in a Thai prison. (Mark and Bridget are finally reunited by Mark's diligent work – he's a human rights lawyer, you know! – to free her from said Thai prison.)

Bridget Jones: The Edge of Reason is not a very good film. It is not a very good film for a lot of reasons – problematic to the modern viewer! – but to me, at thirteen, it was a bad film for one reason: *why would anyone choose*

Bridget over Rebecca? Rebecca seemed to me some kind of exquisite goddess: perfectly at ease in the boardrooms, on the ski slopes, wearing a ball gown. Bridget, it was clear, was chaos.

In my early teens, watching our single scratched DVD on repeat, I was rendered speechless by the unfairness of this.

I was also rendered speechless by the revelation that Rebecca was, in fact, a lesbian – and in love with Bridget too. "Every time I see you I— I light up," she tells Bridget. "I thought you were just— you know— lying," stammers Bridget. "Was every look I ever gave you a lie?" Rebecca murmurs. We cut to a series of glowing Rebecca smiles, all huge brown eyes and swishy hair, now recast in this new light of love. She leans in, and kisses Bridget. And Bridget kisses her back. It's a nine-second kiss, which I could have told you without looking it up. (I watched it a *lot*.) How could Rebecca love Bridget? When Rebecca was so perfect? And what had chaotic Bridget done to deserve both perfect Darcy *and* perfect Rebecca?

It is a truth rarely acknowledged that the sexiest person in romantic fiction is often the love rival. It is, perhaps, a truth only acknowledged by rural teens with limited access to queer media. But it remains, I think, broadly true.

By "love rival", I generally mean the hero's ex-girlfriend, sometimes current girlfriend if we meet her in the early pages. Sometimes she is merely the hero's friend or sister, but there has to be a little plausible deniability there: the heroine, at least, has to *think* she's the love rival.

She is always extremely beautiful. She is usually clever – although if the heroine is, say, an academic with insecurities about how unsexy her job is, the rival will be adorably vapid. If the heroine is grumpy, the rival may even be a lovely person. She is, in every way, the opposite of the heroine – whatever the heroine isn't, she is. Whatever the heroine hasn't, she has.

If the heroine is short, she is tall; if the heroine is all curves, the love rival is teeny-tiny with a waist as wide as a matchstick. If the heroine is petite and gamine, the love rival is Jessica Rabbit. If the heroine is a fun-loving blonde eating Twiglets and always running late, the love rival will be a sleek brunette, probably a doctor, maybe even a children's doctor, who doesn't snack. And vice versa. If the hero has historically been married to sparky chaos, the heroine must be a quiet, shy girl with a bob who knows she can't match up to the ex (but oh, she can and must!).

A love rival is never introduced through the eyes of the hero, always the heroine. (Otherwise we would know straight away that she was no real threat.) And the heroine sees *perfection*.

If I am ever feeling despondent about myself I try to imagine what would be said about me if I was the love rival in a romance book. Specifically, I try to imagine what would be said about me if I was the love rival in a Jill Mansell book. To imagine yourself as the heroine is just too easy and ineffective: the heroine, of course, gets to describe herself (even if it's in third-person perspective). She is self-critical to a fault: the heroine is clumsy or chubby or skinny or awkward. The heroine knows her own flaws too well. But she knows none of the love rival's flaws. She sees only the rival's charms. She sees only what she herself is not. Even when she's hating the rival – even when the *text itself* hates the rival – the attention paid to the rival elevates and lifts her into something special, above and beyond other characters. (Think Caroline Bingley.)

What is good about this strategy, from a self-esteem point of view, is that you can really make it work whatever you look like simply by imagining that the heroine is your exact opposite. Of course, the heroine *will* end up with the hero in the end – but most romantic rivals don't end up alone. We might judge their decisions, but they don't usually wind up unhappy. It doesn't actually matter for your purposes, anyway. You, in your self-esteem-boosting, self-appointed role as love rival, simply need to imagine the one single snapshot in which your rival, the heroine, catches a glimpse of you and is rendered utterly helpless.

This strategy is also, of course, *profoundly gay*.

It's gay in the execution – the female gaze triumphs! – and it's also gay for that to have been the thing I most remember from my early forays into romance reading: women observing women.

Which is not merely symptomatic of my own latent queerness, but of something broader: the fundamental lack of queer romances in the mainstream history of the genre.

I watched the Rebecca–Bridget kiss over and over, as a teenager, because I had never seen anything like it. It was shot – soft light, rain – like the ending of a romcom. If you didn't wait until they both come up for air, you might think it was a perfect ending. "Thank you very much," Bridget says. "That was lovely." She pauses. "Really lovely ... If I ever do decide to, you know, bat for the other side, there's no one else. Only you." But Bridget, as we know she must, chooses Mark Darcy. Of course she does. This was twenty years ago, and even now it would be a stretch: a big-budget Hollywood queer movie that isn't sad? A big-budget Hollywood movie where the girl gets the girl in a shower of soft rain? (*But I'm a Cheerleader* being the only possible exception, and that came out, whisper it, more than a quarter of a century ago.)

Mainstream romance is, broadly, straight romance. Or, at least, mainstream romance with a happy ending.

This is almost as true in literature as it is in the movies: mainstream art about queer people tends to be extremely depressing. Most straight people, it seems, don't like to read about happy queers: it makes them wonder if they chose their lives too fast. It makes them think too much about other possibilities. (I joke. Mostly.)

"Publishable, but worth it?" scrawled E. M. Forster on the manuscript of his gamekeeper–posh boy romance *Maurice* in 1932. Ultimately, it was *not* worth it to Forster: the novel was only published posthumously, in 1971. Even in 1971, the happy ending, in which the gamekeeper and posh boy become woodcutters together, was widely derided. The critic C. P. Snow called the ending specifically, "artistically quite wrong": the *Daily Telegraph* declared that Forster had "wasted his time" writing this "plea for homosexuality".

Perhaps if the gay main characters had ended up broken and alone, the *Daily Telegraph* might have given it five stars.

Mills & Boon didn't publish an explicitly queer title until – this is unbelievable – 2020. "Gay characters have featured in our books before," said a spokesman, proudly. "But not as the *main* characters." (A textbook example of the Disney model of inclusion: keep the queers where they belong, in the back.)

"There is a growing market for LGBTQ [novels]," the American trade magazine *Publishers Weekly* said, that same year. "Romance lists look a little different this season." I can't get past the temptation to add an exclamation mark to the end of that sentence. *Romance lists look a little different this season!* Dungarees are *in*, caps are *in*, fifties skirts are *out*, and I think you'll find the S/S 19/20 silhouette to be, in short, adorably gay.

If, as Philip Larkin tells us, sexual intercourse began in 1963, then did queer literary sexual intercourse begin in 2020? (If 1963 was late for Larkin, imagine how the rest of us must feel.) The answer, of course, is that there have always been queer books – as there have always been queer people. What those queer books have not historically been is very *fun*.

As a teenager I scrabbled around for queerness wherever I could find it: joyful queerness I clung onto like a life raft. I used to meet people on the internet, other teenagers, caught in the same quest: we would post each other collages of neatly copied-out fragments of the letters of Vita and

Virginia and I would pin them up around my bed frame. The best words – the queerest words – I remember in gold gel-pen:

Yes yes yes I do like you. I am afraid to write the stronger word.

Or: *I am reduced to a thing that wants Virginia.*

Or: *What can one say – except that I love you.*

It was a romance novel; it was an epistolary novel; the tragic ending loomed over us. The ending of *Orlando* was much more satisfactory: planes, moon spiders, the future, joy.

And yet the real-life ending – cold clear water, heavy stones, the letter to Leonard – did not seem out of place. It seemed completely obvious that Virginia and Vita were never going to be together. That wasn't how books ended. That wasn't how women who loved each other ended. Not in real books, by real people.

It was also not how men who loved each other ended, either. When, in my first term at university, I found Alan Hollinghurst and *The Line of Beauty*, I read it on repeat. It had the beats of a romance novel to me, if none of the trappings. It felt very magical: a Cinderella story, a Hot Billionaire story combined with the coming-of-age social-outcast stories I have always loved.

Nick Guest lives as a kind of lodger in the Notting Hill home of the wealthy family of his beautiful friend Toby. Toby's father, Gerald, is a Tory MP under Thatcher. Nick is gay, half in love with Toby, and hooking up with hot strangers in the gated gardens of the Notting Hill house. It is an incredibly fun book. It has an ending to make you cry. But of course. But of course! That was how gay books were supposed to end, because – to be very fair – that was how serious books were supposed to end. You weren't supposed to get happy endings in literary books, not often, and I didn't need them. I loved *Tess of the d'Urbervilles*! I loved *The Great Gatsby*! I understood the deal.

The difference, I suppose, was that I had romance novels to give happy endings to straightness. I had romance novels to give *lightness* to straightness. I had, quite literally, thousands of books like that, and I hadn't had to try to find them at all. They gave a balance to my reading, and to my thinking.

It took me, quite literally, decades to find this kind of easy literary queerness on bookshelves – and it was, if a little earlier than the 2020 mark decided upon by the publishing industry, certainly not as early as it might have been. (Thank god for fanfiction.)

When I stumbled across the extraordinary *Beebo Brinker*, it felt like the eponymous heroine had been hidden from me on purpose. Where had she been all my life? Where had she been hiding for half a century? Who was the author Ann Bannon, and how had she been so far ahead of the publishing industry? Beebo is as perfect now as she was in 1957, when she first appeared in print: a tall, handsome butch new to New York. Also perfect: Jack, her gay roommate, who clocks her instantly as a too-drunk closeted lesbian who won't get far by herself. "Someone did this for me," he explains, as he buys her dinner. This is not small-town Wisconsin. This is the big city. "Just so you know," Beebo warns him, agreeing to crash on his couch, "my father taught me how to fight."

"Beebo, my dear," Jack says. "You could throw me twenty foot through the air if you wanted, but you won't have to. I don't even have any etchings to show you."

Beebo throws up; Jack holds her hair back, and lends her a pair of pyjamas. ("Scarlet and orange cotton flannel. 'I like flashy sleepers,' he explained.") She sleeps soundly for fourteen hours, then wakes up to a note on the pillow. *"I'm at work. Home around 5.30 ... White pills in medicine chest for head. Take two and LIVE. You're a devil in bed. Jack."*

Jack can't work out why Beebo won't come out to him in return; it's a shock to him that she doesn't seem to know herself. "People don't want me around, like I'm a nudist, or a vegetarian, or something," she says, frankly. "They think maybe some of it will rub off on them, and they can't imagine anything worse." She's almost there! She's so close to being able to see it! But her small-town shame is in her eyes like smoke.

Jack gets her a job as a delivery boy ("Can you drive?" "I can drive, but can I be a boy?" "You can wear slacks."), and takes her to gay bars and introduces her to his friends. They make fancy cocktails in their apartment and talk about how terrible men are, and about an "absolutely gorgeous"

(Beebo's words!) girl, who Beebo has seen at the store. Her name is Mona, and Jack believes her to be a total nightmare.

> "There's a word for [girls like] Mona," Jack said. Beebo tensed up. "Bitch." He threw her a grin and made her laugh in nervous relief. "Actually, Mona loves girls," Jack went on, speaking in a smooth, casual flow, a conversational tone that bespoke no shock, no disapproval, nothing but ordinary interest. He deliberately looked at the newspaper as he spoke. "Lesbian. Want to freshen this up for me, pal?"

He clarifies, later, that "some of the staunchest Puritan ladies I know are double-dyed bitches, and just because Mona is a bad apple doesn't mean all the gay girls in the world are full of worms. Mona would be bitchy anyway, gay or straight."

Beebo is staggered. "Does it ever happen that a nice girl is a Lesbian?" she asks. "All the time," Jack tells her, without looking up from the paper. "I've met most of them."

Beebo Brinker is both the last and first book in Ann Bannon's five-book series the Beebo Brinker Chronicles: the last to be published (in 1962), but the first to feature Beebo's arrival into New York. When Beebo Brinker appears on the page in book one, *Odd Girl Out*, she is kind, sexy and almost six feet tall: as Bannon remembered her in a later interview, "she was just quite literally, the butch of my dreams". A 1950s housewife obsessed with Radclyffe Hall's *The Well of*

Loneliness, but longing for a happier ending, Bannon turned to secretly writing lesbian "potboilers". "It was not in my nature to do what was essential in those days," Bannon explained, "[either] kill one of them at the end or have one of them go crazy."

Asked by a journalist in 2003 whether she had "felt part of an underground group", Bannon replied briskly that she didn't just "feel" it: she knew she was. "I have no doubt that somewhere there lurks an FBI file from the 1950s with my name on it," she tells the interviewer. "I was genuinely shocked at the prospect of that kind of 'outing'. I had two little children and no intention in the world of abandoning them or subjecting them to anxiety about possibly losing their mother's care."

Bannon was married – the pen name "Ann Bannon" was chosen to protect her husband and children – and remained married for many years. Her own sexuality – "Nobody is totally one way or the other" – remains guarded: she was married to a man; she romanced women in Greenwich Village bars; she wrote lesbian books about lesbians. She was, she wrote in the introduction to the reprinted edition of her first book, "convinced of nothing in the world so deeply as the beauty and passion of same-sex love". The Wikipedia debate rages on: *can* we put Bannon in the canon of lesbian writers? If she never explicitly *said*? If, in fact, she made it clear she felt that "one of the problems of settling on a label is other people ... think they know everything about you"?

But would it matter? Would it matter at all? Would it matter a lot? Does it matter how I identify, writing this now? It might: to write about queer politics is to write about identity, and to write about identity is to write, always, in some ways, about yourself.

And over the last decade, it has seemed to matter intensely. The sexualities of writers of queer romances – in all forms – have been studied to the point of unease: how can Casey McQuiston, a "straight woman", be permitted to write *Red, White, & Royal Blue*? Is it fair for Becky Albertalli or Elle McNicoll to write flagship books with queer characters, when they, too, surely must be "straight women"? Can Alice Oseman really write *Heartstopper*, and can Kit Connor really star in the adaptation of Oseman's work, if we don't have absolute sign-on-the-dotted-line confirmation of their sexualities? All of these creators have been publicly outed – or forced to out themselves. Faced, for instance, with an angry librarian brandishing a copy of *Some Like it Cold*, Elle McNicoll found herself on the end of a barrage of questions. Why had McNicoll written a bisexual protagonist? Why did McNicoll feel entitled to write a bisexual protagonist? Was *she* even bisexual? McNicoll admitted that yes, she was. Well, how was the librarian supposed to know? McNicoll wasn't "wear[ing] a flag pin".

"It's just private. I was born under section 28," McNicoll wrote in an open letter on the subject. "Some things I like to keep sacred." She is far from the only author to face a similar dilemma. Live your life as you wish to live it? Keep your private things private, and your sacred things sacred? It seems like a reasonable request.

The alternative, I suppose, is to accept that unlimited access to your soul may be the price you pay for access to people's hearts. Literature is a bit of a two-way street – and romantic literature in particular, I think. Writer and reader forge a connection based on a shared understanding, not of sexuality, necessarily, but of the universe: a shared language, a shared sensibility. Is there any validity in needing to know that we both came by this language honestly? Is there any validity in the desire to know that this new world was built on something real?

It's complicated. In a 2014 essay, Jamie Fessenden (author of *We're Both Straight, Right?*, *A Viking for Yule*, and other romances of the old-school Harlequin type) explored the complex fact that "M/M romance may be about gay men, but it isn't really ours. Many gay men have difficulty writing them. Not only that, but many gay men have difficulty reading them."

This is because, he says, modern M/M romance is not really related to mainstream queer literature at all: it is, instead, a direct descendant of fanfiction, specifically "slash fiction". And slash fiction has, at least historically, been chiefly written by straight women. Or, at least, people who are read – by the outside world – as straight women.

It's true that many writers of online slashfic, particularly those in the fanfic spaces, were (are!) assigned female at birth, and often in relationships with straight men. Many of

In Love with Love

them were (are!) married, with children. Some of these writers have gone on to flourish in commercial and mainstream publishing spaces. It is very boring to me to wade into this (largely online) discourse; nonetheless, there are vital questions at play here: can authors write about anyone they choose? Should authors write about anyone or anything they choose? Do authors have a duty to write about people like themselves, or do they have the right to do anything they want with their own words? Do authors owe us, the readers, their imaginative lives outwith their writing?

Do writers owe us anything outside of the text that we buy or are given? Do writers owe it to us to live lives in accordance with their works? And do they owe it to us to know everything about their sexualities, genders and private selves before they begin to write?

If these authors have remained the same *people* they always were, they have not, I think, always remained "straight women". They have become, in many cases, queer women. Or queer men. Or stepped outside the bounds of sexuality and gender, in ways less easy to categorise than a simple semantic shift. By writing, by reading, by living – we change. We know more about ourselves than we did before. We *become* more.

What *is* queerness in this context? What is queerness in any context? If queerness is everything outside straightness (as the wild is everything outside the walls of the house), then to firmly define the boundaries of that "outside" seems to me to be almost like putting a fence around a little portion of the wilderness, and pretending you haven't made the house a garden.

It is, or should be, obvious to most people that to convincingly write queer love, you must at least love queer people. It is, or should be, obvious that the writing of good queer love is in itself an act of queer love. This is not to say that everyone who writes queer romance must be queer, but it is to say that to engage in queer romantics is *to engage in queer romantics*. This engagement doesn't need to change anyone's identity, or orientation, but it is obviously (if dangerously) true: writing gay stories is a gay thing to do! To imagine oneself as a gay person is a gay thing to do! People write; people think; people live – and people change. Especially, I think, people who have spent a lot of time writing and thinking and living about queerness. As (angel) Alex Claremont-Diaz puts it in *Red, White & Royal Blue*: "*straight people probably don't spend this much time convincing themselves they're straight.*" It becomes obvious, then, why policing the sexuality of romance novelists is absolutely inappropriate.

Yet it is equally clear why a queer community, so recently freed from those FBI files Bannon speaks of, would feel uneasy at the prospect of an outsider making financial and social gains on the backs of the lost, the bruised, the dead. Homophobia is not historical: it is an ongoing, present reality. It is still illegal to be gay in more than a third of the world's countries. Recent far-right gains in previously liberal nations may (will) make things worse. The AIDS epidemic left immeasurably deep scars through the queer communities of the world; not to mention the ongoing risks of suicide, self-harm, homophobic violence and social stigma. When you are under siege from all sides, a fenced-off garden can feel safer than the call of the wild; founding principles, in this conception, coming second to phlegmatic pragmatism.*

What does it mean to write about queerness? What does it mean to be queer? Judith Butler's "discursive limits of 'sex'" have never felt more relevant: how do we draw a line between the idea and performance of identity, and the actual realities of sexual identity? How do we make a distinction – and when do we draw a distinction – between how we feel, and how we live? How do we draw a line between Ann Bannon's beautiful butch inner life, and her engineer husband and two small girls? Must we draw the line at all? These questions have no answers, or I have no answers for them – but it's hard to read queer romantic fiction and not wonder.

Social scientist Lucy Neville, in her article "The Tent's Big Enough for Everyone", discusses a study she conducted into the way that slash fiction acts as "a safe space for women to

---

* It's interesting to consider this in light of the number of men writing romance novels: in this genre mostly for women, do the facts that it was only made illegal to refuse to serve a drink to a woman in 1982; that a married woman only had the right to be taxed independently on her income in 1990; and that marital rape has only been a crime since 1994 make a difference to how willing we are to accept men into this one safe world? Do we, as women, resent the idea that men might make financial and social gains on the back of our own female suffering? Is this why so few men write romance?

explore their sexualities and gender identities, [and] how these insights connect to women's real-world lives". "Insights into slash fandom have typically consisted of theorists discussing *their* ideas of why women slash and what it means," Neville writes. As a writer of M/M fiction herself, she is able to survey more than five hundred writers of this kind of work. As anyone involved in that space might have guessed, three-quarters of these women felt that their writing had changed their real-life perceptions of sexuality and gender; almost 70 per cent felt that their writing was political.

"I've been awash of sexuality and gender confusion since forever," wrote one participant. Through the queer romance community, specifically the M/M community, they "found people on the trans spectrum who helped me ... feel less alone. [It] was a huge relief – because if there's a word for it, it's a thing, you know? I'm not the only person who feels this way. I didn't make up this way of thinking."

Jack, tucking a drunk Beebo into bed, longs to "explain that she wasn't alone in the world, that other people were different in the same way she was". "*You have company!*" Ann Bannon said, once, when asked the message of her books. "*You are okay!*" She quoted Max Ehrmann's prose poem "Desiderata": "*You are a child of the universe, no less than the trees and the stars; you have a right to be here.*"

The Beebo Brinker Chronicles were, like most lesbian romance of the time, chiefly marketed towards straight men. It is somewhat baffling to wonder what straight men made of these books. Their covers – featuring, in Bannon's own words, "beckoning sexy little twinkies" – feel so very gay, to me: sexy, for sure, if you are a woman who likes women, but for a man interested in women? The description of the straight men in the novel is borderline grotesque: Beebo's employer, asked to leave by his wife, apparently does so, but Beebo notices, a moment later, that "the fingers of his left hand were [still] curled around the door frame: five orphaned earthworms searching for the dirt". And yet, the fact remains that most lesbian pulp romances were actively sold to men. The covers were designed to appeal to men. They were sold widely, in small towns and big cities, not to appeal to an undercover queer market, but because men might want to buy lesbian porn in any drugstore in the country. The existence of these books, in their radical love, community and friendship, cannot be unpicked from straight fetishisation of queer culture and sexuality. Might the same be true of slash fiction?

To put it in very simple terms: if W/W romances were originally published for and by men, and M/M romances were originally published for and by women, what does that tell us about the ways sexuality might, in the world of romantic fiction, be more complex than it originally appears?

Academic Guy Mark Foster, in his (perfectly titled!) essay "What To Do If Your Inner Tomboy Is a Homo", talks about the "psychic mobility" of romantic fiction readers: the ability to identify with more than one main character at a time. Foster is writing specifically about M/M romance, but I think his point speaks to something more generally: romantic fiction, particularly the trend for dual perspective POV, *invites* these shifting perspectives. Where else would the third-act crisis come from? Juliet never sees Romeo's note, but if we, the audience, had no idea what he'd been up to in her absence we'd be too surprised to be sad when Romeo suddenly sits up from the slab. Most romance novels do not end in a double suicide, but many have this structure – a misunderstanding, crossed wires – and this psychic mobility allows us to really *feel* it. We have to be both. We have to understand both.

"I am sure you are right about it," Freud wrote to a friend, on bisexuality. "And I am accustoming myself to the idea of regarding every sexual act [between two individuals] as a process in which four persons are involved." (Four at least, Freud. Four at least!) Straight sex, Freud thought, is not just a question of man-as-man and woman-as-woman basic animal copulation: it's a psychological exploration of the male and female, dominant and submissive, power play possibilities inherent within all of us.

I try my best not to bring a bisexual bias to the table, but there *is*, I think, something inherently bisexual – or more properly, pansexual – in the fluidity of romantic fiction.

Sometimes I even fear that most romance novels about women who have sex with women are essentially escapist fantasies for bi women married to men, both in the writing and the reading. (I say this as a bi woman married to a man, who happens to read a lot of WLW romance.) Beebo-esque butches — almost six foot, strong, handsome, with good fighting skills — almost never make an appearance, even now, in most mainstream lesbian romantic fiction. Nor does the word "lesbian", not really: the word "sapphic", sometimes "queer", has largely replaced it in the marketing materials. (Discuss.) "Sapphic" romances tend to involve at least one bisexual woman, and both women tend towards being obvious (and male-gaze-compliant) beauties. Even when a character is described as "butch", the cover art reveals her — looking at you, *Delilah Green Doesn't Care* — to be curvy, long-haired and wearing skinny jeans. "Butches are for litfic," my lesbian friend said, sadly. "You *never* get good butches in romcoms."

"Sometimes I think that straight women just like to think about what it would be like to have two clean, soft people in one bed, and the sex *has* to be imaginative," said my friend. (It *is*, you must admit, a lovely thought.)

My friend and I were on a road trip. We had both, once, been straight girls reading gay fanfiction, and we had both read a lot of queer literature about gay men. (More, certainly, than we had ever sought out about queer women. Or, perhaps, than we had been able to find.) Now we were both queer women ourselves, and we had been driving for five hours. "Is all sex ... gay?" I said, staring out at the flatland all around us. "Is that the answer?"

It sounded insane. It sounded true. We had been driving for too long. We rang a gay friend.

"Is all sex gay?" we said.

There was a long pause.

"If you mean that all sex that is not for reproductive purposes is, in some way, queer," our phone-a-friend said, carefully, "then you might be onto something." (A patient and thoughtful man!)

"Is all sex gay?": it felt like a mad thing to say. Nonetheless, it stuck with me. It stuck with me because it is just as heretical, biblically speaking, to have non-reproductive heterosexual sex as it is to have non-reproductive homosexual sex: to *lie with a man as with a woman* is punishable by death, as is *spilling one's seed upon the ground*. In fact, Onan's refusal to impregnate his wife – a simple question of the withdrawal method! – is so appalling to God that he strikes him down, to death, on the spot. (Worth noting here that no named gay people are actually put to death in the Bible. The sins of Sodom, from which we get the word "sodomy", and for which the Sodomites were slain, were only much later associated with homosexuality. The Sodomites' original crime seems to have been lack of charity, a surfeit of pride, and possibly plain old regular heterosexual sex outside of marriage. Extremely close same-sex friendships, of the Saul-and-Jonathan they-were-lovely-and-pleasant-in-their-lives-and-in-death-they-were-not-divided type, are not only permitted, but celebrated.)

If sex is for reproduction, then all recreational sex is dangerous. Reproductive sex (pregnancy, birth, childrearing) is physically dangerous for women; therefore, *all* sex is dangerous for women.

In Love with Love

Straight men in romance novels used to win at sex by force: a ravishing, a deflowering, an overwhelming assault which the heroine succumbs to and adores against her will. She has no power at that time: she gains power, emotionally, through repeated sexual contact. It's rape, Jim, but not as we know it. It's rape reimagined in such a way as to reinvent the power structures of the patriarchy. He rapes her; later, he will be on his knees begging to give her everything. He rapes her; it's not the end of her life. The worst thing that can happen to her happens, and she gets a happy ending anyway. It's a fantasy to unpack a fear, but it's a fantasy that's not always easy to read. (Let alone critique.) He is some kind of ship's captain, or cartoon sheikh, or – in the case of the notorious *Seven Brides for Seven Brothers* – one of seven brothers who live at the top of a mountain, all of whom seek a strong and attractive wife. (This 1954 musical is based on a short story, *The Sobbin' Women*, which is in turn based on, unbelievably, *The Rape of the Sabine Women*. This, itself, was a historical event in which many women and girls were raped and kidnapped in the eighth century BC, which was – to be fair, if we must – a long time ago. The musical, though, was nominated for four Oscars. And as late as 2006, was named as one of the best musicals ever made. Startling!)

And so, the man, who was a strong and masculine man, won at sex by being the strongest and most masculine of men.

Straight men in modern romance novels appear to win at sex by a simple three-step procedure: two pages of passionate cunnilingus, a brisk paragraph of mostly doggy style, and a generous post-bonk cuddle. (Bonus points will be given for a nickname which, while absurdly generic, has never previously been applied to the heroine: Red, for instance, or Honey, Sunny, Baby, Sweetheart, Tiny, etc.) What is really remarkable about these sex scenes is that it took reading four romances a day as research for this book for me to notice how alike they are: it is, as usual, a tribute to the romance writer's craft that each time it feels new and exciting.

It is extraordinary, too, that so many sex positions sound like they have stepped straight out of a Zane Grey ranch romance: the missionary, the cowgirl, and their ever-loyal doggy. These names carry with them such heavy connotations that it is almost as if they are stereotypes in themselves: a kind of fiction writing or storytelling with the human body. A missionary, of course, carries the sense both of righteousness and pomposity; a dog has an animal sense of unconscious degradation, disgust, freedom and pleasure. And the cowgirl, as psychoanalyst Dianne Elise noted, has the tomboy's sense of gender-swap freedom. Elise writes, specifically, that both "cowgirl" and "tomboy" act as markers to dis-identify the woman in question from both her own mother, and the role of mother in general. How could a cowgirl be a mother? How could a boy? How could a tomcat? Even words like "spooning" carry a cosy, domestic connotation (the opposite being that favourite of the dreaded lesbian, "scissoring", sharp and dangerous). What can a spoon hold? What can a scissor slice? The sequence of sexual positions, both in life and in the sex scenes of a romance novel, has an imaginative narrative attached. Who is in charge? Who owns who? Is this natural, unnatural, joyful or dutiful?

If the sex you are having is supposed to go one particular way – to tell one particular narrative – and that sex is always dangerous to you, it makes sense, perhaps, that you might want to consider other possibilities. Heterosexual romance, told from the perspective of a straight female protagonist, has one basic narrative: you can write towards it, or against it, but fundamentally the narrative is one of submission. You are always writing against and towards and around the patriarchy. You are always writing around the fact that men have power, and women have less.

In M/M romance, then, women can play out vulnerability in men: men can be vulnerable with other men, but not with women. In straight books you get one (1) moment of vulnerability: an apology, a humbling, he's on his knees begging for forgiveness. There is a duality of masculinity in gay romance that permits the woman writing, or reading, a degree of freedom that is strictly limited in straight books: a vulnerable man is not allowed to be sexy to a straight woman, *but what if he were? What if we could see what that might look like?*

What stories might we be allowed to tell then? What desire might we find? What danger?

Writing about sex that is foreign to us allows us to conceptualise the idea that all sex is foreign. All sex is a journey into the unknown, one way or another.

Queerness acts as a way for straightness to approach the transgressive wild act of pleasurable and useless sex. Eileen Myles writes, in their poem "Peanut Butter", that their thoughts about their lover are *"not exactly/ forbidden, but/ exalted because/ [the thoughts] are useless"*. Useless, unproductive sex is exalted because it leads only to pleasure. It leads only to joy. *"It's more/ like a playground/ where I play/ with my reflection/ of you,"* Myles goes on, *"until/ you come back/ and into the/ real you I/ get to sink/ my teeth"*. Play, thought and action are mirrors of each other: they trace each other's shapes, over and over again, with no point but joy. Perhaps we can say that the straight woman writing queer romance is playing with reflections, too. Perhaps we can say that it is *because* of the fluidity found in romance that it is a genre that should be exalted; it is a genre of possibility, and there all things, and all lives, are possible.

Michel Foucault says that there are always "real places – places that do exist and that are formed in the very founding of society – which are something like counter-sites, a kind of effectively enacted utopia in which the real sites, all the other real sites that can be found within the culture, are simultaneously represented, contested, and inverted." They are "outside of all places, even though it may be possible to indicate their location in reality". He calls them "heterotopias".

I thought for a long time that a heterotopia was a utopia for heterosexuals. Incorrect! Then I looked it up and discovered a heterotopia is a place that is, like heterosexuality, interested in the other. If "utopia is a place where everything is good [and] dystopia is a place where everything is bad," writes theorist Walter Russell Mead, then "heterotopia is where things are different." A heterotopia is a place that is real and unreal; for example, if you look in a mirror, the world you see is both obviously real (it's all around you!), but obviously not real (you can't touch anything that's in the mirror and it's all the wrong way round!).

Boarding schools are heterotopias; a ship is a heterotopia. They are little worlds inside the big world. A garden, Foucault says, is a heterotopia: it is "the smallest parcel of the world and then it is the totality of the world". A motel room where someone goes to have an affair is a heterotopia: it's a place outside of everything where anything can happen.

Romance novels, it seems to me, must be a kind of heterotopia too: the whole community, with our desire to simultaneously police the boundary and open the boundary, with all our many contradictory, multifaceted conventions, tropes, ideas, comments, traditions, must also be a kind of heterotopia. It's like the world, but not the world; it's like literature, but not like literature in that it subverts the need for a new and exciting plot every time. It's a place unto itself. It's Romancelandia.

So, if sex for pleasure is fundamentally transgressive, then writing about sex becomes doubly transgressive; women writing about sex is triply transgressive; women writing as, or about, men having sex, takes us even deeper into the unknowns of transgression. The Love Train has gone off the rails. The horses are running free. The wild is calling. The wind is tousling the long hair of the ex-girlfriends of our lovers. The butches are back from the 1950s. Anyone can be anything. Orlando, who is Vita, written by Virginia, as a boy as a girl as a boy, stands on the hill waiting for her (his?) lover and husband. Pearls glow like moon spiders. The aeroplane is a wild goose is an aeroplane. The stars spin. Time moves. We are somewhere else now, and it looks a lot like home.

11

The Infinite Weird

Anything can happen in the world of romance.

Or rather, romance can happen in the world of anything.

This *is* the genre of possibility, after all. From the furthest reaches of the galaxy – *Ice Planet Barbarians! Pride and Prejudice in Space!* – to the depths of the ocean, you can set a romance pretty much anywhere you want, and cast the characters in any way you want, provided it obeys the beats of the story. We'll know where we are. We'll know what to do. All possible tastes – all possible imaginations – are catered for.

Worlds can happen in the anything of romance: everything is here. Whole universes you have never previously imagined are here.

In the spirit of the internet's famous Rule 34 – *if it exists, there is porn of it* – we might also say that *if it exists, there is romance for it*. If something has been imagined – there is romance for it, about it, within it, of it.

It is, perhaps, the element of romantic fiction most difficult to talk about to people who don't read romantic fiction. A Hot Billionaire is reasonably easy to explain, if a trifle humiliating from a feminist perspective; there can be barely a woman alive and living in a city who doesn't understand the pull of the wide open skies of the Hot Cowboy. The Hot Single Dad is easy to explain to people with no children – in my experience, parents find this one almost impossible to grasp – and even something like a Brandon Birmingham Hot Captain Slash Pirate is not a hard sell to the general reading public. Even a dubcon or bully fantasy has enough crossover with mainstream pornographic interests that it's possible to handwave it away. "He's really mean to her and she's into it" is close enough to "he only pulls your pigtails because he *likes* you" that while people might raise an eyebrow, they won't turn away entirely.

It's when it gets weirder – even just a little weirder – that it starts to become tricky. Infinite possibility leads, inevitably, to infinite weirdness. The infinite number of monkeys on their infinite number of typewriters might eventually write *Bleak House*, but they are going to write an awful lot of stranger things first.

It's when play crosses a line from financially sensible (who doesn't want to fall in love with someone with either lots of money or lots of freedom?) to entirely freewheeling that people start to wonder whether anyone can be both adult enough to enjoy sex, and childish enough to enjoy this kind of play.

Adult play, even (especially) the non-sexual kind, is trouble.

Play is always, essentially non-productive. It is, according to a *New York Times* interview with play expert Jeff Harry, *clearly and by definition* "an action you do that brings you a significant amount of joy without offering a specific result". Perhaps as with sex, so with life: if it's not profitable, if it does not result in reproduction and cannot itself be reproduced, it sits outside the material confines of capitalism – and therefore is irrelevant.

reproducible joy is hardly joy at all says the poet Kaveh Akbar in his poem "For You I've Started Sleeping" (itself, I think, a perfect example of romantic fiction): sex for pleasure, like reading and writing for pleasure, makes clear that there are things in the human experience that cannot be easily quantified.

And yet, of course, romantic fiction is a hugely profitable market sector of an industry built, like all industries, for profit. The reason that publishers offer vast sums of money, plus a classy logo on the spine, to entice successful self-publishers into their ranks is because this kind of writing for joy, about joy, *makes* vast sums of money. It makes vast sums of money for the self-publishers, too. Writing with no purpose but pleasure is astoundingly lucrative when it hits the right spot. (And hits it, as we have seen, repeatedly.)

This is the kind of paradoxical statement that is such a feature of romantic fiction: it's a one-way ticket to Contradiction City if you want to ride the Love Train.

Is it feminist to know your own desires, if your own desires involve an unfeminist longing to be spanked by a big strong daddy? Does the fact that we always know the ending mean we should stop wanting to turn the pages? Can we police our own joy, our own longing, our own wants, our own happiness, and still experience them? How can we talk about our desires when our desires might be silly or strange or stupid or dangerous? And here, now: *if romantic fiction is play, and play has no specific purpose, then how does it change our relationship to that play once we acknowledge that our play is the byproduct of the specific purpose of capitalism?*

Fantasy, too, shares some of this quality: it might be embarrassing for a grown-up to admit a fondness for dragons or space travel, and yet it's an enduringly solid market. People want to have fun. This should make romantasy doubly embarrassing, and yet – perhaps due to the brazenness with which it embraces and explores both genres? – it thrives. The moral of this story, I suppose, is if you're going to do something, do it hard. *Find out who you are, and do it on purpose*, as Dolly Parton may or may not have said.

Fourth Wing, by Rebecca Yarros, and the clear *Fourth Wing* inspiration, Anne McCaffrey's *Dragonriders of Pern*, are classic examples of the hugely successful romantasy genre: they ride dragons! They love dragons! They are spiritually, and in some ways sexually, bonded to dragons! They remain on the bestseller chart for literal years!

There is a truly fantastic novel called *The Pisces*, by Melissa Broder, in which a woman falls in love (and lust) with a merman. ("The tail starts below the dick.") I loved it: I handed out my dog-eared copy, much like *The Other Boleyn Girl*, to my dearest friends. We talked about it like schoolgirls. *The bit where she's in the hotel toilets?* we said. *The bit*

The Infinite Weird

where she wheels him in the little trolley? We could not believe it. It was so clever, so funny, so ridiculous – so real.

Later, I was in a meeting at another office. Someone had propped a copy up on the bookshelf in the meeting room. I was eyeing it up – could I pinch it to replace mine? – when the person I was meeting with came into the room. She saw me looking at *The Pisces* and raised her eyebrows. "Have you read that?" she said. "Yes!" I said, happily. She visibly recoiled. "A bit ... weird, isn't it?" I thought about the bit in the hotel toilets. "Er— yes," I said. She shook her head as if to shake the whole book and Theo's thick scaly tail ("I thought about eating it with garlic butter while we kissed") out of her mind. "*Not* my kind of thing," she said, removing it from the display shelf with a delicate flick of a disgusted wrist, like a woman picking up a dog shit. The meeting was not a great success. I was too humbled to think straight.

And I have thought about that, on and off, for the best part of a decade: it's hard for me to think about romance novels without thinking about that encounter. It was, I suppose, the response I have always associated with romance novels, and it was interesting – and destabilising! – to feel it happen with something dressed up in a literary jacket. (It had tricked people into reading it, and some of them loved it and stayed forever, and some of them did not.)

Her disgust at *The Pisces* was driven by the same factors that fuel the more generalised disgust for mainstream romantic fiction: proximity to sex, proximity to bodies, proximity to weirdness and depravity and desire. It was because women, writing and reading these things, are to be avoided. They do not make for polite conversation.

And yet non-human romance novels are, I think, among the few romance novels to cross over into mainstream literature. They don't seem to register as romance in the same way; they seem to pass, stealthily, into Real Books without a single beat changed. Re-jacketed, adorned with a tasteful literary quote, they move from pure joy to tender, serious meditation on the human condition with a flick of the marketing wand.

Consider Marian Engel's *Bear*, published originally in 1976. The 2016 reissue features a Margaret Atwood quote – "a strange, and wonderful book" – and a solid green serif typeface, set into thick, textural bear fur, with a hand sinking into its depths. The original cover features a watercolour of a woman, nude to the waist, long hair barely covering the nipples of her perfectly spherical breasts, eyelashes like mink half-closed over drowsy, sex-heavy eyes. She lolls back in the arms of – who else? – a bewildered-looking and very large bear. "THE SHOCKING, EROTIC NOVEL OF A WOMAN IN LOVE," blares a banner over the title. The title is gold, all-caps, swirling. The book itself, of course, exists somewhere between the two covers. Is it erotic to fuck a bear? Lou, a librarian, has come to a remote Canadian island. On the remote Canadian island is a bear. Lou sits by the fire, reading a biography of Beau Brummell. "The Beau was dominating duchesses. The Beau was on the make. How she disapproved of him, how she admired him." She caresses the bear with her bare foot. She lies naked for him by the river. "What didn't I do?" she thinks, later, coming to her senses as if she had forgotten something. Then: "Oh, God, *what did I do?*"

It's fascinating to compare *Bear* with Rachel Ingalls' *Mrs. Caliban*, published in 1982 and named by the British Book Marketing Council in 1986 as one of twenty best post-war American novels. "So deft and austere in its prose, so drolly casual in its fantasy, an impeccable parable," reads a jacket blurb – by none other than John Updike. Published as a high-end literary horror (you can tell from the huge green eye and spiky, spooky, luminous green font that dominates the cover), it makes you wonder why *Bear* got the full pulp treatment, and this something quite different. *Mrs. Caliban* tells the story of a suburban housewife who falls into an instant sexual affair with an escaped frogman. "His head was quite like the head of a frog," the narrator tells us, looking closely as the frogman removes her dressing gown and applies himself to her pleasure. "The mouth was ... like a human mouth ... The hands and feet were webbed ... and as for the rest of the body, he was exactly like a man – a well-built large man – except that he was a dark spotted green-brown in colour and had no hair anywhere." The line between disgust and desire is paper thin. He is like a man-shaped oyster; slippery, strange, poisonous if taken wrongly. *Mrs. Caliban* is as weird, sexy, dark and light as *Bear* – and many other romance novels, then and now – but was received, on first publication, very differently.

In Love with Love

It is interesting to think about *Mrs. Caliban*, *Bear*, and to an extent *The Pisces*, in conversation with what I think of as *actual romance novels*. How would these books fare in a community built around certain tropes, certain beats, certain expectations? How would they hold up against, to pick an example completely at random, one Lillian Lark's *Deceived by the Gargoyles*?

Deceived by the Gargoyles: A Love Bathhouse Monster Romance is the first in Lark's *Love Bathhouse* series: Rose Love is the best matchmaker in the world, and she works out of a magical bathhouse disguised as an old video rental shop. It is, we're told, the "premier place for paranormals of certain appetites to indulge in their sexual desires". But Grace, our heroine, is merely there to find love. As she will do, almost immediately, with a gargoyle named Elliot. And Elliot's two gargoyle boyfriends. The gargoyles, you'll be glad to know, have slightly thicker skin than humans, but are still very up for the whole business of love. It has a cover almost identical to *Bear*'s original cover, except that this time, the woman is blonde and clothed, and instead of a bear, it's a spooky silhouette. (The title font is equally flouncy.)

There is something very precious to me about these kind of books: something much more endearing, something much more tangible. Of course, *Mrs. Caliban* and *Bear* both gain readers and respect from their glossy glow-ups – but it's hard for me, a romance reader, not to feel like something has been lost as well. It is, I think, something to do with that sense of community: that sense of something secret, silly, under the covers. It is the fun of a flirtation. It is the illicit thrill of a crush. It is the real ridiculous joy of giving in to a taboo, and so I turn with a sense of gleeful relief to *Unhinged*, by Vera Valentine: a romance novella about a woman and her front door. "This story contains door knob insertion," warns the first page. (Also: "*voyeur, secret underwear theft, deliberate food drugging, alcohol use, allusions to an orgy, gun violence, shooting 'death', wood putty use, sex toy use, condom use, working with police, talking with police, erotic humiliation (very light), fetishistic enjoyment of commands, lubricant use, female domination (with aftercare), male submission (aftercare is supplied)*".) The door, you will be pleased to know, does "turn into a guy". (After the "knob insertion". Goodness.) He is, astonishingly, not only a door, but a son of Zeus. (Sample dialogue: "A favor, huh? So, what, do you want me to oil your hinges?")

For the curious: it kinda works! It really kinda works.

It can't be denied that *Unhinged* fits neatly into a long history of gods transforming into inanimate objects and other animals for sexual purposes. The Greek gods, in particular, are only too delighted to become a swan or a bull or a shower of gold coins. (How sex works, when you are a bag of gold coins upended on someone's bed, I don't pretend to know. Nonetheless, it does work for Zeus. Perseus is born nine months later.)

The ancient Greeks, in fact, offer a rich seam for romantic fiction – particularly where non-humans are concerned. The success of Madeline Miller's (delicious) *Circe* and (double delicious) *Song of Achilles* speak to our unending love affair with the idea of deistical romance: an affair with a god (or demigod) is all the other romance tropes rolled into one. A God might be the ultimate Hot Billionaire, but they are also wild: a Hot Cowboy on steroids, able to walk where they choose, unafraid, all powerful. And with that wildness comes Hot Alien strangeness. You must, and will, surrender. You must, and will, be a pawn in their games – no matter how depraved, how dark, how helpless you feel.

Gods can change themselves; they can also change you. They can impregnate you against your will. (Even when they are gold coins.) They can transform you into their slave, or their prisoner. They can make you into something beautiful, something dead, something trapped, something rich and strange.

"*To all of the women who were ever made to feel lesser, this one's for you,*" writes Wren K. Morris, in the dedication of her 2022 novel *Surrendering to Scylla*. Then she goes on: "*To all of the men who ever made us feel lesser, if I could have legally eaten you, I would have.*"

There are many mythological origins for Scylla: in Morris's telling, she is a nymph transformed. Glaucus, a sea-god, loved her; Circe, of Madeline Miller fame, loved Glaucus. So Circe poisons Scylla's bathing pool, and she is changed forever. Instead of legs, ten tentacles; from her waist, above the tentacles, the six vicious jaws of six vicious hounds. "I was a nymph before," Scylla thinks to herself, "but in this new form? I was a monster. Monstrous. It had always seemed so unsavory, so undesirable, but now it felt powerful." Scylla wrecks ships; she consumes men whole; she takes their gold; sets their skulls, sucked clean, on the ledges of her cave. Men don't have to have wronged her to be punished. She is wild, elemental. She is a force to be reckoned with. She owes nobody anything. It is the ultimate Sylvia Plath wish fulfilment: to eat men "like air".

But Scylla is lonely. Monsters almost always are. (Just ask Grendel's mother.) When she finds she has left one man alive from a shipwreck, she decides to keep him. He sleeps, and when he wakes, he sees only Scylla's own face: a beautiful, youthful nymph. He asks how long she has been there; she tells him she doesn't know. He asks if she is hurt; she tells him it would take too long to say. He calls for her to flee the monster. "*'As for the monster,' Scylla continued, the human-woman-like voice cold as it caressed my cheek with one of those sickening limbs, the suckers of it nibbling at my flesh, 'I'm right here.'*"

The monster is, from the earliest introduction, a sensual thing: the tentacles that can feel every grain of sand, every tiny stone, every crevice of the cave; the dog heads that lick their lips, that taste, that whimper. (Classic tentacles.)

For example: *My Tentacle Romance – A Tantalizing Time with a Tentacle Monster: An Egg-filled Happily Ever After*, by Amber Fox. "Perhaps the anything-but-ordinary date will end in an explosively sexy way, and filled with gooey tentacle eggs!" reads the blurb, adding, hopefully: "Maybe it could even lead to the heart-melting happily ever after that Tess craves with all her being." This was, I have to say, a step too far even for me, although it does offer the perfect example of how this genre has no need or obligation to surprise. The word "tentacle" is in the title *twice*.

Tentacles are obviously phallic: they twine, they thrust, they choke. They sometimes even fuck. Freud, faced with Fox's Tantalising Time, would not so much as have a field day, as a field year. A tentacled woman, then, is doing something new with gender: a tentacled woman has the godlike power to be *both*. A tentacled woman is as fluid as it gets.

Consider briefly Ursula the Sea Witch. The apparent villain of Disney's *The Little Mermaid*, Ursula is tits on top and tentacles on the bottom. She offers Ariel everything she's ever wanted, then steals her voice in exchange. She offers possibilities that nobody in the mermaid kingdom has ever dreamed of; she offers a whole new world. The price, of course, is that Ariel will never see her family again – and she will never again be able to speak her truth.

"That's right," Ursula purrs, to a nervous Ariel. "But you'll have your man. Life's full of tough choices, isn't it?"

Physically half drag queen Divine, half octopus (with the creature's "seductive, scary gait"), Pat Carroll based her Ursula's intonations and inflections on those of Howard Ashman, the gay Broadway lyricist who wrote the original script. Carroll saw the character as "an ex-Shakespeare actress who now sold cars"; it's easy to understand why so many others see the character as a queer icon. The romance of *The Little Mermaid* may be between Ariel and Prince Eric (two manifestly unsuited lovers), but the *sexual tension* of *The Little Mermaid* is between Ariel and Ursula: power, danger, seduction and betrayal. It's Bluebeard and Charming; it's Heyer Hero Mark I and Heyer Hero Mark II. I cannot tell you – and probably don't need to – how much Ursula erotica there is out there.

And yet, of course, it's clear that this reading of Ursula is contrary to the way the film is *supposed* to be viewed. The story is between Eric and Ariel; Ursula is not given a happy ending.

The scarlet-lipped, purple-skinned mistress of the strange, the uncanny, the sexually deviant, the inhuman, Ursula is the monstrous feminine writ large. (Very large.) And the monstrous feminine is so rarely, canonically, the love interest in romantic fiction. The monstrous feminine, like the Hot Billionairess, is a queer thing. The patriarchy has no place for large, powerful, disgusting women. The patriarchy is no place for strange women.

And yet even for ourselves, in a female-dominated genre – where women write the characters, and women read, and love, them – there are still far more male monsters than female. He was the door; the frog; the merman. The minotaur at the milking farm. Sometimes I think this is because of the male gaze: that internalised, patriarchal shame system which keeps us in our place. Other times I think differently.

Through history there have been dozens upon dozens of sexy female monsters: it feels strange to me that they so rarely have their stories reimagined. The succubus! The *lilim*! The Greek baby-killers *empusa* and *moromolyce* and *gylou* and *abyzou*! The *lamia*, with no eyes but enormous testicles, explicitly female, who – not content with eating babies – also ate the young men whom she seduced! She doesn't just feed the baby; she drips milk over its lips until it drowns. She doesn't just kiss the man; she devours him. She consumes as much as she creates. All explicitly female; all explicitly monstrous – and yet, where their male counterparts might easily become the troubled hero of a modern romance, the terrible women of myth rarely rise up and know themselves.

She is, I suppose, a male fear rather than a female fear – perhaps this is why, in such a gendered genre, we don't need to deconstruct her. Perhaps it's not comforting, or even pleasant, to run through yet *again* the ways the world still feels women will fail. We struggle, mostly, to romanticise female monstrosity – and perhaps it's because we don't want to tame them.

A search for this kind of thing – the female monster, reclaimed and reworked – even in romance where truly every taste can be catered for, turns up far fewer hits than you might expect. Some, for sure: "*Seattle succubus Georgina Kincaid's life is far less exotic. At least there's her day job at a local bookstore – free books; all the white chocolate mochas she can drink; and easy access to bestselling, sexy writer, Seth Mortensen, aka He Whom She Would Give Anything to Touch but Can't.*"

It's worth noting, too, that there are far more, and far more highly recommended, reads for the gender-reversed *incubus*. Women, perhaps, want to be seduced more than they want to seduce; or, at least, they want to read more about being seduced than seducing. Women are afraid that men are powerful and dangerous; women are afraid that men will have sex with them while they sleep. Women are afraid that men will rape them. This is one of the ways that we play with those fears.

The line between fear and arousal, like the line between disgust and desire, is thin and shifting. It's also true that the line between power and submission is thinner than people might think: the person who submits is the person who should have the power. The person with the most to lose sets the limits. (This is why, of course, it's vital that Ana Steele never signs Christian Grey's NDA; and it's why the *only* good scene in the movie is the one in which they negotiate the contract.)

If we are writing, we're in charge. If we are writing books about the ways we give in, in some very real ways, then we're not giving in at all. We're the people running the show; we are the gods of the universes we create. *Have your cake*, as Henry de Tamble says, *and eat it too*.

We struggle to romanticise female monstrosity, but do we really need to? Might female monstrosity exist as a space where we don't need to interpolate the male gaze? Might this explain why, perhaps, the only great *lamia* romance novel is 150 years old, and as queer as it gets?

In Love with Love

Is it a romance? It's hard to say, but it's certainly both very gay and very, very sexy. "My strange and beautiful companion would take my hand, and hold it with a fond pressure, renewed again and again," Laura, the narrator tells us:

> blushing softly, gazing in my face with languid and burning eyes, and breathing so fast that her dress rose and fell with the tumultuous respiration. It was like the ardor of a lover; it embarrassed me; it was hateful and yet over-powering; and with gloating eyes she drew me to her, and her hot lips traveled along my cheek in kisses; and she would whisper, almost in sobs, "You are mine, you shall be mine, you and I are one for ever." Then she had thrown herself back in her chair, with her small hands over her eyes, leaving me trembling.

This is *Carmilla*, by Sheridan Le Fanu, and it's hard not to feel that *Dracula* stole her thunder. The story of a sexually threatening, gender non-conforming, ageless demon-thing, who takes active pleasure in the bodily fluids of others, Carmilla is a vampire. She lives forever, feasts on the blood of young women and, to top it all off, can become a sexy cat, as Dracula, twenty-five years later, can become an enormous dog. (A real score for people who understand that all cats are girls and all dogs are boys – but let's not get into what this might mean for black cats and golden retrievers.)

Her first appearance in the novel is as an absence: a warm empty space.

Laura, waking from a dream of seeing a beautiful woman's face, reaches out to "lay [her] hand along that hollow in the bed; someone did lie there". The hollow was still warm, she notes, caressing it gently. There is an obvious sexual connotation here – as tentacles are phallic, surely warm empty hollows must mean *something* – and twelve years later, she meets again the face she saw in a dream. It is Carmilla, and Carmilla tells her that she dreamed of Laura too. She dreamed, she says, that Laura's "looks won me; I climbed on the bed and put my arms about you, and I think we both fell asleep".

Laura is drawn to Carmilla, and repelled by her. Carmilla is very beautiful, and very charming, and adores her; but she also does decadent things like "come down very late, generally not till one o'clock", or "take a cup of chocolate, but eat nothing". Also, everywhere Carmilla goes, young women die.

"I have been in love with no one, and never shall," she tells Laura, "unless it should be with you." It is explicitly queer, and while Carmilla is clearly the kind of predatory lesbian stereotype that the twenty-first century might frown upon, it's hard not to root for her forthright sexual agency. She has no fears, no shame; she has only desire. Unlike, say, Scylla, she has no need of others for their minds: just their bodies will do. The novel is directly, unabashedly sexual – although, to quote someone on a forum: *it's not the most explicit unfortunately* :((The little sad face absolutely kills me.) I, too, can't help wishing Le Fanu had given us something more than warm hollow places, and heaving chests, and tumbling silky hair! I'm with you, *BumbleBee2568*! More sexy Victorian women in their own words!

"Why can't they let a girl marry three men, or as many as want her, and save all this trouble?" Lucy Westenra asks, at the beginning of *Dracula*.

Like *Carmilla*, *Dracula* is a novel preoccupied by sexual power. Lucy, naturally, is surrounded by men who want to marry her, and who will later come together to kill her. The three vampire women are all tits and teeth, like stage darlings. And even Mina, wife of the hero and all-round good egg, is found lapping blood from the Count's chest "like a kitten forced to drink milk".

It is a truly, remarkably horrible book, and – if you're into epistolary stories or monstrous men – I recommend it. "You may go anywhere you wish in the castle, except where the doors are locked, where of course you will not wish to go," Dracula tells the hero in the first chapter. This is, of course, a classic Bluebeard move. And Jonathan writes in his journal that "this diary seems horribly like the beginning of the 'Arabian Nights,' for everything has to break off at cockcrow."

This is a retelling, a romance in the way all fairy tales are romances, monstrous in the way all fairy tales are monstrous. Monstrous, I suppose, in the way that sex is monstrous.

We write to understand our fears; we write to find solidarity in our fears. We write to understand the relationship between our longings and our terrors; between our public face and private heart; between what we say and what we mean. We write in order to have these relationships understood. We write in the hope that one person will hear the thing we can't say aloud.

"How dare you touch him, any of you?" the Count tells his vampire brides. "This man belongs to me!"

Bram Stoker, himself, was married to a woman – though the woman, Florence Balcombe, was an ex of Oscar Wilde's, and Stoker and Wilde were themselves close. As, too, were Stoker and Walt Whitman: Stoker wished, he said, to be the wife to Whitman's soul.* Wilde was arrested, and imprisoned, while Stoker was writing *Dracula*. His own marriage to a woman did not stand against the charge of homosexuality: bisexuality, in any case, would have been no defence.

"Your girls that you all love are mine already," Dracula tells the men of the novel. "And through them you and others shall yet be mine – my creature[s], to do my bidding." It's a bisexual dream! "Lord forgive me," wrote Bram Stoker, in a

---

* Did you know that Whitman and Wilde almost certainly slept together? I am unable not to tell you this. They drank a bottle of "elderberry wine and ... [went] upstairs to his 'den' on the third floor." There, as Whitman put it, they became on "thee-and-thou terms". They discussed "nothing but pretty boys, and of how insipid was the love of women". A veil descends over the third-floor den. The next day Whitman said he had had a wonderful time, and that Wilde was a "great big, splendid boy". Wilde, for his part, told everyone that he had 'the kiss of Walt Whitman still on [his] lips." Now you know!

letter to a friend the week *Dracula* was first published. "I am (now?) quite shameless."

Shameless! Is *this* why we write? We write to *become* shameless: hopeless romantics reckoning with the deepest truths of the self. We write to be free of the thing that stalks us; the thing we don't see coming up behind us in the mirror, but whose presence we feel nonetheless. We write to understand the shape of the invisible things all around us. Lesbians looking for lesbian pulp novels in the 1960s couldn't rely on the covers: all pulp romances had the same kind of covers, and few publishers dared say openly what might be within. Instead they looked for secret clues in the titles: words that would make visible the invisible. Words like "shadow"; words like "whisper". Words like "twilight".

Twilight, said Kristen Stewart in 2024, *was such a gay movie*.

"I can only see it now," she said, cropped hair, wide tweed suit. "The fact I was there at all … it was percolating," she added. The gayness was percolating. Stewart, of course, is Bella Swan: the clumsy teen heroine of Stephenie Meyer's *Twilight* series.

Twilight came to Meyer in a dream: a vampire, sparkling in the sun, and a human girl, in love. The vampire is overcoming his natural urge to bite. The girl is begging to be bitten. (He will not bite her until they are married.) It is purity culture with the barest rags of a story hanging over it. It is a story about repressed longing; about wanting what will kill you; about the closeness of sex and death. And yet, after years of Anne Rice-inspired queerness, Stephenie Meyer came as a shock: these were vampires with the teeth removed. And people loved it. It's hard to overstate the cultural impact of *Twilight*. The series sold over 160 million copies, and was translated into 49 languages; it spent 235 weeks on the *New York Times* bestseller lists.

All around the world, then, girls and women were having the same arguments that every girl I knew was having: who would you choose? Would you choose the self-controlled, ageless vampire? Would you choose the wild, warm werewolf? Were you Team Edward, or Team Jacob? We need to know.

It is fascinating, in hindsight, to see this as the point where mainstream culture began to shift back towards the participatory. If the writers and readers of pulp romances had always been the same people, the rise of glossy hardbacks had, for a time, pushed readers and writers into different spheres. Now, with Team Jen vs Team Angelina fresh in the cultural memory, romance became, once again, the possession of the reader. A fresh wave of fanfiction; a fresh wave of midnight launches in bookshops; a fresh wave of the kind of stories that people couldn't stop talking about.

It made the genre new again, by the same means that romance will always keep renewing itself: sex and death, death and sex, the only two things that really matter.

If romance writers are always on the cutting edge, that's because sex always has to be one step ahead to be exciting, and death is always the unknown. If romance writers are always rewriting and retelling, that's because death and sex are the two constants for all living things. This is the beginning and the end.

And somewhere in between, there's love: love, and everything that happens on the way.

Epilogue

What If We Kissed at the Funeral Home?

There was a period last year when I seemed to read almost exclusively romance novels set in and around funeral homes. This can't actually be true, but for a while there, it felt like every romance novel I picked up either kicked off in a funeral home or featured a sexy ghost. Not a spooky ghost, I hasten to add; this was not a paranormal phase. No gargoyles or tentacles, just ... regular old death. And the aftermath. These were not generally vengeful ghosts; they were ordinary ghosts, often with corporeal forms that seemed more real to the second-sight protagonist than the whole rest of the living world. *The Dead Romantics*, for instance! Or *Rules for Ghosting*!

It was strange how much I loved these books, given how much I hate to read books about grief. And yet what I loved was that death in these books was real, it was present: it was a part of things. People love to say that grief is the price we pay for love. I think they are the same thing. And *love*, as Daisy Bacon says, *is not a part of living that can be shut off from the rest of the world.*

We were, we are – romance readers, romance writers – like people around a campfire: tell us again about what we fear, and what we yearn for. Tell us again about longing. Tell us again about danger. Tell us again about death, and the opposite.

Tell us again about the endless mutations, endless adaptations, of hunger and death and desire and love. Tell us about power, and who wields it. Tell us about what we know to be true. And make the ending happy, *because* we know – we all know – that happy endings are only happy for a time.

This is not because happiness isn't real, or lasting. This is because there aren't, in real life, any real endings.

There is only the point where you choose to stop telling the story.

And why not, then, choose a perfect moment?

Why not end with sweetness?

People laugh at romance novels because we want a happy ending; people laugh at romance novels because they think that we think that a happy ending can overcome everything that came before, and smooth out everything that comes after. No. What would be the point in that? We want a happy ending because of everything that came before, and everything that will come after. Romance readers know how strange and harsh the world can be. And this is why we insist upon the light.

The wild is all around; we live on a tiny bright speck in oceans of vast darkness; and we are alive, in cosmic terms, for the briefest of possible moments. Why not, while we can, end with joy?

Endnotes

22 '... the way they know something adults have forgotten.', "A Note from the Desk of a Newborn Adult", 7 November 2016; https://www.facebook.com/lordemusic/posts/1398988346785548.
25 '... *from ordinary existence.*', *Reading the Romance*, Janice A. Radway, Verso, 1987, Table 2.1, pp. 60–61.
25 '... *or the "romance like the heroine's"*', Ibid, p. 61.
33 '... *it was the worst of times...*', *Hard Times*, Charles Dickens, Bradbury & Evans, 1854.
33 '... *the "blurst of times"...*', "Last Exit to Springfield", *The Simpsons*, created by Matt Groening, written by Jay Kogen and Wallace Wolodarksky, ep. 4.17, 1993.
28 '... *the Labour Party's plan to clean up Britain's waterways...*', Instagram, UKLabour, 22 June 2024; https://www.instagram.com/uklabour/reel/C8gofOjtSmq/.
33 '... *need more friends.*', *Financial Times*, 14 March 2025; https://www.ft.com/content/f510bdaf-14e6-4a0f-90fc-e5ebb54e86bd.
34 '... *business class flights, and pension schemes.*', "The Enduring Legacy of Jane Austen's 'Truth Universally Acknowledged'", "Fresh Air", *NPR*, 25 July 2017.
36 '... *more akin to a modern romance novel.*', *Why Jane Austen?*, Rachel M. Brownstein, Columbia University Press, 2011.
39 '... *the year that* Fifty Shades *got big.*', *Washington Post*, 10 February 2015; https://www.washingtonpost.com/news/wonk/wp/2015/02/10/sex-toy-injuries-surged-after-fifty-shades-of-grey-was-published/.

Endnotes

43 '... "*nobody has read in decades*".', *And Then? And Then? What Else?: A Writer's Life*, Daniel Handler, Oneworld Publications, 2024, p. 123.

43 '*The "death of the author"*...', "The Death of the Author", Roland Barthes, *Aspen*, no. 5–6, 1967.

44 '... *full of universal inherited ideas.*', *The Archetypes and the Collective Unconscious*, Carl Jung, Pantheon Books, 1959.

38 '... *that fits the "romantic fiction" template.*', As quoted in "Exclusive Q&A with British-Nigerian Author, Bolu Babalola", Thobeka Phanyeko, *Glamour South Africa*, 29 May 2024; https://www.glamour.co.za/lifestyle/exclusive-q-and-a-with-british-nigerian-author-bolu-babalola-baf6504c-cd92-4f5f-9c6a-9d4f5c979788.

47 '... *and the beloved ones* – Bridget Jones's Diary.', *Pride and Prejudice and Zombies*, Seth Grahame-Smith, Quirk Books, 2009; *Bridget Jones's Diary*, Helen Fielding, Picador, 1996.

47 '... Mr. & Mrs. Fitzwilliam Darcy...', *Mr. & Mrs. Fitzwilliam Darcy: Two Shall Become One*, Sharon Lathan, Sourcebooks, Inc., 2007.

47 '... *holding out the whole time.*', *Pride and Prometheus*, John Kessel, Saga Press, 2008; *The Other Bennet Sister*, Janice Hadlow, Pan, 2020.

48 '... *Fitz Darcy as a neurosurgeon).*', *Eligible*, Curtis Sittenfeld, The Borough Press, 2016.

48 '*(who* hates *Liz's listicles).*', *Just as You Are*, Camille Kellogg, Random House, 2023.

48 '... *all by herself.*', *Pride/Prejudice*, Ann Herendeen, Harper Paperbacks, 2010; *Pride and Prejudice and the City*, Rachael Lippincott, Simon & Schuster, 2023.

48 '*does what it says on the tin.*', *What Kitty Did Next*, Carrie Kablean, RedDoor Press, 2018; *Her Summer at Pemberley*, Sallianne Hines, Grasslands Press, 2020; *The Scandalous Confessions of Lydia Bennet, Witch*, Melinda Taub, Arcadia, 2023.

50 '... *and the world we have.*', *Reading the Romance*, p. 61.

Endnotes

53 '*. . . gives the people what they want.*', *Wild Love*, Elsie Silver, Piatkus, 2024, p. 1.

59 '*. . . and I write about the situations we all deal with.*"', As quoted in "Danielle Steel falls out of love with romance", Alison Flood, *Guardian*, 23 September 2010; https://www.theguardian.com/books/2010/sep/23/danielle-steel-romance-fiction-novels.

65 '*. . . Mark II, "suave, well-dressed, [and] rich".*', *The Private World of Georgette Heyer*, Jane Aiken Hodge, Arrow, 2006.

65 '*. . . and Type C: Knightley.*', "Georgette Heyer and the Uses of Regency", E. R. Glass and A. Mineo, in *Georgette Heyer: A Critical Retrospective*, Mary Fahnestock Thomas, PrinnyWorld Press, 2001.

72 '*. . . for her to be hit with a belt.*"', As quoted in "Shirley Conran: all hail the queen of the bonkbuster", Rachel Cooke, *Guardian*, 29 July 2012; https://www.theguardian.com/books/2012/jul/29/shirley-conran-interview-lace-republished.

75 '*. . . and above all, his constant patience.*', *Gaudy Night*, Dorothy L. Sayers, Victor Gollancz Ltd, 1935, p. 305.

77 '*. . . as the "odalisques did for Suleiman the Great".*', *A Company of Swans*, Eva Ibbotson, Macmillan, 2020, p. 310.

77 '*They just worked very hard at love – it was all they had.*"', Ibid, p. 384.

79 '*. . . per person per annum.*', "High income improves evaluation of life but not emotional well-being", D. Kahneman, and A. Deaton, Proc. Natl. Acad. Sci. U.S.A. 107 (38) 16489-16493, https://doi.org/10.1073/pnas.1011492107 (2010).

89 '*. . . "Fleabag's Heartbreaking Confession To The Hot Priest Turns Into A Steamy Moment".*', YouTube, 5 February 2024; https://www.youtube.com/watch?v=68Q9El7b1b8.

99 '*Consent culture is "suspicious of tentativeness".*', *Tomorrow Sex Will Be Good Again: Women and Desire in the Age of Consent*, Katherine Angel, Verso, 2021, p. 17.

99 '*They must, then, also know what it is that they want".*', Ibid, p. 7.

100 '*. . . the baby wants his home.*' *The Morning Gift*, Eva Ibbotson, Random Books, 1993.

Endnotes

101 '. . . *they do things differently here.*', *The Go-Between*, L. P. Hartley, Hamish Hamilton, 1953.

102 '*. . . in a piece about the series.*', "Out of the Cave", Tammy Oler, *Slate*, 6 May 2014; https://slate.com/culture/2014/05/clan-of-the-cave-bear-and-feminism-dystopian-precedent-to-the-hunger-games.html.

103 '. . . *as Heather settles into life with Birmingham.*', *The Flame and the Flower*, Kathleen E. Woodiwiss, Avon Books, 1972, p. 99.

107 '. . . *just like that.*', "Harlequin Enterprises ULC: A Global Success Story", Harlequin.com; https://www.harlequin.com/shop/pages/harlequin-enterprises-limited-a-global-success-story.html#:~:text=Harlequin%20sold%20131%20million%20books,licensee%20arrangements%20and%20multilanguage%20exports.

108 '. . . *and* The Lord's Maddening Miss.', *Compromised into Marrying the Duke*, Lucy Ashford, Harlequin Historical, 2025; *His Unlikely Countess*, Helen Dickson, Harlequin Historical, 2025; *The Lord's Maddening Miss*, Lucy Morris, Harlequin Historical, 2025.

108 '. . . *and* Snowbound with the Brooding Lord.', *Wedding Night with Her Viking Enemy*, Lucy Morris, Harlequin Historical, 2025; *A Naval Surgeon to Fight For*, Carla Kelly, Harlequin Historical, 2024; *Wedded to His Enemy Debutante*, Samantha Hastings, Harlequin Historical, 2024; *Becoming the Earl's Convenient Wife*, Louise Allen, Harlequin Historical, 2023; *Their Inconvenient Yuletide Wedding*, Joanna Johnson, Harlequin Historical, 2023; *Snowed In with the Viking*, Lucy Morris, Harlequin Historical, 2024; and *Snowbound with the Brooding Lord*, Sarah Mallory, Harlequin Historical, 2023.

108 '. . . *and* Billion Dollar Ring Ruse . . .', *Crowned for His Son*, Maya Blake, Harlequin Presents, 2025; *Expecting the Greek's Heir*, Lucy King, Harlequin Presents, 2025; and *Billion Dollar Ring Ruse*, Jadesola James, Harlequin Presents, 2025.

108 '. . . *the full monthly package.*', *The Surgeon's Relationship Ruse*, Louisa Heaton, Harlequin Medical, 2025; *Flirting with the Florida Heart Doctor*, Janice Lynn, Harlequin Medical,

Endnotes

2025; and *Surgeon in a Tux*, Carol Marinelli, Harlequin Medical, 2014.

109 '. . . *bright blocky colours.*', *Much Ado About Hating You*, Sarah Echavarre Smith, Harlequin Afterglow, 2025; *Unlikely Neighbours*, Renee Daniel Flagler, Harlequin Afterglow, 2025.

109 '. . . The Teacher's Forever Family?', *City Doc for the Single Mom*, Kate MacGuire, Harlequin Medical Romance, 2025; *Finding a Family Next Door*, Louisa Heaton, Harlequin Medical Romance, 2025; *Reunion with the Single Mom*, Linda J. Parisi, Harlequin Heartwarming, 2025; *The Teacher's Forever Family*, Laurie Batzel, Harlequin Heartwarming, 2025.

109 '. . . *doing in Medical?*', *The Firefighter and the Single Mum*, Laura Iding, Harlequin Medical, 2016.

109 'All In with the Maverick.', *The Maverick's Promise*, Melissa Senate, Harlequin Montana Mavericks, 2025; *Sweet-Talkin' Maverick*, Christy Jeffries, Harlequin Montana Mavericks, 2024; *All In with the Maverick*, Elizabeth Hrib, Harlequin Montana Mavericks, 2025.

111 '. . . *the title topics.*', "The Texas Billionaire's Pregnant Bride: An evolutionary interpretation of romance fiction titles", Anthony Cox and Maryanne Fisher, 2009, *Journal of Social, Evolutionary, and Cultural Psychology*, 3(4), pp. 386–401.

113 '. . . *the place of Mormon women*".', *Riders of the Purple Sage*, Zane Grey, Harper and Brothers, 1912, p. 1.

116 '. . . *she'd never be tamed.*"', "Ranch Romances", Mark Boardman, *True West*, 1 November 2006; https://truewestmagazine.com/article/ranch-romances/.

116 '. . . *his future unknown*". . .', Ibid.

116 '. . . "*one of the great fiction editors of all time*". . .', "Black Mask Magazine, Steve Fisher, and The Noir Revolution", Keith Alan Deutsch, *Something Is Going to Happen*, August 2012 edition.

117 '. . . *with a palette that can make many pictures.*', *The Ogden Standard-Examiner*, March 1941; https://pulpflakes.blogspot.com/2016/12/fanny-ellsworth-article-on-writing.html.

Endnotes

118 '. . . *her detailed editorial feedback.*', "*Ranch Romances*: The Last of the Original Pulps", Michelle Nolan, The Pulp Magazines Project; https://www.pulpmags.org/content/info/ranch-romances.html.

118 '. . . *in The Ogden Standard-Examiner in March 1941.*', *The Ogden Standard-Examiner*, March 1941; https://pulpflakes.blogspot.com/2016/12/fanny-ellsworth-article-on-writing.html.

119 '*Everything at once.*', *St. Mawr*, D. H. Lawrence, Martin Secker, 1925, p. 6.

120 '. . . *or even death".*', *To Whom the Goddess: Hunting and Riding for Women*, Lady Diana Shedden and Lady Apsley, Hutchinson & Co., 1932, p. 19.

121 '. . . *correct use of aids.*', Ibid, p. 45.

123 '. . . *(if it is her ambition to master the horse, to perform on it . . .*', *Normality and Pathology in Childhood: Assessments of Development*, Anna Freud, Routledge, 1989.

123 '. . . *far from it."*', *If Wishes Were Horses: A Memoir of Equine Obsession*, Susanna Forrest, Atlantic Books, 2012.

123 '. . . *Is that Freudian?"*', "Jilly Cooper's very English fantasies", Tanya Gold, *New Statesman*, 17 October 2024; https://www.newstatesman.com/culture/books/2024/10/jilly-coopers-very-english-fantasies.

124 '. . . *risk taking, courage".*', *If Wishes Were Horses*, pp. 309–310.

125 '. . . *"soft hands, and a firm seat".*', *To Whom the Goddess*

125 '. . . *at the same moment."*', Ibid., p. 64.

126 '. . . *He could control a horse."*', *Have His Carcase*, Dorothy L. Sayers, Victor Gollancz Ltd, 1932, Chapter 16.

127 '. . . *cast yourself as inviolable".*', *Tomorrow Sex Will Be Good Again*, p. 36.

127 '. . . *and over everything."*', *Lady Audley's Secret*, Mary Elizabeth Braddon, Tinsley Brothers, 1862, p. 166.

128 '. . . *but a miracle."*', *Gaudy Night*, Dorothy L. Sayers, p. 166.

128 '. . . *"—is buying someone a horse."*', "Jilly Cooper's very English fantasies", Tanya Gold.

128 '. . . *"like a Zane Grey book jacket".*', *St. Mawr*, D. H. Lawrence, 1925.

Endnotes

129 '... *every part of myself.*"', *The Wild Other: A memoir of Love, Adventure and How to Be Brave*, Clover Stroud, Hodder, 2018 p. 169.

129 '... *Elsie Silver told an interviewer in May 2025.*', "Elsie Silver is redefining Western Romance – one country boy at a time", Christelle Lujan, Shereads, 1 May 2025; https://shereads.com/exclusive-interview-with-elsie-silver/.

129 '... *It just makes sense.*"', *Barbarian's Taming: A SciFi Alien Romance (Ice Planet Barbarians Book 8)*, Ruby Dixon, Berkley, 2016, p. 92.

130 '... *But it's something big...*"', *St. Mawr*, D. H. Lawrence, 1925.

131 '... *and* The Atlantic Monthly *rolled together*".', *The Writer's Yearbook*, A & C Black, 1941.

136 '... *or be hiding a secret*".', *Queen of the Pulps: The Reign of Daisy Bacon and Love Story Magazine*, Laurie Powers, McFarland, 2019, loc. 1330.

136 '... *could live without it*".', Ibid., loc. 277.

138 '*(only counting those delivered to the* Love Story *offices).*', Ibid., loc. 1019.

139 '... *bookselling industries*".', *Reading the Romance*, loc. 443.

139 '... *"with the introduction of the Kindle".*', *Love in the Time of Self-Publishing: How Romance Writers Changed the Rules of Writing and Success*, Christine Larson, Princeton University Press, 2024, p. 16.

139 '... *planning a dinner!*"', Grace Hopper quoted in *Cosmopolitan Magazine*, 1967, from "'It's like planning a dinner': How they tried to attract women to computer programming", Charles Miller, BBC Academy, 6 July 2017; https://www.bbc.co.uk/blogs/academy/entries/0adeb6bf-6a6e-4d5c-9d2a-a44c37bfb775 1967.

145 '... *power and relinquishing*".', *Tomorrow Sex Will Be Good Again*, p. 100.

147 '... *a more hopeful time*".', "The Complicated Origins of 'Having It All'", Jennifer Szalai, *New York Times*, 2 January 2015; https://www.nytimes.com/2015/01/04/magazine/the-complicated-origins-of-having-it-all.html.

Endnotes

147 '. . . *just a little one")*.', *Having It All: Love, Success, Sex, Money, Even If You're Starting with Nothing*, Helen Gurley Brown, Simon & Schuster, 1982.

148 '. . . *children's lunches"*.', *Sex and the Single Girl*, Helen Gurley Brown, Bernard Geis Associates, 1962.

149 '. . . *determined to fall in love.*', "Helen Gurley Brown, Who Gave 'Single Girl' a Life in Full, Dies at 90", Margalit Fox, *New York Times*, 13 August 2012; https://www.nytimes.com/2012/08/14/business/media/helen-gurley-brown-who-gave-cosmopolitan-its-purr-is-dead-at-90.html.

151 '. . . *upon the background.*'', *Love Story Editor*, Daisy Bacon, 1954, p. 66.

152 '. . . *she sold it.*'', Ibid., p. 70.

154 '. . . *and it didn't exist.*'', *A Novel Love Story*, Ashley Poston, Berkley Books, 2024, p. 2.

157 '. . .The Little Ice Cream Shop by the Sea.', *The Café at Beach End*, RaeAnne Thayne, Canary Street Press, 2023; *The Beach Café*, Lucy Diamond, Pan Macmillan, 2011; *The Little Beach Café*, Sarah Hope, Boldwood Books Ltd, 2018; *Summer at the Ice Cream Café*, Jo Thomas, Penguin, 2023; *Summer at the Cornish Café*, Phillipa Ashley, HarperCollins Publishers, 2016; *The Little Ice Cream Shop by the Sea*, Lizzie Chantree, Nielson, 2021.

157 '. . . Wishing Well Lane.', *Little Beach Street Bakery*, Jenny Colgan, Sphere, 2014; *The Little Bakery on Rosemary Lane*, Ellen Berry, Avon Books, 2017; *The Little Bakery on Wishing Well Lane*, K. T. Dady, Kindle, 2023.

157 '. . . The Little French Café.', *The Little Bicycle Bakery*, Su Young Lee, Kindle, 2020; *The Canal Boat Café*, Cressida McLaughlin, HarperCollins, 2016; *The Little Village Bakery*, Tilly Tennant, Bookouture, 2016; *The Little Italian Bakery*, Valentina Cebeni, Abacus, 2018; *The Little Brooklyn Bakery*, Julie Caplin, One More Chapter, 2018; *Summer at the Little French Café* and *I'll Be Home for Christmas*, Karen Clarke, Bookouture, 2019.

157 '. . . Rosie's Little Café on the Riviera.', *Rosie's Little Café on the Riviera*, Jennifer Bohnet, HarperCollins Publishers, 2017.

Endnotes

157 '. . . Little Wedding Shop by the Sea.', *Secrets at the Little Music Shop*, Jane Lovering, Choc Lit, 2024; *Christmas Promises at the Little Wedding Shop by the Sea*, Jane Linfoot, One More Chapter, 2017.

157 '. . . The Vintage Dress Shope in Primrose Hill.', *The Vintage Dress Shop in Primrose Hill*, Annie Darling, Hodder & Stoughton, 2023.

161 '. . . *I knew nothing about horses*".', "The Book That Changed My Life: Jill Mansell chooses Riders by Jilly Cooper", Novelicious, 10 February 2014; https://web.archive.org/web/20140703133914/http://www.novelicious.com/2014/02/the-book-that-changed-my-life-jill-mansell-chooses-riders-by-jilly-cooper.html.

162 '. . . Mansell told a journalist.', Ibid.

166 '. . . *"pieces of love sent"*.', *Confusion*, Book III of the *Cazalet Chronicles*, Elizabeth Jane Howard, Pan Macmillan, 2024.

168 '. . . *for what purpose the story is being narrated"*.', "POV disorder", Rebecca Makkai, SubMakk, 20 February 2025; https://rebeccamakkai.substack.com/p/pov-disorder.

172 '. . . *or the corpse?*"', *84 Charing Cross Road*, Helene Hanff, Grossman Publishers, 1970.

175 '. . . *any notice of them"*.', *Daddy-Long-Legs*, Jean Webster, Puffin Classics, 1912, loc. 94.

177 '. . . *so long to reach out. A.*"', *Dear Aaron*, Mariana Zapata, Mariana Zapata, 2017.

178 '. . . *someone's job"*.', *Attachments*, Rainbow Rowell, Dutton, 2011, p. 5.

180 '. . . *you turned up.*"', *This Is How You Lose the Time War*, Amal El-Mohtar and Max Gladstone, Arcadia, 2019, p. 7.

181 '. . . *or not to kill yourself.*"', *Still Life With Woodpecker*, Tom Robbins, No Exit Press, 2001.

183 '. . . *wrote Samuel Johnson.*', "A letter to Mrs. Thrale", Samuel Johnson, 27 October, 1777.

186 '. . . *he wrote, desperately.*', "September 1, 1939", in *Another Time*, W. H. Auden, Faber & Faber, 1939.

189 '. . . *when we see each other.*"', "Maya Angelou at the 2nd Annual HRC National Dinner", YouTube, 28 May 2014; https://www.youtube.com/watch?v=BybZZM881Tw).

Endnotes

190 '... *probably picks up.*"', *Where the Heart Roams* [film], produced, directed and edited by George Csicsery, 1982.

190 '... *where they live.*"', "Csicsery: Math Films, Yes - But So Much More", Doniphan Blair, cineSOURCE, 9 March 2010; https://cinesourcemagazine.com/index.php?/site/comments/csicsery_math_films_yes_but_so_much_more/.

191 '... *it is all too "sad and ineffable".*', "'Where the Heart Roams,' About Romance Novelists", Vincent Canby, *New York Times*, 19 August 1987; https://www.nytimes.com/1987/08/19/movies/film-where-the-heart-roams-about-romance-novelists.html.

192 '... *of the story, electric.*', *Love in the Time of Self-Publishing*, p. 98.

193 '... *in her biography.)*', Chelley Kitzmiller, Amazon.com, 30 July 2025; https://www.amazon.com/stores/author/B003ZODFLY/.

199 '... Beautiful Bastard.', *Sempre*, J. M. Darhower, Gallery Books, 2013; *Beautiful Bastard*, Christina Lauren, Gallery Books, 2013.

200 '... more sweet in Lilliput?"', "Mary Gulliver to Captain Lemuel Gulliver. An Epistle", in *The Works of Alexander Pope*, Alexander Pope, Wordsworth Editions, 1995.

203 '... *negotiation of fear.*"', *Tomorrow Sex Will Be Good Again*, p. 100.

206 '... *outwith the law;*', *Love in the Time of Self-Publishing*, p. 95.

207 '... *unique to romantic fiction.*', Ibid., p. 30.

215 '... *"artistically quite wrong"*', C. P. Snow in the *Financial Times*, 1971.

215 '... *"plea for homosexuality".*', Walter Allen in the *Daily Telegraph*, 1971.

216 '... *that same year. Romance lists look a little different this season.*"', "A Wider Embrace", Rachel Kramer Bussel, *Publishers Weekly*, 2020.

217 '... except that I love you.', *Love Letters: Vita and Virginia*, Vintage Classics, 2021.

219 '... *my father taught me how to fight.*"', *Beebo Brinker*, Ann Bannon, Mills & Boon, 1962.

220 '... *the butch of my dreams".*', "Beebo's Significant Other", Susan Caba, *Stanford Magazine*, March/April 2010; https://stanfordmag.org/contents/beebo-s-significant-other.

Endnotes

221 '... one of them go crazy."', Ibid.
221 '... *their mother's care.*"', "Out of the Shadows: An Interview with Ann Bannon", William Dean, *Clean Sheets Erotica Magazine*, March 2003; https://web.archive.org/web/20071004174241/http://www.cleansheets.com/articles/dean_01.08.03.shtml.
221 '... *one way or the other"...*', "Beebo's Significant Other", Susan Caba.
221 '... *same-sex love".*', Ibid.
221 '... *everything about you"?*', Ibid.
222 '... *"wear[ing] a flag pin".*', "a letter I never thought I'd have to send", Elle McNicoll, 14 September 2024; https://www.instagram.com/ellemcnicollofficial/p/C_5WzAWAE33/?hl=en.
223 '... *reading them.*"', "My take on women writing MM Romance", Jamie Fessenden, 28 June 2014; https://jamiefessenden.com/2014/06/28/my-take-on-women-writing-mm-romance/.
225 '... *convincing themselves they're straight."*', *Red, White & Royal Blue*, Casey McQuiston, St. Martin's Griffin, 2019, p. 112.
227 '... *real-world lives".*', "'The Tent's Big Enough for Everyone': online slash fiction as a site for activism and change", Neville, L. (2018), Gender, Place & Culture, 25(3), 384–398. https://doi.org/10.1080/0966369X.2017.1420633.
227 '... *you have a right to be here.*"', "Desiderata", Max Ehrmann, 1927.
228 '... *little twinkies"...*', "Out of the Shadows: An Interview with Ann Bannon", William Dean.
228 '... *one main character at a time.*', "What To Do If Your Inner Tomboy Is a Homo: Straight Women, Bisexuality, and Pleasure in M/M Gay Romance Fictions", Guy Mark Foster, 2015, *Journal of Bisexuality*, 15:4, 509–531, DOI; https://www.bowdoin.edu/profiles/faculty/gmfoster/pdf/what-to-do-if-your-inner-tomboy.foster.pdf.
229 '... *four persons are involved.*"' *The Complete Letters of Sigmund Freud to Wilhelm Fliess, 1887–1904*, Belknap Press, Harvard University Press, 1985, trans. Masson, J. Moussaieff, p. 364.
235 '... *and inverted".*', "Of Other Spaces: Utopias and Heterotopias", Michel Foucault, 1967.

Endnotes

236 '. . . *where things are different*".', "Trains, Planes, and Automobiles: The End of the Postmodern Moment", Walter Russell Mead, 1995, *World Policy Journal*, 12:4, pp. 13–31.

241 '. . . *a specific result*".', As quoted in "How to Add More Play to Your Grown-Up Life, Even Now", Kristin Wong, *New York Times*, 14 August 2020; https://www.nytimes.com/2020/08/14/smarter-living/adults-play-work-life-balance.html.

250 '. . . "*seductive, scary gait*"),', "Interview: Ron Clements and John Musker of 'The Little Mermaid'", Nell Minow, Moviemom.com, 30 September 2013; https://web.archive.org/web/20160304192125/http://www.beliefnet.com/columnists/moviemom/2013/09/interview-ron-clements-john-musker-little-mermaid-disney.html.

252 '. . . Give Anything to Touch but Can't.'", *Succubus Blues*, Richelle Mead, Transworld Publishers Ltd, 2007.

254 '. . . *leaving me trembling*.', *Carmilla*, Sheridan Le Fanu, 1872, p. 29.

258 '. . . was such a gay movie.', As quoted in "How Kristen Stewart Became a Queer Trailblazer", Adam B. Vary, *Variety*, 11 January 2024; https://variety.com/2024/film/features/kristen-stewart-coming-out-twilight-gay-sundance-sex-scenes-1235867627/.

261 '. . . the rest of the world.', *Love Story Editor*

Acknowledgements

A book like this could never be comprehensive. The books I have written about in these pages are simply the ones that best illustrated the points I wanted to make: lots of my personal favourites can be found here but by no means all – there are too many. To try and make a comprehensive book about romance books would be truly impossible, and/or about ten thousand pages long. (I suppose I could have done it, but it would never have been published.)

All this to say that I owe a huge, huge debt to the romance writing community, and the romance reading community. There are so many of you. There are so many fantastic books, and fantastic people who write and read those books, that I had no space to really get into. My biggest acknowledgement, therefore, must be to everyone I left out of this book: some forever friends, some beloved colleagues, some total strangers whose absence nonetheless makes my heart ache. Thank you, thank you, thank you. Thank you for your work without which this book would never have existed.

Thank you also to everyone who saw me through the third-act crisis. I am extremely lucky to have friends so unrealistically lovely that any good editor would cut them from

Acknowledgements

the plot: thank you. I am extremely lucky to have a family with such a rich seam of beautiful and complex side characters that they, too, would probably also be excised for distracting from the main narrative. Thank you. Thanks, especially, to my parents, who never took a book away from me. A childhood of being allowed to read anything you can reach is probably the fastest way to an adulthood of reading and writing for a living. I am very grateful for this and many other things. Thanks to my sisters, to whom this book is dedicated. Thanks to Daisy; thanks to Charlotte; thanks to Caro, the driving whip behind my galaxy-brain big horse; thanks to Monica for early support; thanks to Katya for Friday afternoons; thanks to Tash and Andy for the house to write in; thanks to Kate, the mastermind behind the machine; thanks, though that seems a deeply inadequate word, to Rich.